SIDE SQUEEZE

JASPER FALLS 6

LYDIA MICHAELS

Side Squeeze

Jasper Falls 6

DEDICATION

For the Wades,
Who somehow always deliver comfort in life's
most confusing moments of chaos.

SUGGESTED PLAYLIST

"The Scientist" by Coldplay
"Ho Hey" by The Lumineers
"Thinking Out Loud" by Ed Sheeran
"Say You Won't Let Go" by James Arthur
"Lost Boy" by Ruth B.
"Don't Give Up on Me" by Andy Grammer
"Come and Get Your Love" by Redbone
"Daddy's Little Girl" by The Mills Brothers
"I Won't Give Up" by Jason Mraz
"A Million Dreams" from *The Greatest Showman*

CHAPTER 1

"*D*on't fuck up. Don't fuck up. Don't fuck up." Mariella flipped open the mirror on the overhead visor and glared into her chestnut eyes. "Do *not* fuck this up. Everyone deserves a second chance. The past is in the past. Who cares what they think of you? It's time to set the record straight. You're smart, professional, and more than capable. You've got this."

Flashing her teeth, she checked for food then smiled, scuffing a smudge of red gloss off her incisor before running her tongue under her lips. Her gaze shot to the dashboard clock. Time to go.

Maybe just a few minutes longer. She was early, anyway. She waited in the heat of her Volvo, questioning her sanity. This interview could go a long way in healing old wounds, or it could massively humiliate her.

She stared up at the towering hotel, designed to look much older than it was. The building boasted a level of fancy Jasper Falls had been missing for years. Maybe something *too* fancy for their little backwoods town, because beneath the mayor's revitalization projects, their town was nothing more than a blue-collar lumberyard.

A few government grants spurred small businesses to set up shop, and those businesses triggered a slight boom in their little economy that enabled the town to progress from a dial-up state to something less Podunk. But nothing was as impressive as the Brick Hotel.

The Brick Hotel had nothing to do with grants or government incentives to rebuild. It had everything to do with the funding provided by the very wealthy and successful Gage King, now husband to Perrin Harris King.

Jasper Falls never had an upscale hotel before—just a crusty little Motor Inn on the outskirts of town. Truckers needing a hot shower and high school students looking for a hideout to drink or hook up made up most of the clientele.

Like everyone else who grew up in Jasper Falls, that Motor Inn reminded her of a time when fun was free and consequences were too far off to worry about. Adulthood was different. Messing up as an adult in a small town had a way of scarring a woman for life, and for the past few years she'd been trying, unsuccessfully, to outrun her past.

Mariella's bad reputation wasn't even her fault. Well, not all of it. Bran had played her for a fool. He'd strung her along, manipulated her, and in the end she'd been just as wounded as the other woman.

Unfortunately, in a small town like Jasper Falls, the gossip moved faster than the Wi-Fi. The town folk loved villains as much as they loved rallying behind their victims. In Mariella's situation, Perrin had the engagement ring, so Perrin was the obvious victim. Mariella had nothing so she'd been unfairly saddled with the label of "other woman", which was not the case at all.

The town didn't realize she'd been with Bran longer than Perrin. They didn't know that Perrin was actually the *other* woman.

For some reason, Bran openly dated Perrin, where he'd always kept Mariella somewhat hidden. Of course the town saw Mariella as the villain in the end. How could they not, when no one knew she'd been dating Bran long before Perrin came along?

Regardless, they fit her with a scarlet letter she hadn't been able to shed since. And poor Perrin got everyone's sympathy. It wasn't fair but it was also one of those unresolvable unfortunate situations. People loved their gossip.

Mariella had waited for the rumors to fade and something bigger to come by, but little towns had damn long memories. And she wasn't sure the locals would ever forget her supposed role in the Perrin-Bran breakup, so she decided it was time to face her past head on.

She glanced at the clock. Now, it was definitely time to go. She shut off the car and climbed out, the cold a rejuvenating slap in the face that made any chance of hysterics impossible.

Outside of the toasty Volvo, frigid wind froze slush into ice. The walks leading to the impressive Brick Hotel were shoveled and salted but still slippery. A gust of chilly air cut through her clothes, stealing a good bit of her confidence with her body heat.

Today was all about her future. It was about affirmations and opportunity. It was about change, and earning a seat at the table where she rightfully belonged. She was done wearing labels she didn't deserve.

She was through measuring her value by misconstrued past mistakes. Regardless of what others might think of her, she was not a terrible person. She had a moral compass and her worth had yet to be defined. This was a chance to prove herself as a responsible, respectable part of this town.

Yes, the Brick Hotel was built and owned by Gage King, and Gage was now married to Perrin. But that didn't mean Mariella couldn't work there. She was perfect for the manager position and determined to prove so.

Another gust of wind pushed her closer to the hotel and she stepped onto the shoveled walk. No bellman greeted her and she wondered if that was due to the cold or a lack of amenities. It seemed like the sort of hotel that should offer valet and luggage service.

She stared up at the five story, colonial inspired building. Tall pillars braced the sprawling awning and antique style windows glistened against the afternoon sun. Pristine white walls adorned with brick accents lent a degree of elegance that never before existed against the mountain backdrop of their town. The red roof made the structure a stunning landmark without appearing garish, and the details hidden within the moldings inspired thoughts of a golden age.

Mariella smiled, her cheeks chilled but her body warming with a spike of anticipated possibility. It looked like a hotel Hemingway might have frequented. She wanted to work there. She wanted to be a part of her town's forward motion, and this seemed like just the place to start.

There was only one problem. Gage King would be her boss. Perrin most likely told him her version of the Bran breakup. He'd never believe Mariella's side over his wife's, and there was no way she'd bring such drama up during a job interview. She could only make a great impression and hope he saw past her reputation—no matter how unde-served that reputation was.

Her stomach pitched and doubt spiked in her chest, pounding hard as she stepped onto the emblazoned welcome mat outside the grand entrance.

"This is a mistake," she whispered, hesitat-ing. She could go back to the warmth of her car. Call her McCullough cousins and do something else with the day, something that was less likely to leave her feeling like an os-tracized failure.

Her phone buzzed and she dug it out of

her bag. Giovanni's name flashed on the screen. Sliding her finger across the notification, she opened the text message and laughed at her brother's text.

A GIF of Han Solo giving her a thumbs up appeared. *Don't psych yourself out. You'll do great. Just be yourself. Good luck.*

That was Giovanni, always getting behind her goals. She quickly texted out a thank you and silenced her phone. She needed that little reminder that this was just a job interview, not a life or death situation.

Sometimes, she focused too hard on getting everything right and forgot that good things were usually born from chaos. If she hadn't killed a bottle of Jose on Karaoke Wednesday last week at the pub—and performed an inebriated but heartfelt rendition of David Bowie's "Space Oddity" in a horrific British accent while dancing like one of Gladys's pips—she never would have overheard people talking about the manager job at the hotel.

The universe had sent her here for a reason. She should trust that cosmic push and just go with it. Enjoy the journey and stop stressing over the outcome, or some other hippy nonsense that took her out of her ever-Catholic, guilt-ridden head.

She could do this.

Straightening her shoulders, she checked her reflection in the glass doors one last time and took the first steps toward her future. Only, when the sole of her knee-high, leather boot hit the porcelain tile, a chip of ice stuck to her foot and gravity betrayed her.

Her muscles locked as she twisted to catch herself falling through the thin air, her arms pinwheeling and her voice crying out in panic. Her knees crashed against the hard ceramic floor, the impact radiating up to her skull as her palms smacked over the cold tile. The contents of her purse and her résumé went flying.

Dark, ebony hair formed a curtain around her face she desperately needed, as she scrambled for composure. *Nobody saw—*

"Ma'am, are you all right?"

So much for poise.

The heat of the lobby mixed with her scorching mortification, and a clammy sweat broke across her skin. "I'm…"

Was she hurt? She quickly took a mental assessment of her body.

Nope. Just her pride. "…okay," she finished with shaky assurance.

She waited for the embarrassment to ebb as she gingerly tried to stand. Her pencil skirt had hitched up her thighs and her hands stung as she made sure her ass wasn't hanging out.

A chip marred the corner of her freshly manicured nail. *Get off the floor.* Disoriented by the fall, she tried to put herself back in some sort of orderly fashion. The contents of her purse were everywhere. How absolutely humiliating.

Sweeping an arm out, she corralled a mix of cosmetics, tampons, pocket change, and other personal items into her bag as two large, expensive looking male shoes stepped into her vision line. Her stomach flipped, certain they belonged to the owner of the Brick Hotel, husband of the woman who hated her more than anyone else in this town, and the person she was there to impress.

"Let me help you." His deep voice carried an unmistakable air of authority but she couldn't bring herself to look up.

Shaken from the fall and certain she'd just made a complete fool of herself, she only wanted to leave. So much for making a good first impression.

Her eyes burned with frustration and she blinked rapidly. She would not tear up like a big baby, no matter how much she wanted to wail at her unending bad luck.

Locking her jaw and shoving away all signs of shakiness, she dug for any remaining shred of confidence. Forcing herself to lift her gaze, she swept the hair away from her eyes and looked up. "Thank you, Mr. King—"

Her words instantly cut off as her limbs and face went numb. It wasn't Gage King. It was so much worse.

What was he doing there? Where had he come from? How long had he been back? Why now?

As she looked up at those unforgettable blue eyes her soul took another fall, her mind hurtling back in time to a moment when the agony of teenage heartbreak was so poignant it could still sting a decade later.

"Mariella?"

Her heart tumbled into the pit of her stomach as she rasped his name, "Harrison."

His eyes, marked with the fine lines of time, narrowed on her. "Wow. It's been…"

Too long, she thought, her heart pounding against the impenetrable armor she'd encased it in since the day he abandoned her.

"Are you okay?"

Mortified that he saw her fall, she scrambled to gather the rest of her scattered belongings, her motions shaky and her gaze never completely leaving him.

His hair was still thick, but slightly darker than the sun-bleached golden blond it had been in high school. His voice was deeper, and although he was a decade older, his body appeared stronger. Honed and filled out.

Gone was the boy in the letterman jacket. Here, was a man—a devastating man—in a tailored suit reeking of success and authority. And she was the hot mess kneeling on the floor like something a hurricane blew in.

Clambering to her feet in an inelegant twist, she smoothed her pencil skirt over her thighs and quickly tidied her hair. "Harrison," she repeated this time with feigned calm. An unnatural smile trembled to her lips as her heart jackhammered in her chest. "You're back."

For years, she dreamed about all the things she might say if he ever returned. Forgotten fantasies of slapping him rushed to the forefront of her mind, and she curled her fingers into a fist to resist the temptation.

She didn't remember him being so tall. She'd probably miss if she tried to slap him.

On the other hand, the instinct to hurl herself into his arms left her unsteady on her already rickety feet. Every single emotion regarding Harrison Montgomery seemed a perfect paradox of wanting to prove herself a

dignified woman while also wanting to sur-
render every inhibition that controlled her
composure.

She could still recall the feel of his flesh
beneath her tongue and the way his body
trembled and flexed under her touch. A shiver
pulsed through her at the memory of his control slipping and the intense way he would
take her.

"I'm only here for a few days."

Shoving away those inappropriate memories, she locked her knees and met his sapphire stare. "Oh?" She tried for a blasé tone
but grimaced when it only sounded
breathless.

"My dad died."

"Oh." Her façade wilted, instantly replaced
with concern. Ward Montgomery passed
away? This was the first she'd heard. "I'm so
sorry."

He bent down and picked up her résumé.
The mature cut of his hair gave him an air of
sophistication, a direct contrast to the bristle
of his five o'clock shadow.

We could have made the prettiest babies... No.
Her mind could not go there!

"You dropped this." He glanced at her résumé and she suffered a pinch of inadequacy.

He'd obviously moved on from their little

town and found great success. Meanwhile, she was bragging about her time at the community college and experience working at their family's café.

"You're here for an interview?"

She snatched the resume from his hand and tucked it back inside the folder. "Yes," she answered sharply, her spine stiff and posture defensive.

Half of his mouth curled into a smirk. Was he judging her? He had some nerve.

"And I'm late. It was nice seeing you." Blowing him off, she crossed the foyer to the reception desk where the young man watched her with wide eyes.

"Are you okay, ma'am?"

Ma'am? She winced, still feeling like quite the foolish kid despite her age. "I'm fine, thank you. I'm here to see Mr. King."

The desk clerk flushed and his gaze dropped to her blouse. He cleared his throat. "Your um..."

She frowned and glanced at her chest. "Shit." Shoving her purse and résumé on the counter she quickly fastened the buttons that had come loose, wincing as she realized Harrison had also seen her bra. Perfect.

"Are you sure I can't get you some ice?"

"No, I'm fine, thank you." Stuffing down

too many uncomfortable emotions boiling under the surface, she slung her purse over her shoulder and collected her résumé, holding it like a shield across her chest. In the reflection of the mirror behind the reception desk, she spotted Harrison still watching her. "I have an interview with the hotel owner."

"Of course." The clerk lifted the phone to his ear and pressed a button. "Your name?"

"Mariella Mosconi."

She waited, head angled down, but her stare watching the mirror through her lashes. Why was he still there, lingering? Didn't he have somewhere to be?

Harrison proved long ago that he could vanish faster than Houdini. Now would be a perfect time for him to do just that.

The desk clerk spoke softly and set the phone back in its cradle. "Mr. King will be right out."

"Thank you."

She felt Harrison approaching before confirming his nearness with her eyes. Every baby hair on the back of her neck tingled with awareness as her spine tightened and her lungs lost their depth. Shallow breaths added to her unsteadiness.

A large hand—no ring—slid a crisp black business card on the granite counter in front of her, but he didn't stop there. Her breath hitched as the warmth of his body burned through her coat. He stood so close, his clothing caressed hers, the soft brush of fabric whispering erotic memories into her mind.

His presence was so potent she felt his nearness shiver over every inch of her skin.

"I'm in room two-ten." His words were low and discrete, close enough to her ear that his warm breath teased over the sensitive flesh of her throat. "Come see me after your interview. I'll have something on ice. We can celebrate your new job or ice down those knees. Either way, we have some catching up to do."

She shut her eyes and tried not to quiver at the tempting invitation. She wasn't an impetuous teenager anymore, yet her response felt completely juvenile in the most delicious way. Men didn't do this to her. They didn't send jolts of awareness through her belly and leave her panties wet. Only Harrison did that.

It wasn't fair. She didn't want him to have such an effect on her after so many years and after he'd so completely broken her heart.

Long fingers, with nails bitten down to the quick, slid the card closer. Not a business card, but a room card. She couldn't determine if arrogance or an overdue apology motivated him.

She had so many questions. He never even bothered to clean out his locker before he left. He deserted his team, his friends, his entire town without offering a single explanation. But most of all, he abandoned her.

Where had he gone? What had he done for the last ten years? Did he have a wife? A family?

Her heart pinched at the thought.

She stared at the room key, part of her wanting to fling it at him and tell him to go to hell, but her hand covered the card before he could take it away. Even if it was a tawdry proposition, she wanted time to consider what she wanted, and right now, with him standing so close, she could hardly think or spell her name.

Maybe she wanted the overdue opportunity to grill him about where he'd been. *I've got you now, Harrison Montgomery.* He wasn't getting away from her this time. Not without an explanation.

Steady footfalls approached from the corridor off the lobby and Mr. King appeared. "Ms. Mosconi, thank you for coming in."

Harrison stepped back, always an expert

at making a quiet exit. But she felt his withdraw all the same.

She tucked all thoughts of Harrison away with the room key and took Mr. King's proffered hand. "Thank you for taking the time to meet with me."

"Of course. The others are waiting in the boardroom." He waved a hand toward the corridor. "Right this way."

Others? She didn't allow herself to glance back. Her focus was firmly on her future.

The further she moved away from Harrison, the easier she breathed. Until they stepped into the boardroom, greeted by Perrin King's cold glare.

"Mariella Mosconi, this is Mauricio, our banquet manager, Aaliyah, our lead groundskeeper in charge of landscaping and maintenance, and I believe you know my wife, Perrin."

Mariella's hope deflated. She knew, then and there, she wasn't getting the job.

CHAPTER 2

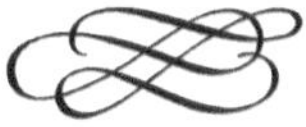

Disguising her discomfort, Mariella flattened a firm hand on her knee to stop the incessant tapping of her foot beneath the boardroom table. Luckily, the carpet muffled most of the sound, but the pitcher of water set at the center of the meeting table quivered with each nervous twitch.

She grinned at the four faces seated across from her. Mr. King provided each of them with a leather portfolio and notepad, emblazoned with the hotel's logo, in case anyone wanted to jot down notes during the interview.

As the orchestrator of the interview and person with the final say, Mr. King made a few notes based on her answers, but his handwriting was too small for Mariella to read from her position across the table. Mauricio asked several questions about her experience with events and her preferences when working with a team. Aaliyah didn't say much, and Perrin mostly glared at Mariella, as if imagining ways to burn her at the stake.

"Outside of your experiences listed on your resume, what kind of proficiency could you bring to the Brick Hotel?" Mr. King asked.

Mariella's resume wasn't what anyone would call extensive, but every bullet point—big or small—had earned her best effort. She was a hard worker who put pride in everything she attempted.

"I know managing a café isn't as elaborate as managing a hotel, but I did that job while earning my bachelor's in business administration. No matter how challenging my classes were or how busy the café was, I never lost my cool. We had diverse customers with different needs, and I met those needs, every day. I made sure the other employees knew how to meet those needs as well. I took great pride in remembering the preferences of our regulars and our…not so regulars. People notice my attention to detail and appreciate it. I think it's important to put others at ease and always make sure the clientele feels valued and heard. That's how you get them to come back."

She didn't see the point in mentioning that the café was owned by her mom and two aunts, a front for their competitive and highly skilled obsession with out-baking each other. Of course, she was the manager. The three sisters knew very little about running a business and would give the inventory away for compliments alone if left unsupervised. Mariella had actually been able to turn a lucrative profit from the place.

Perrin tapped her pen over the closed leather cover of her portfolio. "If a guest requested a service that went beyond hotel policy, what would you do?"

It was the first time she addressed Mariella directly. Mariella wasn't ready to make eye contact, so she focused on the shoulder of Perrin's flannel shirt. Despite being more dressed down than the groundskeeper, she was still intimidating.

"I suppose I would offer whatever was within the hotel policy, based on my training for such situations."

"But this is a very particular, and difficult, guest. We wouldn't want to lose him as a future guest."

"In that case, I'd defer to Mr. King."

"Would you now?"

Her question felt like a trap, so she glanced at her prospective boss.

Mr. King cleared his throat, and Mariella wondered if his wife's interrogation made him as uncomfortable as it made her. He didn't intervene, and Mariella's feet started to sweat inside of her boots.

"Suppose Mr. King isn't around," Perrin persisted.

"I could call him—"

"Have you made a point of contacting past employers at home on their days off?"

"No, I mean, my aunt owned the café, and if there was ever a problem I could always—"

"As manager, the tough decisions won't always allow time to confer. You would be expected to think on your feet. Mr. King might own the hotel, but his presence is needed elsewhere. It would be inappropriate to contact him when his focus is needed somewhere else."

She got it. This woman didn't want her contacting her husband. Message received loud and clear.

"I…" Boundaries were one thing, but Mariella refused to come off as incompetent. "I'm sure there will be adequate training for situations such as the one you described that will help any manager subdue an unhappy guest. Once I know the hotel's policies, I doubt there would be much need to contact or involve Mr. King."

"As your supervisor, he might want to stay informed—"

"I think we're getting off on a tangent." Mr. King mercifully redirected the conversation and neutralized the hostility Mariella sensed radiating from his wife. "I wouldn't hire a manager I didn't trust to make the proper decisions, and a daily email will be more than enough communication, once our staff is fully up and running. Also, Mauricio is a great sounding board, and if there's ever a complication too great to solve between two directors, *with* the hotel's policies in place, I'd hope someone *would* contact me. In all my companies, I pride myself for being available to any level employee."

She appreciated him defusing the situation. It wasn't easy being the target of someone's hate. Nor was it fair. She could have held Perrin just as responsible for her humiliation, but Mariella thought Bran deserved the majority of the blame. They were both victims of the same cheating asshole.

Perrin obviously moved on and married a better, handsome, incredibly successful man.

Mariella had no one. She hadn't even been with anyone since Bran. Couldn't Perrin see she was the winner of this stupid rivalry and back off?

"Do you expect any conflicts between your personal life and holiday events?" Mauricio asked. "Guests often book weddings and parties over holidays, like New Year's Eve, Passover, Labor Day, and so on, to get better rates."

Glad for the simpler question, Mariella smiled. "I don't have a personal life." She blanched the moment the confession slipped out. "I mean, no, that shouldn't be a problem."

Perrin had her so rattled, any attempt at sounding remotely sophisticated had gone out the window. Mauricio smiled, as if she'd made a cute joke, and Perrin's eyes narrowed. It hadn't been a joke, just brutal honesty. But maybe playing it off as a joke made her look like less of a loser.

Already exhausted from pretending she belonged there, Mariella questioned if she even had a shot at this point. Whether Mr. King thought her suitable for the job or not, she bet Perrin had the final say, and there was no doubt the woman would have plenty to say about her husband hiring her nemesis.

Deferred to simple honesty, Mariella gave

them the humble truth. "Look, I still live at home with my parents because I have student loans to pay off. I'm single, so I'm excited to start a career. I want that sort of meaningful commitment in my life. I don't have kids, or a husband, or pets, so if there's ever an emergency at the hotel, or an event that requires my presence, I shouldn't have an issue being here."

"Well, we wouldn't expect any of our staff to totally sacrifice their personal life for their job," Mr. King joked. "We want happy employees, which is why we offer a great personal package. But it's good to know that you're available if needed. I appreciate your flexibility."

And Mariella appreciated his easygoing manner. "I'm only right down the road, and I rarely travel out of town." How could she with the oppressive debt of college looming? She needed to start paying off her loans.

This was the first job she'd found offering a competitive salary with benefits. Not only could she chip away at her debt, she could eventually afford her own place.

"Suppose a guest approaches you because they've been locked out of their room." Perrin's thumb clicked the top of her pen. "The manager has a master key. What do you do?"

Mariella wondered if the boss's wife sat in on all the interviews or just hers. "First, I'd ask them to accompany me to the lobby where I'd run their name and information through the system."

"How would you know if they were giving you their real name?"

"I suppose I could ask for their identification, but if they don't have their key, they might not have their wallet. I guess I'd have to trust my instincts. If everything checked out and I didn't suspect any shifty business, I'd create a duplicate key." It wasn't like Jasper Falls had A-List celebrities or government officials visiting on the regular.

Mr. King nodded, appearing satisfied with her answer. "Such procedures and policies are outlined in the company manual."

All of Perrin's questions revolved around her obvious distrust for Mariella. Luckily, Mr. King appeared unfazed and continued to describe some of the aforementioned policies.

Mariella's mind flashed to the man upstairs. Thoughts of Harrison led her to thoughts of Bran. She truly had a terrible track record with men.

She wondered, if Harrison had not broken her heart so completely, would she have put up with Bran's crap for so long? Bran had always been disconnected, which, in hindsight, looked extremely suspicious. But Mariella had been so determined to protect her heart from breaking again, she used Bran's shady distance as another layer of armor.

Despite the public humiliation and impact on her reputation, the pain of her and Bran's breakup was nothing compared to the absolute agony she suffered when Harrison left Jasper Falls. How could that be? How could a teenage fling come close to comparing with an adult relationship?

The truth was, it didn't. There was no comparison. What she'd felt for Harrison was bigger than anything she'd ever experienced with Bran or anyone else.

She nodded as Mr. King continued to explain his vision for the hotel, but her mind remained on the guest upstairs in room two-ten. In a few minutes this interview would end and she'd have to make a decision.

Harrison was dangerous. He made her feel too many things.

She wasn't a foolish kid anymore, and she needed to think several steps ahead if she wanted to reach her goals. Harrison would only distract her. Not distract her with a relationship, of course, because she wasn't foolish enough to even think such a thing was possible with him. But the pain of losing him again, even after only a split second of seeing him back in Jasper Falls, could send her into a headspace from which it could take months to recover.

Harrison wasn't the sort of guy women should build plans around. He was anti-commitment in every sense of the word. A simple conversation could make him claustrophobic. And she knew better than to think he'd changed.

Glaring at the doorknob-sized engagement ring on Perrin's finger, nestled snugly against the platinum wedding band, a sense of inadequacy swallowed Mariella. What was she even doing here? She was making an ass of herself.

As the boilerplate dialogue carried on, it became clear Mr. King was merely letting the sand run out of the hourglass. Someone with his level of success would know this script by heart. And as he seamlessly wrapped up the interview, never once giving any real implication that she didn't stand a chance for the job, Mariella somehow felt his dismissal down to her soul.

"Do you have any questions for us?" Mr. King finally asked.

A painful throb beat in her knee from

where she'd fallen in the lobby and tension knotted in her shoulders as discomfort transformed into indignation. They knew she wasn't getting the job, so why pretend like she stood a chance?

It wasn't fair. She was as good a candidate as anyone else, perhaps the most qualified person they'd find living in their town, but none of that mattered. At this point, she had nothing left to lose.

She lifted her chin and met his stare. "I'd just like to say, I'm a hard worker and I take pride in every job I do. I love Jasper Falls, and as someone who's lived here all of her life, I know a lot about the area. I want to see our town grow and prosper. I went into the service field because I enjoy putting others at ease, but if that is somehow a drawback for you, then maybe I'm not the right woman for the job. I'm professional and congenial. I bring a warm and welcoming presence wherever I go, which is something I think you'd want in a hotel manager."

She forced her eyes to meet Perrin's stare. "And I'm honest. I know I'm not perfect, and I don't have a lot of experience, but if I'm unsure about something, I'm not afraid to ask questions. I would never intentionally do anything to hurt someone else, including my employer or the company that employs me. That's the truth, whether you believe it or not."

Every muscle inside her body quaked as she waited for some form of response. She wasn't a confrontational person, and she hated the way this interview had gone, but she would not let Perrin leave the others with an undeserved impression of her. Her past mistakes should not define her. And it was Perrin who had been the other woman!

Mr. King closed the cover of his leather portfolio and stood. "I think we have everything we need. Thank you, Ms. Mosconi." He shook her hand when she rose. "You should have an answer by the end of the week."

"Thank you for your time."

"We'll be in touch."

She escaped the room, avoiding Perrin's stare on the way out. As she approached the lobby, she reached into her coat pocket for her car keys, but rather than find jagged metal, her fingers closed around smooth plastic.

She withdrew the black keycard and her steps slowed as she stared at the logo of the hotel. Her heart jittered with uncertainty as warning bells clattered through her mind, much louder than the whispering impulse to do something reckless.

Yet the impulse to heedlessly throw caution to the wind grew louder and louder the longer she stared at the keycard in her hand. After such a disastrous interview, she felt like saying fuck it all.

Harrison said he'd have something on ice, and she needed a drink. She wanted to tune the world out and forget everything for a while, just get lost and not feel this unending pressure to be the mature adult.

She glanced at the elevator door and then at the entrance into the lobby. The desk clerk was on the phone, his gaze focused on the computer. No one from the interview had followed her out of the boardroom.

Before sensibility could step in and ruin everything, she hit the call button and the elevator opened. She rushed inside and muttered, "Some things never change." Her chipped nail stabbed into the button for the second floor just as her stomach dropped down to her toes.

CHAPTER 3

The elevator deposited her on the second floor and the doors closed at her back. Mariella pivoted, instantly regretting her decision, but the illuminated numbers overhead tracked the elevator to the fifth floor.

"Shit." She pressed the call button anxiously and waited.

What was she thinking? She couldn't meet Harrison in his private room. What did she think would happen?

Well, she knew what would happen—*hoped* something might happen—and damn her for falling right back into the same gullible trap she had years ago.

Why wasn't the elevator moving? It seemed stuck on five.

But what if she did go through with it? What if she found his room, knocked, and just kissed him the moment he opened the door?

Her heart misfired about her ribs as thrilling possibilities flashed through her mind. Flesh on flesh. Mouths biting and tongues licking. God, it had been so long since she'd had decent sex.

But Harrison was never just sex. No. With him, it was a form of possession. Almost sacramental, like she was promising her soul to something untouchable and all-powerful.

Jesus, she needed to get the hell out of there. Her finger stabbed into the glowing call button, but the elevator remained frozen on five.

Would he let her? Of course, he would. He was a man. She could picture him lifting her off her feet and kicking the door shut as she wrapped her legs around his hips.

"Shit." Her stare drilled into the numbers above the door. "Come on," she hissed.

She needed to calm down. Forcing her hand into her pocket so as not to break the elevator, she traced her thumb along the edge of smooth plastic. His room key was more than a blanket invitation to contact him. That was a pass into the place where he slept. Because really, what were hotel rooms aside from four walls and a bed?

Her stomach swooped as another collage of sensual images rushed through her mind. Maybe this was exactly what she needed. He was only visiting after all. If she knew from the start what she was getting into, what harm was there in a little dalliance?

She could have control. *She* could be the one to walk away.

Technically, she could call it self-care.

Okay, that was reaching.

She pinched the bridge of her nose and looked up at the numbers. "Are you kidding me?" Still on five. She searched the hall for signs to a stairwell, which carried her deeper down the corridor and further away from the elevator.

She'd never had an official booty call and wasn't sure if she could handle something so casual, even with someone less important than Harrison. It was weird, she and Harrison had never labeled themselves as an official couple, but there had never been anything casual about them. That was why his abandonment hurt so much in the end. She'd always thought she meant more to him than she actually had.

Shame or regret or something equally icky

filled her, and she started to panic. Where the hell were the emergency exits in this place?

As her feet rushed over the tread of the Williamsburg floral carpet, she tried to escape the truth she didn't want to face. He probably hadn't thought of her since the day he left. They were a high school fling, for God's sake. He probably had a dozen women since her—maybe more.

Her stomach soured at the thought.

Or maybe this wasn't about sex at all, and she was reading way too far into his invitation. What if this was just a way to catch up after lost time? It had been ten years. He might not even find her attractive anymore.

He probably remembered her as the little freshman who followed him around moon-eyed until the night she forced him to acknowledge her. Girls weren't supposed to get hung up on the guy they lost their virginity to unless they ended up marrying him.

Long-term commitment had never been what her and Harrison were about. Her lingering emotions for him only proved how pathetic her relationship history was. God, she needed to get out more and start dating again.

Her stomach swooped and her steps halted as she stared at the numbers on the wall. *210.* Subconsciously she knew the stairwell was just around the corner, but she pre-tended it didn't exist. What a funny, fire hazard design for a hotel with absolutely no way out of the second floor except through Harrison Montgomery's room.

Reason had stepped out, and in its place came some sort of Lewis Carroll narrative where she was Alice, far beyond the looking glass. The illogical side of her brain teamed up with her woman parts and flexed, already claiming victory. No denying part of her still wanted him, while the other parts of her—mainly her heart, which had the memory of an elephant—wanted to run away and hide.

Staring at the door, her fist tightened until her knuckles popped.

Knock.

Just do it.

Be reckless. Have fun for a change and forgive yourself.

You need this.

But no matter how much she wanted to let go, her body remained paralyzed, her heart knowing all too well that Harrison Mont-gomery wasn't something she could simply shut off. He was a live wire, a hot fuse, and she would surely end up burned in the end.

So why wasn't she leaving? Surely the ele-vator had returned by now. What was it about this man that made him so magnetic? She was helpless under his spell. Even now, when she knew—*knew*—she could not go down this path with him again.

Harrison had been a star on the varsity football team. Devastatingly gorgeous, with eyes so bright and mysterious, anyone could tell he hid a big secret.

There was something so untouchable about him, something girls wanted to unlock, but he never allowed anyone close enough to fully see the real him. Yet every once in a while, she'd glimpse the raw side of him, so vulnerable and aching, he'd let her soothe him, but only for a moment and then it was gone.

For the most part, he kept himself locked up. But those secrets he hid, Mariella knew they caused him to run away—from his hometown, his high school diploma, his planned future, and her.

Maybe he thought he could fool her, but he never could. Even now, with his purposefully refined clothing and that air of sophistication he put on downstairs, she recognized the intensity boiling under the surface. Some men simply weren't made to be gentlemen, and Harrison Montgomery was one of those men.

Perhaps his private nature was part of the allure. She wanted to unravel him. Did that make her as pathetic as all the other girls that wanted him before?

Looking down at the room key, she considered her three options. Knock, enter, or get the hell out of there before she got hurt.

A vision of her younger self sobbing into her pillow, wondering what she'd done wrong, filled her mind, and she stepped back as if her fingers were just burned.

Forgotten pain knifed through her. This was a mistake.

Backing away from his door, she pivoted just as the handle clicked, and her spine stiffened, sending her shoulders bunching up to her ears.

"Mariella?"

Her breath chilled in her chest. Every muscle froze at the deep timbre of his voice. He had such power over her, she didn't trust her subconscious, thinking she'd purposely come this far so he'd catch her. Some self-sabotaging part of her wanted this to happen so she'd be forced to face him and get the answers she'd waited more than a decade to hear.

A warm hand brushed over her shoulder and down her arm, sending a sharp shiver up her spine. "Were you leaving? Come in and have a drink with me."

Her eyes closed. The word *no* cemented like a boulder in her throat, but she couldn't get it out.

His touch caressed the hand hanging numbly at her side, brushing softly across her knuckles until her fists unclenched and he could lace his fingers with hers.

"Come on, Mariella. It's been too long not to catch up. Come inside."

And that was all it took. Her tension slackened, and she followed him inside like a foolish lamb off to the slaughter.

CHAPTER 4

"How'd your interview go?"

He still wore his suit, but he'd removed the jacket and tie. The pants were a unique slate blue, like his eyes, and his cuffs were French, secured with gold cufflinks in the shape of his initials, HM.

This wasn't the same kid she used to fool around with in high school. This was a man who lived way outside of her pay grade. New inadequacies mounted, compressing the towering old ones that still remained.

She shook her head, feeling like a small-town hick in the shadow of his success.

"That good, huh?" He chuckled and went to the mini fridge. "Well then, how about that drink?"

Her gaze settled on his socked feet. The

men she knew didn't wear dress socks like that. She was in way over her head. "I really can't stay."

He turned and frowned, a small bottle filling his large hand. "Do you have somewhere to be?"

"I just wanted to say it was nice seeing you and…goodbye." While he might not believe in goodbyes, most people with manners and common courtesy did.

"Mar—"

"Goodbye, Harrison." She turned and left the room without rushing. He didn't come after her, which was a relief as much as an insult.

When she reached the elevator, the illuminated numbers said it was on the first floor. She pressed the button and heard it shuttling closer.

"My dad died." His voice was low, but it carried from the far end of the hall and somehow whispered into her ear.

"Not fair, Harrison." There was no way he could have heard her hushed utterance, but he didn't need to. He knew exactly what he was doing, using his father's death as some sort of truce he didn't deserve from her.

He closed the distance and took her hand just as the elevator doors opened. "That's why

I'm back in Jasper Falls," he explained, but she'd already figured out as much—certain his return had nothing to do with her.

Her head lowered. "Harrison…"

"I could use a friend."

They weren't friends. Friends checked in. They called.

Yet somehow their connection went deeper than friendship. Somehow she knew he wasn't telling her of his father's passing to simply state facts. He was confessing the conflicting emotions tied a man whom he did not share any real father-son bond. Why did she know that? And what, exactly, was her responsibility here?

He waited her out in typical Harrison fashion, refusing to communicate in words but implying everything he wanted her to know in the weighted silence they shared.

Ward Montgomery owned the hardware store and had been a beloved member of their community. Kids rarely considered other kids' parents beyond rating if they were mean or nice, boring or fun. Ward came off as nice and boring, just a piece of their town's backdrop, the old hardware store owner.

But through her experiences with Harrison, she had a hunch there was more to the man than tools and a polite, *"Have a nice day."*

Harrison often left his house angry and worked up. He never wanted to talk about it, but as she and Harrison grew closer, she took a protective position in his life.

Mariella didn't have any real reason other than instinct, but she was never as impressed with Ward Montgomery as the rest of the town. And in small towns, there was no escaping a funeral, especially when it honored a longstanding member of the community. So there would be no escaping Harrison.

"I'm sorry for your loss," she repeated, her hand slightly tightening around his.

"I'm glad he's gone." The ice in his tone sent a chill through the air, and her gaze cut to his face.

His cold expression confirmed, once more, that he had problems with his father. He'd left town when it was well known he was meant to take over the hardware store when Ward retired. What would happen to the store now that Ward was gone? Selfishly, she wondered if Harrison would be forced to stay, but his contempt for his father and this town warned that would never be the case.

"I could use someone to talk to."

Did he really want to talk? Or was he asking for something more? Part of her wanted to give him that something more, despite what it might cost her. She wanted to comfort him.

"How long are you here?" If she was going to stay, for even a few minutes, she deserved to know. "The truth, Harrison."

"A few days, tops. Erin wants a funeral, but as soon as that's over, I'm gone."

And nothing would make him stay. Just like before. Not even her.

Maybe this time she'd be more prepared.

His thumb brushed over her knuckles. "I thought about you."

Her eyes closed. "Harrison, you can't say stuff like that."

"Why? It's true."

She didn't believe him, but she also wasn't completely sure he was lying. "Do you honestly think it's wise for us to be alone together?" She still didn't know for sure if he had a wife or a girlfriend or maybe an ex-wife, possibly some children. A lot could happen in ten years.

His stare traveled over her body, dipping to her chest and rising to her eyes. "Honestly?"

She nodded. "Honesty would be nice."

He rubbed the dark golden stubble of his jaw. "Well, honestly, I've been in a murderous mood since my sister called this morning. I thought of all the reasons my dad deserved to die on my drive here but found no relief in finding him gone. It's like he's still alive, even though he's not. And feeling his presence around me makes me want to hit something. I actually considered leaving and letting Erin handle all the funeral shit. But then you came tumbling back into my life, and I stopped thinking about my dad all together."

"Why?"

"Because I honestly can't think of anything other than how much I'd enjoy fucking you in those leather boots and that sexy bra I saw earlier."

And just like that, her panties were ruined. "You didn't answer my question."

He arched a brow. "Do I think it's wise? Yes, Mariella, I think the two of us fucking is one of the wisest things I can do while stuck in this fishbowl of a town. My mouth between your thighs might be the only way of keeping me out of a barroom brawl tonight, because no matter what happens, I plan on getting good and drunk before the hour's up." He gave her hand a gentle tug. "Let's get you out of that skirt."

Her heart tripped as she fell into step beside him. She had not waxed for this.

CHAPTER 5

_H_arrison couldn't believe she was actually coming back to his room. This had been a wretched trip home for a miserable cause.

His sister, Erin, was a mess when he got to the house. He had no choice but to go inside. He'd sworn years ago that he'd never step foot in that place again, but seeing his little sister so distraught and confused did something to him.

He should have protected her better. He should have come back and made sure she got out of there, but he hadn't because he was a selfish prick who couldn't see past his own trauma and pain.

He would prefer setting himself on fire than deal with any of this shit. And no matter how sorry he was that his sister had been exposed to their dad's abuse a decade longer than him, he still considered bailing on her now. That's how fucked up he was when it came to anything having to do with his rotten, bastard of a father.

Mariella had been an unexpected and welcomed surprise. He was shocked not to find a wedding ring on her finger and wondered if she'd been married at some point because he couldn't imagine her making it this long and remaining single.

So many questions. So little time.

"The rooms are nice," she edged her way into the main area without fully leaving the path to the door.

He wasn't sure how it was possible, but she looked better than she had in high school. The roundness of her cheeks had sharpened and her heart-shaped face was more defined. Her sly, smoky eyes and fuller lips left no mistake that she was now a woman.

Of course, she was wiser. It had been more than a decade since he last saw her. He'd be a fool to think she hadn't changed.

His mind flashed to the day he'd left Jasper Falls. He'd been a total jerk, not saying goodbye to her, but he needed to leave and he feared seeing her one last time might persuade him to stay. If he tried to say goodbye and she cried or asked him not to go, he would have wavered.

Back then, he couldn't risk that. He needed to do the dick thing and just go. No goodbyes. No explanations. No excuses.

He figured he'd never see her again, but in the rare chance that he might, he was almost certain she'd never forgive him. Yet here she was.

"So how about that drink?" He could use a strong one.

She lingered by the bathroom, still not fully entering the room. He set two glasses on the coffee table. Maybe she'd be more comfortable if they sat on the sleeper sofa and ignored the bed. Although he'd made no secret of his intentions in the hall.

"Have a seat."

She looked incredible in that professional little skirt that hugged her hips and that blouse that barely constrained her tits.

"The rooms are nice." She slowly stepped deeper into the room, working her way to the window that overlooked the view of Main Street.

The interior design was traditional but contemporary, a nice blend down the middle of modern amenities and colonial charm. Everything still smelled new.

He filled the glasses with ice from the bucket. "So how did your interview really go?"

She slipped off her coat only to fold if over her arm. He wanted her to sit down.

He had a bottle of white wine sent up in hopes that she'd show. He also had a bottle of whiskey delivered in case she didn't.

"It doesn't matter. I won't get the job."

"Oh?" He removed the foil and twisted the screw of the wine key into the cork.

She sighed. "The owner's wife hates me."

He frowned, unsure who owned the hotel. "Who's the owner?"

"Right, you haven't lived here in over ten years. Doesn't Erin keep you up to date on the town gossip?"

"We're not as close as we used to be." That was an understatement.

"Oh, well, the owner is Gage King."

He looked at her in question. Was that name supposed to mean something to him?

"He owns King Construction," she explained.

"The outlet chain?" He recognized the name because his father used to bitch and moan that box stores like King's were going to put their hardware store out of business.

"Yeah."

"What the hell's he doing in Jasper Falls?"

Kings was no small operation. It was a public company, and Harrison owned a few shares for the simple fact that it would piss off his dad.

"He fell in love with Perrin Harris."

The fruity scent of pressed grapes permeated the room as he filled her glass. "He's with Perrin?"

"They're married. She's now Perrin King." She popped the *p* of the other woman's name as if the match didn't impress her.

He frowned. "I thought she was marrying Bran Dawson."

She rolled her eyes and tossed the coat on the bed. "I'm not surprised that story somehow reached you. Her and Bran broke up. Turns out he was cheating on her with someone else."

Small towns always had the biggest gossips. "Who was the other woman?"

She crossed to the sitting area and accepted a glass, frowning at the cubes floating on top. "Ice?"

"It didn't come chilled."

Their fingers brushed, and she took a step away.

Okay, she wanted to take things slow. He could do that, but he wanted to get to the real conversation so they could shed the awkward niceties.

She took a sip then met his stare. "It's been a decade. Are we really going to waste time talking about Perrin?"

He paused, remembering how little Mariella cared for small talk. Or was it small talk? He grinned, her bitter tone spiking his interest. "You don't like Perrin."

"I like everyone. But *Mrs*. King definitely doesn't like me."

He smirked and lowered to the sofa. "Now I'm intrigued." He waved a hand inviting her to join him on the small settee. "What did you do to make her dislike you?"

She opened her mouth, and he anxiously awaited whatever flippant comment might come, but then all playfulness left her expression. "It doesn't matter. No matter how I explain it, I look like the bad guy." She sat down, taking a long sip of wine and it clicked. Mariella was the woman that broke up Perrin's engagement. But that wasn't her. There had to be more to the story.

"Try me."

She blew out a breath and pressed her back into the cushion, getting more comfortable. "Well, after you left, Bran and I sort of became a thing."

"He's not what I would consider your type, but okay." He'd hoped she hadn't been too broken up over his leaving, even though he despised the thought of her with anyone else.

She laughed without humor. "Well, that was the problem. According to Bran, I wasn't his type either—not for big things anyway. He wanted to sleep with me, but he had no interest in marrying me or bringing me home to meet his family. He spent years making excuses and I spent years gobbling them up."

"I'm afraid to ask where Perrin comes in."

"She comes in a few years later when I was preoccupied with college. He started to date her behind my back, but after a while, when he realized Perrin had something I didn't, she somehow became the front runner, and I became his dirty little secret." She swallowed back the rest of her wine, and he graciously refilled her glass. "Then he proposed to her."

"He asked Perrin to marry him when he was still dating you?"

"That's right. But no one knew he was dating me."

"What an asshole. Did you know he proposed to her?"

"I didn't even know they talked. I had suspicions there was someone else, but I always assumed they were meaningless conquests or women from the next town over."

"Why would you tolerate that?"

She shrugged. "I was too busy to care. Or too lazy to make a fuss. My mind was focused on school, and I figured I'd eventually deal with his deception, never once expecting he flat out asked someone else to marry him. I mean, I thought he had major commitment issues."

"So how did you find out?"

She laughed coldly. "I found out the same way everyone else did, when I read the announcement in the paper. Then, I was just..." She shook her head and looked down at her lap, her soft brow slightly pinching. "I was the mistress."

"But you weren't. Not really, if you were dating him first."

"That didn't matter. Everyone else saw it differently. Gossip traveled like brushfire and now women hold their men a little tighter when I'm around."

Mariella had never been one to care what others thought of her, but this one seemed to really get to her. It seemed unfair that she might wear a label she didn't deserve.

"Hey." He scooted closer, looking into her dark eyes. "You're too good to be anyone's mistress."

"But still not good enough to be someone's wife."

He winced, figuring this was why she still wasn't married. "Perrin Harris doesn't have anything you don't."

"Oh, please. Everyone in Jasper Falls knows she's the prettiest—"

"Hey." He lifted her chin with his knuckle. "She has *nothing* on you, Mariella. Bran Dawson's a tool. He deserved to lose you."

A soft blush covered the high arch of her cheekbones. "You're sweet." She sipped her wine, the motion removing his hold of her face. "What about you? Any marriages or mad love affairs in the past ten years?"

"I had a few close calls with some gold diggers and a two-year relationship with a woman who never knew much more than my phone number."

"Is that your way of telling me you're successful?"

"I do all right."

She glanced at his pants, inspecting the

material with a quick brush of her fingertips. His cock twitched.

"How much was your suit?"

"What?"

"Your suit. How much?"

He chuckled. "I don't know."

"Liar."

"I really don't." He tried not to laugh, but, for some reason, she always made him feel a little lighter, like nothing was really that serious. "My personal shopper picked them up."

"Oh, my God, you have a personal shopper? Gross."

"What can I say? I'm *bougie*."

"Well, I can't even afford knockoff labels."

"I don't think Jasper Falls is much for designer labels, so I think you might be safe there."

"You'd be surprised. We're really moving up in the world. Last month we got our first Uber driver, and we're on the short list for another cell tower. Pretty soon, we'll be able to get rid of our land lines like the rest of the world."

"I stand corrected." He couldn't resist the opening. Reaching for her ankle, he lifted the heel of her knee-high leather boot to his lap, tipping her back onto the settee. "And what about these?"

"Those old things? I think I bought them on consignment at the church rummage sale a few years back."

His hand traced over the leather until his fingers found the warm flesh of her thigh. She sank deeper into the settee, not bothering to stop him. "They look designer."

She raised a brow as if to say they would never know then asked, "So what happened to the two-year woman who didn't know more than your phone number?"

"Her time was up. I lost interest and moved on."

"Just like that?"

"Just like that."

Her gaze cut away. "I guess some things never change."

"Mariella, it wasn't like that with us."

She sat up and flattened her skirt over her knees. "No, I'm sure she got a goodbye."

When she put her glass on the table beside the ice bucket, he caught her hand. "I was young."

"You were older than me."

"I was stupid."

"You were cruel."

Her words cut through the air like a guillotine and he released her hand. "I never intentionally meant to hurt you. That was the last thing I wanted to do."

Her lips pressed tight, and he hated the quiver of her chin. If she cried, it would be his penance. He deserved that and worse for ghosting her like he had, but he wished there was a way to make her understand why he needed to go without explaining all the terrible things he'd been trying to escape.

"I'm sorry I hurt you."

She looked at him, the whites of her eyes no longer as clear. "It still hurts when I think of that little girl lying awake at night wondering what she did wrong."

"You did nothing wrong. There was nothing you could have done to make me stay."

She choked out a laugh. "Wow. Is that supposed to make it hurt less?"

"I mean, you didn't do anything to make me go. It wasn't about us. It was about me. It was something I just needed to do. And if I would have come to you to say goodbye, you would have asked questions I couldn't answer. You would have asked me to stay, and I couldn't. Please believe me when I say I had no other choice."

"Can you answer my questions now?"

Tension knotted in his shoulders. He

thought about his father's cold body laid out in the county morgue. If the bastard was finally dead, why did his demons seem more alive than ever?

It was this town. He hated this tiny, picture-perfect town where everything appeared fine on the surface but nothing more than bullshit lies rested under the surface.

"No, it's not meant to make it hurt less. I hurt you, and I'm sorry. Nothing I say now can undo what's been done."

She scoffed. "So why say anything at all? I mean, it's been a decade. Moment's over, Harrison."

If it was over, he wouldn't feel the heat of their lingering chemistry now. "Because I despise knowing my selfish choices caused you a second of pain. If there had been any way to avoid that, I would have, but there wasn't. Not at the time."

She was silent for a long moment but then she nodded, accepting his apology. She slid her wine glass closer to the bottle, silently requesting another refill. He topped off both their glasses, emptying the bottle.

"Do you want to talk about your dad?"

"Not even a little. Do you want to talk about your interview?"

"Nope."

His hand lowered to her thigh, slowly gathering the soft suede of her skirt. "How's your knee."

"It hurts."

"I can put some ice on it for you."

She looked at him with a knowing smirk. Swiping her glass off the table, she sat back, knees cocked open in invitation. He reached into the ice bucket and fished out a cube, pressing it to the area of her knee that bore a slight bruise.

Her skin was hot, melting the ice as he dragged it upward. Her lashes lowered as he followed her inner thigh, his hand disappearing under her skirt.

"I meant what I said at the elevator."

She looked at him, her cheeks flushed and her eyes heavy. "I didn't say no."

"So is that a yes?"

Her brow twitched and her gaze never left his. She scooted lower, only opening her mouth to sip her wine. She was as sexy as he remembered—more so. Adulthood suited her.

Nudging the coffee table back, he lowered to the carpet and fit himself between her legs. The ice melted to nothing and he grinned, reaching into the bucket for another cube. His soft caress explored her flesh, finding something so familiar in touching her but also something new and exciting.

They weren't kids anymore. No curfews. No finals tomorrow. No impending doom of having to decide their entire future by graduation. No fear that they couldn't handle a *complication* if one should arise. They could do whatever the hell they wanted, and he wanted to fuck her six ways into next week.

He traced a cool line up her other thigh, the ice cube nothing more than a chip of cool slush under the heat of his touch at this point. When he grazed the hot seam of her panties, she gasped.

"I should tell you no."

"Then tell me no."

She laughed, her body languid and melting under his exploring touch. "I never could."

"Are you telling me to keep going?" His finger traced the damp silk separating him from heaven. He wanted nothing more than to sink his body into hers, fingers first, then his tongue, and eventually his cock.

"Yes, but you better make it worth my while."

He growled, fisting the wet gusset of her panties and yanking her forward. He rose on his knees, stealing a kiss from those tempting lips and showing her without words how much he wanted her.

How had he forgotten how good her mouth could taste, how wild her hungry eyes could drive him? Mariella was never like the other girls in high school. There was always something potent and intense hiding beneath her calm surface. Back then, she didn't do things the way others did at their age, and now she didn't kiss him the way most women kissed.

He kissed her full lips with bruising force and she welcomed it. Mouth gasping, her tongue swept across his in teasing invitation, as her fingers fisted his hair. The pristine façade of any reserve shattered as she bit at his mouth, yanking him closer and greedily meeting his desire head on.

Clothing shifted as his fingers searched urgently for more. He meant what he said about keeping the boots on, but the panties had to go.

"Rip 'em. I don't care." Her body shifted closer, her narrow skirt hiking up her hips.

Snapping the fine material of her panties, he shoved her knees wide. Glistening pink flesh called to him and he dove forward to steal a taste.

The seating area was too cramped for him

to have her the way he wanted. And she was over dressed. Biting at her plush inner thigh, he tugged at her blouse.

"You have too many clothes on, and this sofa is too damn small." He wanted her naked, in only the boots, and he wanted her now.

Her laughter tickled his ears, teasing and mocking his struggle as he tore at her clothes. He yanked her off the settee and hoisted her over his shoulder, smacking a hand over the round curve of her ass as he carried her to the king size bed.

"How is it that you're even sexier than you were in high school?"

"I could say the same for you."

He tossed her down on the coverlet. "Clothes. Off. Now." They both stripped quickly. "The boots stay on."

Kicking off her skirt and scraps of her panties she lay back, completely naked except for those stiletto leather boots she bought on consignment. A cloud of ebony waves encircled her smiling face. Curves of flawless olive skin begged for his touch.

Jesus, she was perfect.

How was it, that in all his exploits with the opposite sex, he'd never seen another woman as pretty as she? He swallowed tightly, overcome with some sort of nostalgia or déjà vu.

He wasn't prepared for whatever feelings she was triggering.

"Harrison?"

He cleared his throat to hide the effect she was having on him. He thought it might be awkward revisiting this part of his past, but nothing had ever felt so natural.

"Goddamn, you're sexy." He caught her booted foot and brought it to his shoulder, pressing a soft kiss on the tender flesh of her thigh.

Her smile softened and she stretched languidly beneath him, not a single reservation in her whiskey brown eyes. Crawling over her, bending her body beneath his, he traced his tongue along her throat.

A fist gripped in his hair, demanding his attention, and he looked at her. "Don't hold back, Harrison."

He never could when it came to Mariella. "I won't."

He gripped the tender flesh of her ass and squeezed, dropping his mouth to her breasts and sucking her nipples into hard points. Her body was familiar, and there was a sense of nostalgic homecoming that unraveled as he explored and relearned her curves. He savored every exposed inch of beauty laid out before him, and she responded in kind.

Their bodies came together like lyrics of a song, harmonizing with perfect memory. He filled her and she surrounded him, every inch of his skin buzzing with the awareness that this was Mariella in his arms again.

Very little could soften the nostalgic pain of this place, but *this*—he and Mariella—that had been what he missed most when he'd left. That had been the hardest temptation to leave behind.

Her body was a symphony he conducted. Every sway of his hips and strum of his fingers brought about a new song of pleasure from her lips. She preened and purred for him, begged for more and wept in delight when he delivered.

She was the only instrument he'd been born to play, and after all these years, he still knew her by heart. They moved like poetry, sometimes frantic and hard, other times slow and indulgent.

Their palpable connection filled his chest like a heavy breath, lodging in his throat until he could barely breathe. What was it about Mariella that made her so different from all the others?

She got the real him. The raw him. The side other women didn't know or take the time to find. There was something unique about her that drew out his secrets, unraveled his vulnerable sides, and let him simply exist exactly as he was. No facades. No false promises. Just them.

When she held his face and looked into his eyes, he didn't shy away. For some reason he let her touch him that way, despite the sharp sting of intimacy or the fear that she might see something cowardice or ugly inside of him.

Maybe he allowed it because he knew she'd looked there before. He believed she sensed the secrets he'd kept hidden, but she also respected his need for secrecy, then as much as now.

"I've missed you," she whispered, the delicate confession a fragile truth he wanted to handle with care.

"I missed you too." He hadn't lied when he said he thought about her. But she was a memory he didn't easily allow. Of all the things he ran away from in Jasper Falls, Mariella was the one temptation he struggled to leave behind.

Their connection startled him, though it shouldn't have. There was always something more about them. Something right. It was like they were a part of each other, and ten years apart had done nothing to change that fact.

He rolled their bodies, pulling her over him. Cradling her on his lap, her sweat-glistening skin pressing tight to his, he held her close and kissed her hard as she rode him. Chest to chest, there wasn't much space to move, but he wanted that restrictive contact, needed to feel her with him, tight and tense, her welcoming body against his hard edges.

They could stretch out or reposition, but that wasn't how he liked it with her. Unlike with the others, when it came to Mariella, he wanted her as close as possible. He wanted to consume her and be consumed.

No one else had ever been able to give this much to him. Or was she taking? Either way, he fucking loved it.

"God, I missed this." He squeezed her closer, biting her shoulder.

Her nails scraped over his back and raked through his hair, sending chills from his scalp down his spine. "It's so good between us."

"We're great like this." He caught her hips and pulled her down on him, holding her in place. "Feel that, how perfectly we fit together. I want to die like this."

She laughed, her breathy chuckle a sensual tease along his flesh. "Please don't. I'm not finished yet."

He kissed her hard and toppled her to the bed. "Oh, I'm far from finished."

Their mouths collided in desperate need, a million lost minutes to make up when they only had this fleeting moment available to them. She was a rush, a euphoric chill, an endless quiver that mimicked all a man could feel on the precipice of ecstasy.

They went at it for hours, never completely pulling apart but eventually falling asleep in each other's arms, her body wrapped tightly around his, locked as one.

Harrison hadn't slept so soundly in years.

But when he awoke, the bed was cold. "Mariella?"

He shot up, thrusting the covers aside and bolting off the bed to search the bathroom. She was gone. He didn't have her number and wasn't sure where she was living. That meant, if he wanted to see her again, he'd have to show his face in town and track her down.

"Fuck," he groaned, scrubbing his hands over his bleary eyes and grinning at the lingering scent of her covering his skin. She wasn't getting away from him that easily.

CHAPTER 6

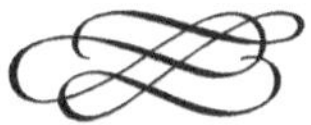

Jasper Falls seemed so big when Harrison was a little boy. With mountains that disappeared in the clouds and green horizons as endless as oceans, the town seemed to have no limits, no chance of escape. But as he grew older, he sensed a better life beyond the city limits, and that thirst for something different, something better, had driven him away from everything familiar into a world of the unknown.

And somehow, despite the higher crime rates and pricy cost of living, those unknown parts of the world felt safer. He never felt a familial pull to return to Jasper Falls, so he never questioned the rightness of his escape. However, he also didn't let himself think too hard about those he left behind.

Erin was a tricky part of his childhood. They had grown apart, and now when he thought of her, his chest burned with regret. He should have done better where his sister was concerned, but he hadn't. Those unexamined regrets still filled him with discomfort, and the only simple cure seemed to be continued distance.

Out of sight, out of mind. But in a town as small as Jasper Falls, there was nowhere to hide.

Seeing his sister and Mariella filled him with uncomfortable emotions best ignored. Soon enough, he'd be back where he belonged, and Erin could do whatever she wanted with the store and the house. She'd be fine. And Mariella…

Well, he had no doubt Mariella would eventually get married and spit out a few babies. The bittersweet thought turned his stomach no matter how easily the modest image came to mind.

How was it that everything in Jasper Falls looked so tiny? The houses were smaller, the yards nothing but postage stamps, and the streets were too narrow for cars to park *and* drive. Living in New York for more than a decade gave everything in Jasper Falls a hokey make-believe feel, like he was driving through a television studio or visiting *The Truman Show* set.

But even small things could be lethal. The sight of his father's rinky-dink hardware store sank like a bullet into his chest, rattling around and pinging off old memories he wished would stay hidden.

Sometimes, in a nightmare, a person scraped the surface of consciousness enough to know they were only dreaming. Yet the instinct to run and hide doesn't wane. Seeing his father's store was along those lines. The man was dead, on a slab in the morgue, yet Harrison battled an urge to run away from his ghost all the same.

"Fuck you," he breathed, eyes narrowing on the darkened storefront as he slowly drove by.

Ward Montgomery was a corpse. Harrison was a grown man—a far better man than the bastard who hardly raised him.

He had a condo in Manhattan, women at his beck and call, and enough money to buy and sell this town twice over. It was time for those cowardly memories and fears to die with the man who created them.

Rather than park and check on the store, he continued driving down Main Street. Everything looked strangely the same, but different. Some stores had fresh paint on the original, tired old signs, while others had been completely transformed.

Street lights were newer, and lampposts had been newly installed to look older. The town looked unmistakably better, sort of revitalized like it had been given a second wind and an injection of vitality. Younger generations could do that, he supposed, unsure why he expected everything here to look older when it appeared the exact opposite.

Even though there were drifts of snow everywhere, people still walked the sidewalks and visited shops. Pink and purple wreaths decorated the lamp posts. Hearts, perhaps for Valentine's Day. The picturesque quaintness pissed him off for reasons he didn't understand.

Everything looked a little too storybook for his liking. He preferred things at face value. That was one of the reasons he'd always been attracted to Mariella. She was always direct and honest.

His thoughts steered his car away from Main Street and down a side road until he was winding in and out of neighborhoods close to Mariella's parents' house. He wasn't exactly sure which house was theirs, but he knew it was in this general area.

There had been a blizzard a few nights ago, and while the roads were plowed, they were still slick. His car wasn't meant for joy riding in the snow, and he didn't have four-wheel drive, but he headed north anyway.

He took a detour up the mountain, and followed a bumpy country road to the McCullough acreage—McCullough Mountain. Stale resentment boiled back to life as he recalled how much he envied the big family. Erin had been closer to them. She even dated Finn for a while, but Harrison supposed that hadn't worked out. Pity, because it would have been nice to see his sister with a good family like the McCulloughs.

Navigating his way up the pockmarked thoroughfare, he steered clear of any mud or icy patches. Once again, the familiar roads appeared smaller than he remembered.

He'd read somewhere that Luke McCullough never made it pro, which pissed him off. Luke got the scholarship that should have been Harrison's ticket out of Jasper Falls. When his father learned there would be no free college ride, it had caused the fight that changed everything.

The road disappeared for a moment and all Harrison could see before him was his father's blotchy complexion as he tried to choke the life out of him. He could still recall the pain of struggling to breathe and the fear that his father might actually kill him. No matter how many times he'd been hit, knowing his father could end him without flinching hurt most of all.

His tire rocked into a crater and his focus returned to the bumpy road.

"Shit." He shouldn't be this far up on the mountain. The roads were hardly plowed. He followed the divots other tires had left and looked for a place to turn around, driving back toward the suburban neighborhoods below.

He hadn't waited around for graduation. It wouldn't have mattered anyway with no scholarship or any place to go. Instead, he cut out early and ran, no high school diploma, barely any money, and no lifeline in case things went wrong, which they had in the beginning.

It was amazing the things people would do to survive. That had been his main goal, survival. He'd been desperate to make something of himself, determined to never return home again.

He'd sold just about every bodily fluid science would buy just to keep a warm roof over his head that first winter. By the following spring, he'd landed a job at a mechanic's garage where he learned a thing or two about fixing cars. He'd come from such a sheltered background, he would have been content to continue living a blue-collar life, but one day, an old Bentley broke down by their shop and his life changed for the better.

Larry Dunbar—founder of Dunbar Associates, lover of classic cars, blacklisted from eighty percent of Nevada casinos, and a dangerous card shark only a fool would bet against, rolled into Harrison's life on a flat tire, saw potential in him, and pulled him out of poverty in a black limo.

"You're gonna make me money, kid. I know it in my gut," he'd told him the day they drove into Manhattan.

Harrison knew the man had the power to change his life for the better, so he trusted him and learned as much as possible. At first, Dunbar treated him like a protégé, advising him on everything down to how to tip a waitress and what shoe laces to buy.

Over time, Harrison realized Dunbar didn't work on Wall Street, Wall Street worked for him. He was a genius when it came to investment, and Harrison wanted to learn every possible thing he could teach him about success.

Dunbar was his father's age, but he didn't look like the older men he'd grown up around. His clothes were nicer, his skin less leathered, his eyes shone brighter, and his car was purchased for pleasure rather than functionality.

It was love at first sight. Not only did Harrison want to know his secrets, but he also wanted to live his life. He wanted to be Larry Dunbar.

That first trip into Manhattan stole his breath away. The towering sight of skyscrapers reminded him just how small and unworldly he was. For a moment, he was scared enough to return home, but then something changed. He saw kids his age bustling down the busy streets, fearless and focused on some destination, and Harrison swore he'd only look forward and never look back.

"The country's for agriculture," Dunbar once told him. "Things grow and die on farmland. The city is for steel. Everything strong goes into these buildings and they're made to rise."

Harrison wanted to rise. He wanted to reach the top and live in a penthouse like the gods, overlooking the rest of the world.

Within one year he'd earned enough

money to buy and sell his childhood home. Why that number mattered, he wasn't sure. He had no interest in purchasing the house. It haunted him for years, even after leaving Jasper Falls. But part of him needed such a measuring stick for his success, a sort of metric to prove he'd accumulated—*in a short time*—more than his father ever could.

Back then, the more he earned and learned, the more Dunbar expected of him. Harrison needed to prove his father wrong. He wanted change, and he wanted it fast. This worked perfectly for his mentor, who often used Harrison's personal vendetta to drive his ambition toward success and the success of the company.

Harrison had a knack for investing money in the right markets. He became obsessed with rates and investment opportunities to the point that he sometimes dreamed about numbers. Within a couple of years, he was given a corner office and a private parking space for his own collectible car.

He knew then, if he'd stayed in Jasper Falls, it would have eventually killed him.

Yet here he was, back again.

His car idled in front of his childhood home, and he cringed. While none of the houses screamed new construction, there was something vacant and hollow about theirs. No shutters like the others, no welcome mat or wreath on the door. Just a cold, lifeless shell.

Why had his sister stayed? She'd left for a while when she took a job for the mayor, but when that fell through, she couldn't afford rent and had to let her apartment go. He should have helped her. He could have sent her money or…

God, he was a shitty brother.

He beeped the horn, alerting her that he was there.

They had a meeting with the mortician at eleven so Erin could go over all the details of the funeral. Why they needed a ceremony to celebrate the life of a man who made their childhood a living hell was beyond him. This was her decision, not his.

If it had been up to Harrison, a can of lighter fluid and a match would have done the trick. But Erin begged for a funeral, and he couldn't tell her no.

She said she needed closure and claimed the funeral would be better for the town. The town never gave a shit about them, so he had a hard time caring what any of the locals might need or think. Still, there was little he could deny his sister, and for reasons he couldn't understand, she was pretty torn up over the whole thing.

The front door opened and she came skipping out of the house looking much better than she had the day before. The moment she got into the car, he could smell traces of his past on her clothing. Traces of their father's cigarette smoke and the tinge of emotional poverty swirling in the air.

"Hey."

"I wasn't sure you'd show."

He frowned. "I told you I'd be here."

She shrugged and buckled her seatbelt. "I know, but I thought you might have changed your mind."

She expected him to bolt. The thought had crossed his mind, but here he was. "Where is this place?"

"Head to Main Street. I want to grab a coffee first."

Once Erin had her coffee, she directed him to the funeral home. Despite the thirty-degree day, he rolled down the window to let in some fresh air. The unwanted stench of his childhood home was destroying the leather scent of his car.

"Are you hot? It's freezing outside."

"I just want some air."

She turned up the dial that controlled the

heat. "We have to come up with something to write in the obituary. I wasn't sure if you remembered any of Dad's—"

"I told you, I'm not doing any of that. I'm just here to cut the check."

Her brows lowered as she frowned at him. Her judgement needled, but he didn't care. "Harrison, you might regret—"

"The only thing I regret is not leaving sooner, Erin. I'm doing this for you. I don't need any of it."

His sister let out an audible breath and sat back in the seat. "Then why'd you even come?"

"Because you asked me to."

"I also asked you not to leave, but that didn't stop you."

"You could have left, too. I'll never understand why you stayed here or why you moved back home." She'd been on her own. She could have toughed it out. "It's like you just gave up—"

"Don't. I haven't got the strength to argue with you about events that can't change."

He wanted to know why she stayed. Didn't she realize there were countless opportunities out there. She could have started over a dozen times, but she stayed stuck in this damn town.

"Was it because of Finn McCullough? Is he why you stayed?"

"Jesus, Harrison, drop it. And my relationship with Finn ended years ago. He's married and has half a dozen kids, now."

"It just doesn't make sense."

"I could say the same about you vanishing out of our lives. You had a family here."

His shoulders tensed with the weight of unshakable guilt. His mother had left a few years before him. And as far as family went... He had a sister. That was it.

"I should've called more. Checked in to see if you needed anything."

"Well, I'm fine."

It bothered him, that the softness he remembered in his little sister was gone. She was harder now, jaded and calloused by time. Had his absence contributed to making her that way?

A hundred questions raced through his head. Did their dad ever ease up? How bad did it get after he left? Why did she help a man who only ever abused them?

Was she sad? Was she happy? Was there something wrong with him for feeling relieved now that their dad was dead?

How could he do better by her? Did she hate him? Did she need anything?

Rather than voice a single worry, he kept his eyes on the road and his mouth shut.

When they reached the mortician's, everything was pretty cut and dry. He let Erin do the talking. She only deferred to him when the funeral director asked which day they wanted the burial.

"The sooner the better," Harrison said.

When they wrapped everything up, he cut the check for all but the headstone. No way he was paying to immortalize that son of a bitch with some sort of statue. If Erin wanted to go that far, she could pay for it herself. To his thinking, even a plastic grave marker was too much.

On the drive home, she mentioned something about hiring a priest again, but he didn't see the point. However, he wasn't going to stand in her way if that was what she needed to 'find closure'.

He parked in the driveway but didn't shut off the car.

"Do you want to come in? We could order pizza and watch a movie. I have some boxes of—"

"I can't."

Disappointment flashed in her eyes, but he had to put his own mental health before hers in this case. Today had stirred a lot of unwanted emotions, and he needed some space to clear his head.

"You'll have to eventually go through—"

"Whatever's left is yours. I don't want any of it."

"I can't do all of this on my own, Harrison."

"Just…let me know what you need, and I'll pay for it." He'd hire cleaners to come empty the house if that's what it took.

She scoffed and shoved open the door. "Thanks." Her tone lacked any hint of gratitude.

As soon as she went inside the house, he sped out of the driveway and drove as far away from his childhood home as possible, but there was no escaping the unwanted memories that kept surfacing.

He wanted to keep going. He wanted to leave everything behind again, but he couldn't because he had to stick around for the fucking funeral.

"Fuck!" He slammed his palm into the steering wheel as he waited at a stop light, unsure if he'd go straight toward New York or turn right and return to the hotel.

The light changed and he hesitated. A horn honked, spurring him out of his thoughts, and he jerked the wheel, heading back to the hotel.

He still wasn't breathing right when he reached Main Street. The thought of being caged in a tiny hotel room made him want to ram his fist into something. He needed to blow off some steam.

Pulling into the parking lot of O'Malley's Pub, he decided to have a beer rather than devour the bottle of whiskey tucked in his suitcase. There was no sense of homecoming when he stepped into the tavern. He'd left town when he was only eighteen, still too young to drink in the state of Pennsylvania, so this was one place blissfully free of memories—so long as he didn't look at the clientele.

He took a stool at the far end of the bar when none other than Perrin Harris appeared. "What can I get you?"

Jesus, he hated small towns. "I'll take a beer."

"Holy shit, *Harrison?*"

"The one and only."

"Wow, I haven't seen you in—God, it must be more than a decade, now." Realization flashed in her eyes. "I'm so sorry about your dad. First round's on me."

He gave a tight smile. "Whatever's on tap is fine."

He watched her as she filled a pilsner. Perrin Harris had always been pretty, but she wasn't his type. That blonde pixie look was cute, but he preferred women with darker features who were a little fuller in the hips. She had nothing on Mariella's beauty.

He needed to find out where Mariella lived. If he found a McCullough or a Clooney, he could possibly get some answers. Perrin probably knew, but after everything he learned about their little rivalry, she wasn't the person to ask.

"Here you go." Perrin placed the beer on a cocktail napkin. "Did you want to look at a menu?"

"Sure."

She plucked one out of her apron and set it on the bar. "So where are you living?"

"New York." He glanced at the menu. "I'll take the house burger. Medium rare."

She typed his order into the computer. "You staying with family?"

What family? He and Erin barely knew how to speak to each other anymore. "I'm at the Brick Hotel."

Perrin's eyes lit up with a smile. "That's our hotel! My husband, Gage, just opened it. How do you like it so far?"

"It's nice." He had no energy for a Yelp review.

"They're still a little under staffed over there. We're interviewing for managers."

It was the closest thing to an opening he'd likely get. "Find anyone good, yet?"

"Meh." She dried a glass and hung it on the wine rack with the others. "I'm still holding out hope."

A woman barreled in from the back and delivered his burger. "Perrin, girl, you better scoot if you plan on meetin' Gage for your date. It's almost five."

"Shoot." Perrin untied her apron. "Just charge him for the burger. His first beer was on the house."

"Go," the woman ordered.

"Nice seeing you, Harrison."

He gave a nod and pulled his burger closer.

Once Perrin was gone, the woman turned to him. "What'd you do to get a free beer?"

"Nothing."

"Bullshit. Perrin counts every penny around here. You must've done somethin' right." She lifted a stack of papers out from beside the register and set one in front of him.

He frowned at the sheet. "What's this?"

"Jukebox bingo. Stick around and play. It's fun."

He doubted that. "How does it work?"

"Don't worry. The rules get explained before we start. Your burger's gettin' cold."

She was a pushy little thing, but the burger was well worth eating hot—cooked to perfection and just what he needed to settle his stomach.

"Sorry I'm late, Sue." A woman appeared and shoved an enormous bag behind the bar. She tied back her hair. "The kids were driving me nuts. I never thought I would get out of there."

"No Finn tonight?"

"He's on his way. His mom was telling him something, and I didn't want to hold you up."

"Plenty of time," the bartender, Sue, said, refilling Harrison's beer without being asked. "Here you go, sugar. I'll put that one on your tab."

The other woman looked at him and smiled, cocking her head. "Hi, I'm Mallory McCullough. I don't think we've met."

She wasn't one of the McCulloughs he remembered. "Harrison Montgomery. Did I hear you mention Finn?"

"Finn's my husband. Do you know him?"

"We went to school together."

"Montgomery?" she said slowly as if playing a mental game of connect the dots. "So you must be Erin's…?"

"Brother."

"I didn't know she had a brother." Her expression softened and she touched his arm, the motion intimate and unexpected. "I'm so sorry about your dad."

Maybe it was a mistake to come here. He could do without all the touchy-feely sentiments. "Thanks."

Her hand disappeared, and luckily, more patrons poured into the bar, requiring drinks and asking when Jukebox Bingo was going to begin.

Harrison recognized a few faces, but kept his head down. He wished Sue hadn't refilled his beer. There was no law that he had to drink it. He tried to flag her down, so he could cash out, but the evening rush had started and by the time he was able to snag her attention the beer was gone.

Reaching into his pocket, he withdrew his wallet and stilled, a flashback filling his memory from his and Mariella's first time together. Every sense came alive, and for a moment, he was back in high school again.

Forgetting what he was doing, he searched the crowd for a dark-haired beauty but didn't see her. He wanted her to appear and wondered if she would, since Jukebox Bingo seemed a big crowd pleaser in Jasper Falls. Maybe he could text her and tell her to shoot over to the bar and join him for a drink. Maybe a few drinks. Then they could go back to his room and…

The woman, Mallory, yelled something to someone across the bar and laughed. The McCulloughs were her cousins, which meant Mallory might have Mariella's number. He pushed his beer forward to get her attention.

"Another one?"

He nodded. "Are a lot of your relatives coming, tonight?"

"A few. The girls like the bingo more than the guys. But Tristan and Luke usually show."

"Tristan?"

"Luke's husband."

He stilled. Luke was married to a man? He hadn't seen that coming. He was shocked Luke settled down at all. He'd been a hound with the ladies back in the day. What other surprises should he expect?

He figured it wouldn't hurt to wait around a while and see if Mariella showed.

Over the next thirty minutes the crowd doubled, as did the volume of the bar. Still no sign of Mariella, though.

Just about ready to call it quits, he reached for his wallet again, only the music cut off and a microphone screeched through the speakers. "Okay, everyone, break into teams and put your phones away!" Sue yelled from the stage. "Mallory is passing around bingo stampers. I'll play snippets of a song, and if the title's on your board, mark it off. Five in a row is a bingo."

He couldn't stomach the corny game so he waved his platinum card at Mallory. "Hey, can you cash me out?"

She looked at his card. "Um, I don't think we take that card."

He fished out some bills from his pocket, praying it was enough to cover a burger and a beer. "This should cover it."

"Not if you expect to buy me a drink."

His heart skipped out of beat, and his head jerked at the soft voice purring in his ear. The stress of the day washed away with just one glimpse of her smiling face. "Mariella."

"I didn't expect to find you here." She slid onto the stool at his right and smiled at the bartender. "Hey, Philly, I'll have whatever he's having."

"Make it two," Harrison said, returning to his seat.

She slid his bingo card between them. "Do you want to be on my team?"

"Under one condition."

Mariella lifted her playful stare. "I'm all ears."

"You give me your phone number, first. I had no way of reaching you, today, and you snuck out—"

"Shh, shh, shh." She slipped her hand into his pocket and fished out his phone. His body instantly responded. "Locked. Who would have guessed?" She angled the screen at his face and the device opened. She entered her contact info and saved it under an emoji of a lemon. "There."

He frowned at the emoji. "A lemon?"

She leaned closer and whispered, "In Italy, the lemon symbolizes longevity and affection. I think we proved last night that our chemistry has some staying power."

"I think it's a theory worth testing again."

"Oh, well, I'm all for experimentation for the sake of science."

Tucking his phone away, he slipped his hand below the bar, resting it naturally over her denim-clad thigh. She stripped off her jacket and a shoulder peeked from the loose white sweater that drooped down her arm.

Mallory delivered their beers, and he casually ran a finger up Mariella's thigh, not stopping until his fingertip slipped beneath the folded material of her sweater. Tucked in the corner as they were, the shadows provided a bit of privacy.

Leaning close, he whispered, "Your place or mine?"

Her lips parted when he teased the warm skin of her stomach. He wanted to kiss the glossy red sheen right off her lips.

"Yours."

Fuck bingo. He wanted her. "Let's go."

She caught his wrist. "Not so fast, mister. I came to win."

So did he, but his mind was on a different prize.

She sipped her beer, looking adorably casual and comfortable in her home town setting. He wondered how she managed patronizing the pub when her and Perrin shared such a strong dislike for one and other.

"I wasn't sure if you'd come here."

She frowned, the game now started and the music and crowd louder. "O'Malley's? Why wouldn't I? It's practically a rite of passage. Locals tithe here as much as they give to the church."

"Doesn't Perrin own it?"

She shrugged. "So does Maggie, and she's a Clooney."

"Wait, Maggie didn't marry Nash?"

"She did, but Nash passed away a few years ago. Now she's married to my cousin, Ryan."

Nash died? It was a disturbing thought to know someone from their generation was already gone. It made his time away feel longer somehow.

"Wow."

Mariella nodded, her lips pressed into a sad smile. "It was really sad. He was so young and talented. And they were so in love." She met his stare. "It's hard to lose someone without having the chance to say goodbye."

His gaze lowered, guilt spreading through his chest like poison. He suddenly realized all the possible ways Mariella's life could have changed. It was a damn miracle he'd found her like he had, still single. But the fact that she'd forgive him, shocked him most of all.

His palm rode up her thigh, affectionately affirming that she was there. He uncapped the stamper and looked at the bingo board. "Let's do this."

She grinned. "That's the spirit. Let's kick some bingo ass."

"That and I plan on being inside of you ten minutes after we win."

Her cheeks flushed with pink as she laughed. "With that kind of can-do attitude, you should probably take off your pants now."

CHAPTER 7

Mariella could hardly catch her breath after the promise he just delivered. A promise she very much wanted him to see through.

She wasn't sure what they were doing or if this was actually going somewhere, but she knew things would likely end the same as before, with her alone and sad and Harrison gone.

Did she care? Last night she had a list of reasons why they shouldn't open this can of worms, but today she was fresh out of logic and holding fists full of can openers.

Screw the consequences. She wanted him too much to turn down a chance to be with him again. Besides, this might be the last chance they had.

Harrison would eventually return to New York, and they would both move on. So long as she understood the temporary circumstances of their situation, she could protect herself from getting too involved.

They might never see each other again. Why shouldn't she take care of her needs while he was here? She was a modern woman. She had a right to feel satisfied and seek comfort from whoever she wanted. They were both single. They knew what they were doing.

"You okay?" His hand squeezed over her thigh sending another wave of desire through every nerve ending in her body.

She slouched into him and smiled. "How do you do that?"

"Do what?"

"Touch me and make my bones melt." He'd always had that hold over her.

"Is that what I do?"

"Don't play dumb."

He chuckled and pushed her hair over one shoulder so he could nuzzle his mouth along the sensitive curve of her neck. Not only did his touch feel amazing, it felt good to be with someone who didn't care about hiding their connection. Bran had always been so private about displays of affection—for reasons obvious to her now.

Mallory caught sight of them and did a double take, then shot her a thumbs up as if she approved. Mariella was going to be a puddle if he kept necking her like that.

Another song kicked on, the recognizable intro to "Don't You Forget About Me" by Simple Minds and she shoved Harrison off her. "We have this one!"

Harrison stood, resting his chin on her shoulder and wrapping his arms around her waist, but she was all business.

"There." She stamped their card, marking off the song and the FREE space in the middle of the card.

"Awesome. Only four more to go."

"Ready for the next song?" Sue asked from the stage and the crowd cheered. She played the next clip.

"The Who," Mariella whispered, searching their board. "Damn, we don't have that one."

"I never knew you were so competitive."

She was grateful she'd worn such a thick sweater. When his front pressed to her back her nipples turned to pebbles. Even when he barely touched her, she somehow felt him everywhere.

"Not competitive. I just really like winning. And I hate to lose."

"Got it."

The next song was a challenge. "It's Coldplay," Harrison whispered in her ear. "'The Scientist.' We don't have that one either."

"Damn it!"

"The game's still young."

At this rate they were going to be there all night, and she really wanted to get back to his hotel room. She took a long sip of beer and hunched over the bingo sheet, as if her positioning might somehow help the probability of a win.

The next song was The Stones, but they didn't have that one either. "Are you sure we're not using an old bingo sheet?"

Harrison's hands cradled her hips, distracting her focus. "How about a kiss for good luck?"

She turned, and pressed a peck on his jaw.

"If that's the best you've got, you deserve to lose."

She glanced over her shoulder at him. "Is that a challenge?"

"I heard you hate to lose."

"Facts."

"Then you better kiss me like you mean it, if you want it to be a lucky one."

Rising to the challenge, she slid off the stool and looked up at him. "You have to bend down a little."

"My pleasure." He only bent his head the bare minimum, but it was enough.

Gripping the back of his neck, she pulled him closer and sealed her lips to his. His tongue teased over hers, and he banded an arm around her back, lifting her to her toes as he took over the kiss.

"Wowzers, here's one for the couple in the back," Sue said, then she played a snippet of Peggy Lee's "Fever."

Mariella recognized the first sultry beat and ripped her mouth away from Harrison's. "We have that one! Where's the stamper?"

Harrison handed her the little green pen and she smacked a blotch over the song title.

"We're back in the game!"

It took six rounds for them to actually win, and several more rounds of beer to keep them hydrated. Jukebox Bingo was thirsty work.

Mariella wasn't sure what Harrison expected as a prize, but the free drink token worked for her.

"We played all night for a free drink?" he asked, stunned and obviously disappointed.

"We played for the glory. Can't you feel that?"

"Feel what?"

"Victory!" She lifted her free beer and clanked it to his. "To us. We make a good team."

"To us." He clinked his pilsner and surprised her by looping his arm around hers like a groom might do with a bride. The motion brought them closer, linking them as one.

Everything felt so right in that moment, she wondered why it had to end. She wondered why they couldn't just stay like this forever.

Time slowed and the people around them disappeared as she looked up at him, seeing everything she still wanted in a man. Everything except his track record of abandonment and disregard for her tender heart.

Didn't he see how easy it could be between them? "What's in New York?" she whispered.

"A big apple," he joked, but she saw in his eyes that he was purposefully sidestepping her serious question.

"Did you ever think about…" There had to be something holding him there. She spent the night with him, but they barely talked. "Do you have children?"

His expression turned unreadable. "No. It's just me."

And, somehow, without having to actually say the words, he told her that was exactly how he preferred his life.

They were so close she could see the golden flecks in his blue irises. It was getting late. A Cinderella-like fear took shape in her heart, spurring her forward as something warned that by this time tomorrow her carriage would turn back to a pumpkin. "We should go. They're trying to close."

He helped her into her coat and paid the tab. Outside, the parking lot was half empty and dusted with a thin veil of freshly fallen snow.

The metallic air nipped at her nose, and she pulled a pair of red knit gloves out of her pockets.

"Cold?" He removed the scarf from his wool dress coat and wrapped it carefully around her neck. The soft cashmere smelled of him, and she never wanted to give it back.

"Thanks."

They stopped midway between her dated Volvo and his swanky luxury sedan. The silent debate went on for only a few seconds before they both spoke at the same time.

"The hotel's not that far."

"We should probably walk."

Glad they were both on the same page after having several drinks, she took his hand as they strolled down Main Street. She liked that he shortened his strides to match hers, and how they could still enjoy each other's presence in silence.

The storefronts were dark and the road was empty. The town was as peaceful and as beautiful as a Christmas card. She liked the pink and purple decorations the town put out for Valentine's Day. Would Harrison still be here on the fourteenth?

After that, the storefronts would turn green, for St. Paddy's. By then Harrison would surely be gone.

The longer they walked in silence the louder reality seemed to scream. There was nothing she could do to keep him here. He was going to leave her again and it was going to hurt like hell, just like it had before.

Her gloved hand tightened around his, and he gently squeezed her fingers. They were already through the looking glass and there was no going back. She might as well enjoy the adventure while it lasted.

CHAPTER 8

The night was too still, like they were walking through a painting on a postcard, a facsimile of a place he almost recognized, a place that looked safe and welcoming, but that familiar itch of discomfort wouldn't wane. Everything seemed too good to be true.

As if reading his thoughts, Mariella glanced up at him. "Does it look different from when we were kids?"

"Smaller. I remember everything bigger."

She smiled, her cheeks rosy and her nose red from the cold. "The mayor did hire a special crew of architects to come in and shrink everything down while you were gone."

"I figured."

Their steps were quiet over the pavement,

the newly fallen snow muffling any noise. At the bar, he could think of little more than getting inside of her. But now, he enjoyed their leisurely pace as he simply strolled beside her. New York was never this quiet or unhurried.

His gaze snagged on something shiny up ahead, resting on the brick walk, just out front of the hardware store. He had no interest in passing his dad's store, but he wanted to see what was sitting on the sidewalk.

As they closed the distance, his thoughts jumbled. A package? No, it looked too flimsy to be a box. Newspapers? Maybe they were stacking up since no one had been by. Then the object came into view and he realized they were flowers.

His feet stopped and his jaw locked. The dated mosaic tile marking the entrance with the letters MH—Montgomery Hardware—brought an unwanted deluge of memories to the forefront of his mind.

"Someone left flowers for your dad." Mariella's soft voice didn't match the turmoil splintering between his ears as he stared down at the wilting bouquet.

They all loved Ward Montgomery.

Visions of his childhood home ransacked his mind as the quiet night screamed with remembered chaos. The echo of his mother's voice shrilled through his mind, sharp with panic and then brave with protective rage. Was that even her voice? She left when he was so young, he could hardly remember.

He heard the whip of his father's belt and a mixture of panicked cries. His mother's pleading as she begged through tears and promised things. Words that would change absolutely nothing about the way his father was.

Then came his father's endless taunts.
Lazy! Useless! Ingrate!
Sorry excuse... Pathetic...Cry baby...
Leech! Selfish! Stupid!
He could hear his father mimicking him when Harrison would sometimes stumble over his spelling words. *"Dar—dar—dar... Sound like one of those morons on the slow bus. No brains and no ambition. I'll have to carry you your whole life."*

Harrison's chest tightened. His hands balled into fists as he wished to kick those flowers away, beat every bloom off every stem and scream for the world to hear what a fucking monster Ward Montgomery truly was.

"Do you want to take them? Maybe Erin would want them."

He couldn't bring himself to touch them. "No. Just leave them there."

The cold winter air webbed across his heart like ice. Glaring at the front door of the store at the still aisles and dark displays of tools inside, he heard his childhood voice shaking with fear as he tried to face down his dad time and time again.

His gaze fastened on the rack of framing hammers, and he remembered his father snatching one off the wall one day and hurling it at him. Mr. McCullough had come by to pick up some chicken wire for his fence that day. Harrison always wondered if that front bell hadn't rung, if his father would done more than thrown a hammer at him.

"Hey, are you okay?"

Her gloved hand curled around the sleeve of his jacket. There was no disguising the tension flexing through every overwrought muscle in his body. He couldn't bear the weight of her touch, so he paced.

Spotting a rock sitting beside the plowed drift, he debated picking it up and hurling it through the front window, but his dad wasn't here to clean up the mess, and any damage would fall to Erin.

Erin.

God.

How many days had he tricked himself into not thinking about her? Not worrying? He was a fucking coward. A decent brother would have done more to protect her.

"Harrison?"

"Why is she having a funeral for him?" he snapped.

He didn't understand why Erin needed this. He wanted to be there for her, but he couldn't stomach her compassion for a man who terrorized and beat them. "She hated him. I know she did."

Mariella frowned. "Your father?"

He shook his head, of course Mariella wouldn't understand. No one would, because like good little victims, they did everything in their power to protect their abuser.

He wished he could spell it out for her, but he couldn't. There was too much. Too many lies. The entire town was brainwashed and blind. Not a single one of them ever looking beyond the flimsy excuses they offered to explain the scrapes and bruises that took time to heal.

"The whole town loved him," he rasped, the words tearing up his throat like blades of glass.

Mariella took a slow step toward him, but his eyes remained locked on the storefront.

"Love's a powerful word, Harrison. True, he was part of our community. We all went to him whenever a screen needed fixin' or something wasn't working right around the house, but very few of us actually knew him. He was a store owner, willing to open on a Sunday if a blizzard was coming. That made him a part of Jasper Falls, but none of us had anything close to a real relationship with him."

"I think about the things people will say, and I want to hit something."

"What are people saying?"

"How great he was. What a good man he was." He ground his molars. "They loved him."

Her brow pinched. "Sometimes, we love the wrong people—people who do very little to deserve our love. And sometimes we don't like the people we love, but we can't stop loving them despite knowing they don't deserve us. We can't beat ourselves up for loving people, Harrison. Better to love than to hate. Hate is a much heavier burden to carry."

Her words were too much, too honest and on the money. While their father made sure everyone else's houses functioned smoothly, their home had fallen apart. Dysfunction seeped from every room, yet no one ever noticed the source of such damage. So why did he feel like Mariella could suddenly see every filthy secret he hid?

He picked up the rock and fisted it in his hand.

Mariella stepped in front of him, now gripping his wrists and demanding he look at her. "Did I tell you what it was like for me when Bran and I finally broke up?"

His brow crimped in confusion, his focus divided between her and the store. "What about it?"

"Everyone kept telling me how pretty I was. Anytime I was sad, or needed to cry, that was their reply. *You're too pretty to cry over some guy. He doesn't deserve you. You could get anyone you want.* None of that was true, though. I couldn't get anyone I wanted. And it hurt to feel so alone and rejected. It didn't matter what shape I was in on the outside. Inside, I was wrecked."

"You did deserve better." He was at least certain of that. She deserved better than Bran Dawson and better than the way he'd left things.

"I know everything isn't always as perfect as it appears, Harrison. People see what they want to see, and they tend to avoid the un-comfortable stuff. The more something hurts, the harder people try not to see it."

Was that what his life had become, a collection of shiny luxuries that blinded him from his uncomfortable past? He had a beautiful Manhattan apartment, several lavish cars, box seats at any game he wanted to see. His life was a rotation of activities that suited his schedule and worked well with his business needs. But when the blinders came down, the truth was too much to bear. Some days he felt like a little kid still trying to outrun the ghosts of his past.

She pried the rock out of his hand and tossed it in the snow. Bringing his cold fingers to her lips, she pressed a kiss to his knuckles. She forced open his fist, pressing his touch along her jaw and smiled up at him.

"Our past is just a memory, Harrison. All the painful thoughts…They're just thoughts. And we have to train ourselves to stop thinking them sometimes, so that we can enjoy the present."

The ice encasing his heart cracked as warmth bloomed in his chest. The fleeting wish that he could take her with him when he left drifted through his mind, but something about Mariella belonged here, in Jasper Falls, and he didn't want to disturb that. New York would change her, and she was perfect just as she was.

"I want to show you something." Maintaining the hold of his hand, she led him across the street.

When they were kids, a small bread factory had occupied this part of town, but now, little boutiques and businesses lined the walk. They stopped under a green awning and she removed keys from her purse.

"What is this place?"

"You'll see."

With the lights off, the shop was mostly dark, but he made out the shadows of tables and chairs. The interior was warm. Fragrant coffee beans and a hint of baked goods scented the air. She hit a switch and the glass displays flickered to life. A café.

Did she work here? Own it?

"It's my family's," she explained, as if reading his mind. "My mom, Aunt Rosemarie and Aunt Maureen do most of the baking, and my younger cousins usually work the counter." She took off her coat and stashed it with her gloves and purse on a chair by the front. "Have a seat."

Unsure where to sit, he preferred to stand.

She moved around the shop with practiced familiarity. Flipping switches, and illuminating various corners and countertops.

A glass plate with a rondure lid displayed

bright green muffins. The handwritten sign said they were pistachio muffins. She plugged her phone into a port on the wall and turned a dial on a large stereo system.

The Lumineers played from the speakers, that catchy song about being together in a sweet home. He knew in an instant this song would always remind him of this moment, remind him of her.

Mariella opened the register, an old brass machine that was a century out of date, and removed a hair tie from the penny slot. In one quick move, she gathered her thick, dark hair and twisted it on top of her head in a knot. His stare traveled the long line of her neck, and he once again wondered how anyone so beautiful remained single for so long.

"Take off your coat." She grabbed an apron off the hook and tied it around her waist, cinching it tight.

"Are you making something?"

She slid open an ice chest and removed a heavy block wrapped in wax paper. "I'm going to bake for you."

Every motion was sweet temptation. He wondered if he was nuts, letting himself get close to her again. This time around would be a million times harder to leave.

She was everything alluring and addicting,

but also dangerous. It was more than sex. They were trespassing on new territory, and it was a lot more complicated than it had been when they were just kids.

He removed his coat and draped it over a chair, slowly crossing the café to come stand beside her and watch her work. She smiled, as if silently saying he stood exactly where he belonged.

She unpacked a neatly wrapped square and set it on the marble countertop.

"What is that?"

"It's croissant dough. I started it yesterday." She smoothed out the parchment paper and set a large block of what looked like butter on the counter. "You can help."

Flattening another sheet of parchment over the butter, she moved behind him and guided his hands over the brick. Her warm fingers slipped between his, pressing over the paper into the cool block.

"Let the warmth from your hands heat the butter to soften it."

It was a novel experience for him, having a woman touch him this way, almost maternally, as she showed him how to do something he'd never attempted before. "Shouldn't we use a stove?"

"No, that's too much heat. Croissants take

patience. Our body knows the exact temperature the dough needs to be." Her hands massaged over his, almost sensually, guiding his touch in a soft, kneading pattern.

Within a few minutes the brick softened. She flipped it and he continued to work the other side.

"This is the part where we get to work out our tension." She handed him a long, marble rolling pin. "Hit it."

He gave her a second glance, then took the rolling pin.

"Go ahead. You won't hurt it."

He tapped the slender rolling pin over the flattened block of butter.

Mariella laughed. "Oh, come on. You can do better than that."

His fingers tightened around the smooth marble and thought about how much damage he could do. A rock. A rolling pin. It wasn't a good time to arm him with weapons.

He set it down and stepped back. "You do it."

She took the rolling pin and showed him how it was done. Whacking the butter into the counter, and leaving several rounded divots in the surface. Then she rolled out the divots, flattened them with the pin as it slid over the paper. She flipped the butter to do the same to the other side.

No matter how aggressively she attacked the butter, there remained something innately gentle about her. Safe. He could see her doing this with children and laughing through a cloud of flour in some perfectly simple kitchen somewhere. The watercolor image filled his mind and he committed it to memory.

Once the butter was smoothed into a thin rectangle, she set it aside. "Now it's getting warm in here."

She removed her sweater and tightened her apron, around a thin bronze camisole that nearly matched the golden tone of her skin.

She worked the dough into a smooth blob, flattening and flipping it, but never letting it completely lose its shape. Every motion was practiced. She knew exactly when to apply flour and when to use her hands versus the rolling pin.

"Who taught you this?"

"My grandmother. In high school, she took me to Italy to cheer me up. We spent a month visiting distant relatives. Her cousin was a pastry chef in France. It's his recipe."

He remembered seeing her grandmother around town. The woman was four foot tall and about eighty pounds soaking wet. Everyone was afraid of her for some reason, and they called her Italian Mary.

"Why did you need cheering up?"

She avoided his stare and placed the flattened butter over the dough. "I…had a dark moment."

Because he left? Or was that a completely narcissistic assumption to think he could have such an impact on her? "When?"

"The summer after you left." She folded the butter inside the dough and used the rolling pin to laminate them together.

His hand closed over hers, stilling her motions. "I should have said goodbye to you."

She wouldn't look at him, but she nodded. "That would have helped, but my heart still would've broken."

"There was nothing anyone could have done to make me stay." He'd meant it when he said his leaving had nothing to do with her. "You only would have made my choice harder."

At that, she did look up at him. Her eyes shimmered like glass. "I doubt that."

"I don't." He traced his thumb along her jaw. "You were the only person I felt…"

He couldn't explain what he felt with her. Safe. Quiet. Still. She was his sanctuary, his escape. The person he missed most whenever he felt homesick.

"You feel like home," he rasped.

She wouldn't understand that his own home didn't stir such feelings for him. She was where he ran to catch his breath when the walls were closing in.

He didn't want to mislead her, but he also couldn't bear the thought of her mistaking their connection for a meaningless fling. "You were what I missed most after I was gone."

A startled look crossed her eyes and she turned away. "I have to preheat the oven."

The break of their connection snapped like a limb falling from an ancient tree. It scared him. He didn't like emotional abandonment, but that was exactly what she'd just done.

He opened up to her and she walked away. Why had he confessed such private things? He didn't even know what he was saying. He'd had a lot to drink and it was late. It had been a long day, and he was rambling.

He glanced at his coat.

"Do you want some coffee?" she asked, returning from the back.

Maybe coffee would sober him up. "Sure. I can make it." He looked at the complicated chrome machines along the wall. "Or..."

She laughed and set a box of German chocolate on the counter. "I'll make it."

He stepped back as she hit switches, ground beans, packed fancy espresso filters, and steamed milk. Whatever she made wasn't quite coffee. It was better.

"What the hell am I drinking?"

"A salted caramel macchiato. They're my favorite."

She returned to the dough and butter, forming it into two separate silken slabs. When the dough got too warm or soft, she chilled that section in the freezer and worked on the other slab for a while, always keeping both at the consistency and temperature she wanted.

When it was finally ready, she showed him how to use a pastry wheel to cut the dough into thin triangles, which she then rolled gently around a nib of chocolate.

"Now, we bake them?" He desperately wanted to taste anything that took this much work.

"Not yet. They need to proof."

"Proof?"

"Sit for a while and rise. If we try to rush the process, it won't work. Good things require time and patience." She carried her coffee mug to the curved booth in the back of the dining room where his coat draped.

He wondered how long she planned to stay at the café but figured they still had a few hours before dawn. He scooted into the booth beside her and sipped his macchiato.

"What's New York City like?"

Her question sent his mind to another place and time. "Loud. Alive. Fast. Gritty on the ground floor, and polished at the top."

"I've never been in the actual city. I've just passed it on the highway."

"You could come visit me." The offer escaped before he actually considered what it was he was suggesting.

"Really?"

"Sure. We could catch a Broadway show, if that's something you'd like, or we could visit a good steakhouse, have drinks on a rooftop bar—whatever you want." He wanted to show her something impressive, something to help her understand the lure, but at the same time he didn't want to overcomplicate his life.

"I bet you look natural there." Her fingers brushed over the sleeve of his cuff. "You're different now. You look like a New Yorker."

"I've changed," he agreed. "But I'll never forget where I came from." He'd tried several times and failed.

Her body rested in the curve of his arm, her touch slowly exploring. "I wish you didn't have to leave again."

Afraid of what he might promise, he kept quiet and turned her face toward his. He hadn't meant to do more than kiss her, but her body welcomed him with hungry invitation as she twisted and sank her tongue into his mouth, demanding he give her more.

Straddling his lap, she deepened the kiss and he cradled her hips. Her hands rode over his dress shirt, searching for skin and pulling at his buttons.

They were hidden in the shadows at the back of the café, but if anyone were to walk by and actually look inside, they would see them.

"I want you, Harrison. Right now."

He yanked down the front of her camisole, freeing her breasts and capturing a nipple in his mouth. Unraveling the apron strings around her waist, he tugged at the knot. She grabbed his hand, guiding it under the material to the front of her jeans where the zipper was already down.

"Jesus, Mariella." Warm heat met his fingertips as she rose on her knees and pressed his hand inside her panties.

Desperate kisses urged him on as she

ground herself against his touch. Her fingers were in his hair, her mouth at his racing pulse, and his cock was about to burst.

"This booth's too small for all the things I want to do to you."

Shoes dropped to the floor and she kicked off her pants. "Plenty of room."

She unlatched his belt buckle with insistent fingers. The tight grip of her hand around his flesh had his hips lifting toward her.

"People might see," he warned.

"Let them. I don't care. They don't exist."

She stroked him greedily, aligning their bodies and rubbing his hard flesh along her most sensitive places. She was a wild riot of feminine moans and heated need. At that first tremble of bliss, her muscles clenched and her head fell back. He hadn't even entered her yet and she was already coming.

Grabbing her hips, he thrust into her heat and growled as her channel clenched and fluttered around his pulsing cock, gripping him tight. "Kiss me."

Her mouth smashed to his and he groaned, thrusting his hips and pounding into her. She cried out, taking every inch of him but it wasn't enough. He wanted more. He wanted all of her. Every moan. Every cry.

Every deeply buried desire. He wanted her fucking soul.

Fisting her hair, he filled her to the hilt and breathed hard against her throat. She was a drug he'd never overcome. He simply didn't know how. Didn't want to.

Drunk on her existence, he reveled in this madness only the two of them could create. She was fire in his arms. Heat in his veins. And the withdrawal he knew would come might kill them both, but goddam, he never wanted to quit her. Not yet.

Loose chestnut waves tumbled around her face, framing her unmatched beauty as she steadied him. How did she do that? How did she always know when a storm was building inside of him and somehow quiet the riot with only a look? Their connection was almost spooky at times, but he loved how fluently she could read him.

He traced his tongue along her throat. "I can't get enough of you."

Her nails scored his chest where his shirt had come open. "You have all of me."

He thrust and the table wobbled. Their coffee cups rolled and shattered onto the floor. Neither of them cared enough to stop. They couldn't.

She was right. Nothing else existed when they were together like this. Just them.

He feared the morning. Feared the days to come. He didn't want a painful goodbye, but he'd eventually have to leave. His life was in New York, and her life was here. It was too much to think about.

"Where'd you go?" Her brow pressed to his as she rocked over him with unhurried strokes. "Stay here with me, Harrison. Don't leave me. Not yet."

He pressed his lips tight to hers, sealing away any promises that might slip from this moment of passion and pleasure. He never wanted to mislead her or hurt her, but he understood he'd never be able to fully avoid both.

<h1 style="text-align:center">CHAPTER 9</h1>

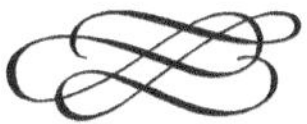

"Who are you?" Mariella stared in the mirror at her swollen lips and tousled hair, unable to recognize the woman in the reflection.

This wasn't her, not a side of her she'd met before. Sure, she and Harrison had always shared off-the-charts chemistry, but they had been horny kids back then. Emotions were always heightened for teens.

Now they were older. She got winded climbing a flight of stairs. Harrison, the grown man, was a completely different animal, and she had no explanation for the unparalleled, wild, totally uninhibited sort of monkey sex they just had.

He unleashed something inside of her she hadn't known existed. Something untamed and unapologetic. He turned her into a woman who shamelessly took exactly what she wanted, consequences be damned.

And, oh, there would be consequences.

She didn't want to think about that now, their inevitable end. But, damn it, she should.

Harrison was temporary.

"Where can I find a dustpan and broom?" he called from the storeroom and she flinched, quickly turning on the faucet and washing her hands.

"Hanging on the wall by the back door."

She needed to pull herself together. Too many emotions boiled under the surface, and if she didn't keep her cool, she might confess something she'd regret or get all sappy and start to cry. This was casual. Casual sex didn't involve sappy emotions or confessions of love.

"Keep it surface," she whispered to her reflection. "Don't be psycho. It's just a side squeeze. Nothing serious."

On her way back to the front, she checked on the croissants, which looked ready to bake. It was getting late and they had to get moving if they didn't want a run in with her mother or aunts, who usually got to the café just after five each morning.

Harrison finished sweeping up the mess

from the broken coffee mugs and dumped the scraps in the trash. When they saw each other, they stilled, and laughed.

"You're wearing my lipstick."

"You're wearing my whisker burn." He arched a brow. "It smells like coffee and sex in here."

"Don't worry. I put the croissants in. That'll cover up the scent of sin." She leaned her elbows onto the counter, simply admiring the undone view of him in his open, untucked dress shirt, wrinkled slacks, and that dark golden, five o'clock shadow.

He paused from tidying up when he sensed her staring. "What?"

"Just admiring the view."

He gave his bicep a little flex for her benefit. "How long until the croissants are done?"

"A few minutes."

"That soon?"

She pushed off the counter and grabbed a rag to wipe down the surface. "Soon is never a word I'd use to describe baking croissants. I started making them two days ago."

"Good things take time." He tossed the wet rag he used to wipe the floor into the sink and pulled her to him. "I'm not sure what was in that coffee you made, but I'm not even remotely tired."

She traced her tongue across his lower lip. "Hmm, should we go again?"

He backed away, and she frowned.

"Harrison?"

"We, uh, were a little hasty."

She frowned at his change in tone, then understanding dawned. "We forgot a condom."

"I'm sorry. I should have—"

"Hey, you weren't acting alone. We were both there."

"Are you…"

"On the pill? No." Why would she be when she hadn't been with anyone since Bran?

"Shit."

"I'm sure we're fine. It's not the right time."

"You're sure?"

Well, she wasn't going to bust out a calendar and calculator, but the app on her phone was fairly accurate and warned her when she was fertile. "Pretty sure."

He relaxed. "It won't happen again."

Because pregnancy led to long term commitments and that wasn't what he wanted. The energy shifted with an awkward silence. A little too much reality for both of them at the moment.

"I should check the oven."

"I'll finish straightening up."

She passed the next several minutes carefully moving the croissants to the cooling racks—a nice surprise for her mom. Unlike Harrison, she was getting sleepy but considered making an espresso just to stay awake with him.

Every second they had together was precious and would be over too soon. The longer he stayed, the less time they had left.

Her heart beat like a ticking time bomb. Inevitable detonation creeping closer until every palpitation felt like the thump of a gong ringing between her ears. No more coffee.

She carried a plate of warm croissants to the front. "Ready to taste?"

He eagerly hovered over the dish, breathing in the sweet, buttery scent of the flaky pastry and melted German chocolate.

"They look too pretty to eat."

"They're not." She scooped one up and bit into the pillowy, warm dough. Her eyes rolled back in ecstasy. "There's nothing quite like a hot croissant." Realizing he watched her, she flushed and covered her mouth.

"Even watching you eat turns me on."

She laughed and fed him a bite. His lips closed over the pastry pinched between her fingers and he groaned, his eyes closing in delight as he chewed.

"Nothing should taste that good."

"Right?"

He peeked through his lashes at her, then bit the last bite out of her hand. "I would weigh a thousand pounds if I worked here."

"That's why God made the good desserts so time consuming—to tame the temptation."

He kissed her with buttery lips and whispered, "I don't feel like pacing myself. Let's get out of here."

They bundled up and she shut off the lights. Knowing her mother would be there shortly, she left a note for her on the register telling her she left a surprise in the back.

It wasn't unusual for her to sneak out and bake in the middle of the night. Insomnia had been an issue for her since the breakup with Bran—too many thoughts tormenting her at night when the world slowed down.

"Someone delivered a stack of newspapers out front." Harrison bent to pick up the small bundle that got delivered each morning.

"Oh, thanks. I'll put them inside." She ran the stack of papers inside and paused, flipping one open and turning to page four.

Ward Montgomery's obituary was at the top of the page. Short and simple, with only the mention of his two children, the hardware store, and the time of his service.

"His funeral's today?" Mariella whispered to herself, the realization hitting like a thousand sobering bullets.

They were almost out of time. Why hadn't he said anything? Warned her? She supposed he had, but she wasn't listening.

Harrison waited out front in the glow of a street lamp, looking as picturesque as Cary Grant in his wool coat already dusted with flurries.

She couldn't move. She wanted to freeze time and stay trapped in this moment forever. But that wasn't an option.

Feeling sick, she set the papers in the rack by the counter and shut off the lights. She tried to fake a smile but failed. Swallowing back the threat of tears, she gathered her purse and keys and met him outside.

She refused to cry in front of him and would not shed a single tear. Their time was too precious to waste in sadness, but after…

Her heart would surely break once more. Maybe knowing what was to come would make it easier to bear this time around.

Now that they were both sober, they backtracked to the bar to get their cars. They didn't speak when they reached the hotel. Harrison merely led her to the elevator and held her hand on the ride up to his floor.

"You're quiet," he commented as he unlocked his hotel door. "Tired?"

"Not really."

"Good. Me neither."

Once inside, he stripped off his coat and hers. She toed off her shoes and he did the same. Piece by piece, they removed their clothes and moved to the bathroom.

Freshly folded towels sat on the counter. The room filled with steam within seconds after starting the shower and she shivered. He pulled her under the spray and wrapped her in his arms, cradling her close as he pressed kisses to her shoulder.

It was one of the most loving acts a man had ever done to her. She thought about all the lies Bran had told her, all the hollow words he said to make her believe his feelings were true. They meant nothing. But this, the way Harrison held her now, this meant something.

If this wasn't love, she couldn't imagine what was.

His hands explored her front, cupping and stroking as he adoringly washed her. She hid nothing from him. Not her scars or her pudgy parts. There was something about him that simply unhinged her sense of inadequacy around him. She wanted him to see her flaws, because deep down she knew they wouldn't bother him.

He loved her. She believed, on some level, he loved her. But she also knew he'd never admit his feelings, and no matter how much he cared, those secret sentiments would not be enough to make him stay.

After drying each other off, he led her to the bed and bundled her in blankets. The sun was coming up. It was officially his last day. Somehow, she knew they wouldn't share another dawn.

"Make love to me, Harrison."

He kissed her softly and a heavy weight filled her chest. Every breath invited the burn of unshed tears.

It was already starting. This was part of his goodbye.

She arched as he entered her, savoring the perfect way his body filled hers. When he looked into her eyes, his stare seemed to travel to the pit of her soul. And when he pressed deep, he held himself there as if trying to imprint a memory.

The moment passed between them, silent and paper thin. The longer it lasted the more she could feel her heart tearing in half.

Their breath mingled as they watched each other through misty eyes, their bodies clinging through the creeping sorrow that somehow fed the beauty of the moment. The pale dawn light filled the room, chasing back the shadows as reality moved in.

This was how she wanted to remember him. Unguarded and peaceful. There was no tension in his stare. No pain banked in his sapphire eyes.

Neither of them mentioned that they forgot a condom again. She selfishly wanted it that way. No barriers.

When they finished, she felt permanently changed, resigned in a way that left the empty parts of her heart eternally caved in so no one else could ever fill that space. As she rested in his arms staring at the hotel ceiling, she wondered how she remained so silent while her riotous heart broke with an earth-shattering crack.

She couldn't help it. One tear slipped from her lashes and she lacked the strength to wipe it away. When she finally found the courage to look at him, his eyes were closed and his breathing level.

She should go. If she didn't go now, she'd never be able to leave. And if she didn't make the choice to leave, he would choose for them. She couldn't bear to suffer the sight of him walking away from her again.

Sliding out of bed, she replaced her body with a pillow, which Harrison hugged to his side. She quietly gathered her clothes and carried them to the bathroom.

Once dressed, she wrote on a small notepad with the hotel's logo at the top.

HARRISON,

It was incredible seeing you again. If you're ever nearby, feel free to call. You have my number.

~M.

IT WAS for the best that she didn't have his number. The ball was in his court.

Taking one last look around the room, she quietly let herself out.

She made it all the way to the elevators before losing the battle with her tears. As she traveled down to the first floor, she dug a tissue out of her purse and blotted her eyes. She wanted her bed and pajamas.

The doors parted and she stepped out, head down, as she followed the pattern of the carpet to the lobby floor. A small voice screamed inside of her, begging her to turn around and go back to him, exist just a little longer in the illusion.

The effort to resist caused her to physically shake. Tears brimmed and she blinked them back. Almost home. As soon as she made it there, she could fall apart in private.

"Ms. Mosconi?"

Startled by her name, she pivoted and staggered to a halt. "Mr.—Mr. King."

His gaze briefly retraced her steps, but he had the good grace not to comment on her entrance point. "I was planning to call you this morning."

"Oh?" Best that she got all the bad news over and done with at once.

"About the interview. The staff felt you made a strong impression. Mauricio and Aaliyah really liked you."

Not what she expected to hear, she frowned. "They did?" He didn't bother to lie and lump his wife's opinion in with the others'.

"Yes. And I agree, you're very qualified for the job."

She was speechless and needed a moment to catch up. "I…I'm sorry—you're offering me the job?"

He grinned. "If you're still interested. We'd

love to have you on our staff. You can start as soon as tomorrow, if that works for you."

"What? I mean, yes!" A stunned smile overtook her face. "Tomorrow would be perfect! Thank you! I can't believe this."

"Great." He shook her hand and she matched his professionalism with over-zealous enthusiasm. "I'm in town for the next few days, so I'll be the one handling your orientation. Be here at seven and we'll start the paperwork then."

"Thank you so much, Mr. King."

"Call me Gage. And welcome to the Brick Hotel."

CHAPTER 10

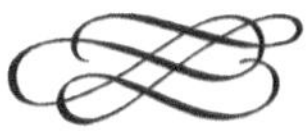

"And now we ask friends and family to say their final goodbyes by placing a flower with Ward as we lay him to rest."

Erin stepped over the muddy path cleared from the snow, and Harrison caught her elbow as her high heel sank into the damp ground. She leaned forward, placing a single rose on their father's casket and then returned to his side.

The priest looked at him expectantly, but Harrison didn't flinch or give any indication that this circus was for his benefit. Ward was dead. Let him rot.

"Now, we invite friends of the family…"

Several townspeople approached the grave and dropped a flower. Each person looked vaguely familiar, but at the same time unrecognizable. The only person he wanted to see was missing. She'd been missing since he woke up that morning to find his bed cold and hotel room empty.

"Your father was a special man. My condolences to you both," an older man said.

It took every ounce of Harrison's composure not to correct such statements and destroy his father's memory by explaining what a vicious son of a bitch the bastard truly was.

This was for Erin, and he didn't want to upset her. His sister still lived here and had to face these people on a regular basis.

The cluster of townsfolk thinned, and he spotted the McCulloughs approaching. "Let's go," he whispered in his sister's ear, but not before Mrs. McCullough got ahold of Erin and pulled her into a bear hug.

"I'm so sorry for your loss, dearie. Your dad will surely be missed."

His stomach turned. The scent of bullshit getting thicker and thicker.

The woman turned to him and he was swallowed in what he could only call suffocating maternal affection. He didn't like having such things offered because there was no source of maternal anything in his life, so he tensed under the foreign affection and she let go.

"Sweet boy. I haven't set eyes on you in years. How handsome you've become."

He didn't know what to say, so he stayed quiet.

Mr. McCullough held out a hand and Harrison shook it. That was normal. Hugs and soft sentiments were languages he couldn't speak.

Finn McCullough approached Erin, and Harrison watched for any signs of old sparks. Erin should have married him. He could have given her a normal life. He'd always assumed they would have ended up together, and he felt like a shmuck for not knowing why or when they broke up. A brother should know such things, especially when he only had one little sister to look after.

Tugging his collar, Harrison cleared his throat. The shirt was choking him.

Where was Mariella? Why wasn't she there?

In the distance, he spotted a man that looked like Giovanni Mosconi. It said a lot that Mariella's brother would come to pay his respects, but she didn't see a point. His jaw locked and he bristled against the cold.

Would things change now for Erin? She'd be all alone once he left. Maybe she'd finally be at peace and do something good for herself.

Was he responsible for her in some way now? What about holidays? With Ward gone, did he have some duty to do something? He didn't celebrate holidays because his family never had. They were just like any other day, but maybe that would change now that it was just the two of them.

Still no sign of Mariella. The pressure in his chest heated and tightened, straining his muscles and making it hard to draw in a full breath.

Would Erin expect him to come back to Jasper Falls? Maybe he could do that now that Ward was gone. It would give him a chance to see Mariella.

No, he should come back for Erin. Family should be enough. But he couldn't picture it, couldn't imagine them doing something normal like carving a turkey as if on the set of some corny sitcom.

And what would happen when he eventually came back and found Mariella celebrating the holidays with her own family? Kids and a husband. Damnit, where the fuck was she?

"Harrison, we're so sorry for your loss," Finn said, shaking his hand.

He nodded, but kept small talk out of it.

When he spotted Mariella's parents, he looked for her again, but she wasn't there. Was that it then? No goodbye?

He supposed he deserved that. He just never expected her to do something so spiteful. That didn't seem like her style.

Because it wasn't. So why wasn't she there? She couldn't spare five minutes?

Unable to take one more condolence, he excused himself. "I'll meet you in the car."

He waited for Erin as she spoke to Mariella's brother. Harrison was anxious to be on his way.

He'd finished what he'd promised to do, and now he was done. Too many unwanted feelings surrounding him here. He needed the noise and rush of the city to drown out those unwanted thoughts.

He still couldn't believe Mariella didn't show.

He watched his sister walk back to the car, her head lowered and her hand swiping about her eyes. Guilt stabbed into him and he wondered if he should stay one more night. One more day wouldn't kill him, would it?

He could leave in the morning, just to make sure Erin was situated and didn't need anything else. Twelve, maybe twenty-four more hours. But this time with no Mariella.

The thought alone nearly made him vomit. Too many bad memories. Too many questions about why she hadn't shown.

As soon as Erin settled in the car and shut the door, he blurted, "I'm leaving tonight."

"What?"

He put the car into drive and navigated over the plowed roads. "The coroner will get you the death certificates and then you can close out all his accounts. I don't care what the will says. Do whatever you want with the house and the store. It's all yours."

He didn't want anything. It made him feel better knowing his sister could have whatever was left. Now she could afford a fresh start.

"You can't put all this on me, Harrison. I need your help."

He was giving her as much as he could offer. "I can't stay here," he snapped, feeling like a cornered animal. "This town, these people… I don't belong here anymore."

"Why is it always about you? What about me? Do you think I want to deal with any of this shit?"

"Then don't. Sell the house, as-is, and start your fucking life, Erin. He's not your excuse anymore."

"Fuck you!"

He deserved that. He was putting a lot on her. But he was done with this place ten years ago. Getting involved now felt like a step backward.

He wasn't like her. He couldn't look his demons in the eye and just shake it off. Those memories reminded him of a person he no longer was.

As he drove down Main Street, he found himself searching for Mariella's car, but he didn't see the Volvo anywhere. Something had to have kept her away today. This inconclusive feeling was suffocating him.

He pulled into the driveway at their childhood home, and his gut twisted. If Erin really needed something, she would call.

The lie singed. Erin had too much pride to beg for help when it wasn't firmly offered.

His neck was sweating. He loosened his tie and unbuttoned his collar.

He should go in and get her settled. Maybe go over a plan to break down the next few steps—no. He couldn't walk in that house again. Ward might be gone, but he still couldn't do it. The fucker's memory was everywhere.

"He's dead, Erin." Harrison wasn't sure if he said the words for her sake or his. "Take whatever he had left and use it to start your life. He at least owes you that."

She scoffed and climbed out of the car, holding the door as she judged him through the dark lenses of her sunglasses. "He *is* dead. At least for me."

"What the hell does that mean?"

"You're the one who can't face this."

"Oh, bullshit—"

"You can't even walk in the house, Harrison! You accuse me of making excuses, but I stayed. I took it. I faced what you didn't have the balls to face."

"I don't have to listen to this," he snarled, jerking the car out of park.

"You left me here and you never looked back. I was fifteen. You knew it would get worse for me with you gone, and you didn't care. I'm not surprised that you're leaving again, leaving me to deal with the crap you can't handle. But don't you dare accuse me of being some willing victim of abuse."

Was that what she thought? That he saw her as weak? His sister was one of the toughest women he knew, all spit and vinegar, a fighter through and through.

But she was right about him. He had run away because he couldn't handle it anymore. He was tired of fighting back when he'd much rather save his strength to fight forward, toward a better future.

Maybe that meant their dad won. Because when Harrison left home, he'd felt truly beaten.

"I fought back the best I could, Harrison. I tried to fix it instead of running away."

Goddamn her. Like he didn't already feel like a total coward. "And like I told you before, you can't fix nasty when it's sewn into someone's soul."

"Well, Harrison, I guess you win then." She slammed the car door, walking away with the last hurtful word.

CHAPTER 11

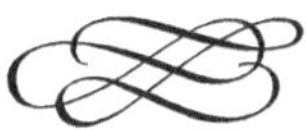

hree Months Later

MARIELLA'S FOOTFALLS clicked over the porcelain tile of the lobby, muffling the moment her heels hit the corridor carpet. Her steps moved fast, motivated by the first thought she had that morning, which—for once—had nothing to do with Harrison Montgomery.

She knocked on Mauricio's office door.

"Come in."

She grinned and set his coffee on his desk. "You're going to love me. I've finally got it!"

"Good morning to you, too." He popped open the lid to the travel mug and sat back in his chair as he took a sip. "Every time you bring me coffee from the café I'm reminded how much our hotel coffee sucks. We need to convince Gage to invest in a better machine." He set the mug down and crossed his arms over his pristine white dress shirt, top button undone as usual.

"Are you ready?" She could barely contain her excitement.

"Hit me with it."

She held out her hands as if reading each word off an invisible marquee. "Salmon pinafores."

"Salmon?"

"Yes! In lieu of gifts, they're making dona-tions to Locks of Love. *Locks!*" She lifted a hank of hair and waved it at him. "Get it? Locks…*lox*." She mimed eating. "It's perfect. And it's pink!"

"You do realize the guest list is mainly six-teen-year-old girls, right? Smoked fish doesn't scream teen aesthetic. I don't care how sophisticated they think they are."

She dropped into the chair across from his desk. "Really? I was so pumped about that one."

"It'll come to us." He slid a box forward. "Here, have a donut."

The box was from the little roadside diner

on the outskirts of town. Mauricio passed it every morning on his way in.

"I shouldn't." But she flipped open the lid anyway and selected a plump, glazed one from the center. She took a big bite and mumbled, "Bathing suit season's just around the corner and I'm going to need a circus tent to cover my ass this year."

"Oh, please." His dark stare traveled over her. "Do you have plans tonight?"

"I have to stop by my brother's place. My cousin, Braydon, is taking some measurements for Giovanni and his wife while they're out of town. I have to let him in."

It didn't escape Mariella's notice that Harrison's sister was now her sister-in-law, but she tried not to think of Erin that way. Erin and her brother were living an exciting life while they toured the country. They were currently in Texas and then off to Seattle. Who knew where Giovanni's fame would lead them next?

Their marriage had been a bit of a shock to Mariella, mostly because her brother had been away for years and proposed to Erin a split second after he returned home. She supposed some guys just knew when they found the right woman. Maybe that was how it worked. It had for Bran.

Her brother and Erin left Jasper Falls shortly after the funeral for Ward Montgomery. Mariella still regretted not attending the service, but that morning had been the start of what would forever be called the worst day of her life. She'd been so distraught over losing Harrison again, she'd made herself physically sick.

There was no dignity in heartbreak, but forcing herself to walk away from Harrison before he walked away from her at least let her preserve the illusion of composure.

She'd earned the right to fall apart in private. And fall apart she had.

Part of her hoped he'd seek her out for a final goodbye, but in true Harrison fashion, he left without a word.

Giovanni's relationship with Erin Montgomery was a curveball to the gut. Suddenly their family was having dinner with Harrison's sister, and then they were hearing wedding bells. They were adorable together, and Mariella was happy for them, but on some selfish level, she couldn't help but wonder why him and not her.

In light of her brother's joy, she kept her heartbreak to herself. Work created a great escape from her lonely thoughts, and Mauricio had become an instant friend, which she needed at the moment. She needed as many distractions as possible. And over time, the pain and loneliness would eventually fade to something she hardly noticed at all.

As long as she went through the motions, she was living. And if she was living, she couldn't possibly be dying on the inside, no matter how sad some days got. Right?

"I can pick you up afterward. You owe me a date," Mauricio said. "How many measurements does he have to take?"

"I don't know. They're remodeling." The house, Erin and Harrison's childhood home, had been on the market for a few months, but they unlisted the property when Giovanni's career took off. Now they were planning on keeping the home so they'd have a place to stay when they weren't traveling. "Maybe they're planning to add a nursery."

Mauricio frowned. "Is she pregnant?"

"Oh, no. I mean, I don't know. I was just thinking a little niece or nephew might be nice."

Her period had been late after Harrison went back to New York, and she foolishly found herself hoping he might have left a part of him behind. In the end, her cycle started, probably just late because of new job stress or all the crying she'd done that month.

She wasn't remotely ready for a baby, anyway. She still had loans to pay off and planned to milk living rent free at her parents as long as possible so she could save some money, whittle away her debt, and one day buy her own place. Not to mention the fact that Harrison had vanished and never called—not the sort of communication you want with a baby daddy.

"I don't know if a baby would fit into your brother's schedule right now. He's always on tour," Mauricio commented.

"True."

It was selfish of her to want her brother to rush into fatherhood just so she could have a little one to spoil, which would be an almost certain distraction from her personal loneliness. Giovanni wasn't ready to be a dad, according to their recent conversations. He and Erin wanted to take things slow, despite their mad dash to the chapel.

Everyone's life seemed so much more exciting than hers. So much for visiting New York, catching a Broadway show, dining at Peter Luger's, or sipping cocktails on a rooftop overlooking the Manhattan skyline. Her phone never rang.

She'd known, deep down, that those things were never going to happen. *I love yous*, marriage proposals, and travel invitations were all meaningless when spoken during or directly after sex.

"How about I pick you up at seven? Does that give you enough time to help your cousin?"

Mariella brushed the sticky, glaze crumbles off her fingertips, and stood. "Sure. And I'll keep thinking of appetizers for the sweet sixteen."

Mauricio chuckled. "Think of a good one. The meeting's at four, and I've got nothing."

"Today?" Her eyes widened.

He cringed. "Today. Who knew an entourage of teens in braces would be the root of my culinary downfall?" He flicked the box of donuts on his desk. "I've moved on to eating my feelings and found Boston creams are a great way to stuff down any sense of inadequacy."

"Aw," she laughed and tipped her head in sympathy. "Something clever will come to you."

"Let's hope so. Which reminds me, scratch the candy station. Mom doesn't want her daughter picking taffy out of her braces all night."

Mariella pulled out her phone and made a note. "So nix the vessel rentals?"

"For now. I'm sure they'll go back and forth at least five more times." Then he added in a dry tone, "I love my job."

She was grateful she mostly dealt with the guestroom issues. Event planning was pure drama. "Well, we can have drinks tonight. Don't fill up on too many donuts."

"Too late."

Walking back to her office, she mentally reviewed her tasks for the day. Now that she had settled in, Gage King was rarely around. He popped in for big picture decisions and used the hotel to sometimes host meetings with investors and shareholders of Kings Construction, but other than that Mariella mostly ran the show.

"Mariella!" Aaliyah jogged down the corridor and fell into step at her side.

"Good morning. How's the puppy settling in?"

"Oh." The tension in her face melted into a maternal glow. "I caved. She's in the bed with us. I tried the crate training, but I can't bear her little cries."

"Do you have new pictures?"

She laughed and pulled out her phone. "Only one or two...*hundred*."

Mariella glanced at the screen and her heart turned to mush. "Oh, my goodness, look at her!" She swiped through the photos, falling head over heels in love. "What name did you settle on?"

"Penny."

She looked like a Penny, with her sweet copper face and dark brown eyes. Maybe she should think about getting a puppy. Then she wouldn't have to sleep alone.

She handed Aaliyah back her phone. "What did you need?"

"I found a beehive near the west exit. I was going to take care of it, but there's a lot of guest activity by that exit, and the hive's bigger than I thought. I think we need to call a specialist."

"Okay." Mariella made another note in her phone where she kept an ongoing to do list. "I'll see who I can find in Center County and set something up."

"Thank you."

By the time Mariella settled in at her desk, responded to her emails, checked her voice mail, and attacked the priority items on her to do list, the day was half over. She had a budget meeting after lunch and needed to review a few points before the call started. Then she planned to pop in on the sweet sixteen meeting at four, if only to offer Mauricio some support and help smooth any feathers of the highly idealistic and mildly spoiled birthday girl calling the shots.

Just another day in the life of a small-town hotel manager. All in all, she loved her job. The hotel was doing great with all the new local tourism in Jasper Falls, and they usually operated at eighty percent capacity on the weekends.

With seventy guest rooms and more than fifty newcomers visiting each week, she had first dibs on checking out the clientele, half of whom were men. Divide that number in half again, deducting wedding bands, other sexual preferences, and men outside of her age range, and that left at least ten possibly single, so-so attractive, feasibly datable heterosexual men. Yes, her social life had turned into a mathematical word problem. And if trains were traveling in and out of Jasper Falls at ninety miles an hour while she still had at least five to ten childbearing years left, she might just crash into one eligible bachelor before hurling herself onto the tracks.

Folding her arms, she dropped her head onto her desk and groaned. It had been months since Harrison left, and she'd met no one. She was lonely, horny, and starting to wonder if she might die a spinster.

Sitting up, she stuffed down those icky thoughts, straightened the name plate on her desk and pulled up a search for puppies.

What the hell was she doing? She couldn't get a dog. Closing the search, she decided to take a walk and check on things around the hotel.

By the end of the day, Mauricio was still without an idea for the sweet sixteen appetizers. Princess wanted something decadent, and Mom wanted something affordable that wouldn't stain fingers, formal wear, or get stuck in braces. The meeting had been tedious, and the menu still had too many kinks that needed ironing out for anyone to claim they made progress. Some days were just tougher than others.

She popped by Mauricio's office on the way out. "Seven o'clock?"

He looked up from the sweet sixteen paperwork. "Huh? Oh, right. Yes, seven o'clock. I'll pick you up at your place."

"Perfect." She hesitated a moment. "Don't stress too much. Everything will work out. You still have time."

"I've coordinated weddings with budgets

twenty times this size, but something about this family has me sweating."

"It's teenage girls. They know exactly what they want, but generally stink at communicating their needs. And they naturally blame everyone else for their problems."

"Don't I know. Little Miss has fangs like a viper and no problem expressing disappointment."

Mariella gave him an empathetic smile. "Drinks on me tonight. See you in a bit."

"Chao."

When she got home, she helped her mother with a few things, and set the table for dinner. Nona made eggplant parm and the kitchen smelled heavenly.

"Colleen, stir the sauce," Nona ordered and her mother rolled her eyes, passing the plates for the table to Mariella.

"You're not eating?" Mariella's mother asked, noting that she put one plate back and only set out three.

"I have dinner plans with a friend."

"A male friend?"

"Not that kind of friend. It's Mauricio, from work."

"A date's a date, Mariella."

"I didn't call it a date."

"Did he?"

"Ma, it's fine. We're just friends. Mauricio knows that."

"Who's friends?" her father asked as he came into the kitchen, pecking a kiss on Nona's cheek. "Col, my lunch box broke again. I think it's time to retire this one."

Her mother snicked and took the lunchbox. "Like it's owner." She opened the junk drawer and dug out a roll of electrical tape. "Try this, Paulie. We're past the age of investing in new job supplies."

Her father goosed her mother. "Only six months left before social security kicks in."

Mariella smirked at the cute way they flirted and grabbed napkins for the table. Her father poured a glass of red from the jug of wine stored on top of the refrigerator and sat at the empty place setting to work on repairing his metal lunch pail.

"You not eatin' with us, Mar?"

"She has a date," her mother said, tossing tomatoes into the salad.

"It's not a date."

Her father raised a bushy brow. "You seeing someone?"

"No. Mom, don't start rumors."

Her mother snickered and shoved two wooden spoons into the salad bowl. "It's that man from the hotel."

"What man?"

"The wedding planner," her mother said.

"He's straight?" her father asked, making a mess of his lunch box as he tried to reconstruct the broken handle with tape.

"He's not a wedding planner," Mariella corrected. "He's the banquet manager. And yes, he's straight. Hetero men can plan events too, Daddy."

He held up his hands in mock defense. "How would I know? Seemed like a fair question. If things work out, at least you'll have a nice reception. I imagine he has some vendor connections and can save us a few bucks."

"Oh, my God," she mumbled, shaking her head. "We're not dating and no one is getting married. See what you started, Mom?" She grabbed her purse and keys off the chair by the wall and kissed Nona's cheek. "I shouldn't be too late."

The days were getting longer and there was still a bit of sunlight left when she pulled into Erin and Giovanni's driveway. Her heart pinched as memories washed over her.

They never hung out at Harrison's when they were young, but she remembered being in his car a few times when he had to swing home to grab something between school and football games and the occasional house party.

She could still hear the echo of his old Dodge idling by the curb. He never parked in the driveway. *"I'll only be a second."*

"Do you want me to come in with you?"

"No. Just stay here. I'll be right out."

Staring at the glowing windows, she'd patiently wait for him to return. Sometimes she heard him arguing with his dad.

He always rushed out of the house, jumping off the porch rather than taking the steps. His mood noticeably changed whenever his father was home, and Harrison would slam the car door and not say a word for several minutes.

She could always tell by his jaw whenever he was tense. She'd learned early on that he didn't like to talk when he was upset.

But she hated seeing him that way, so sometimes she asked anyway. "Is everything okay?"

"Fine," he snapped, cutting the turn close as he raced toward the mountain in the distance.

"Harrison, slow down."

"I should just keep fucking driving and never come back."

The thought of him running away gutted her. "What happened?"

"The same thing that always happens. I'm a

fuck up. I should have done better. I'm just one big fucking disappointment!"

He was shouting, and even though his rage wasn't directed at her, she felt trapped in the cross-fire. The car sped up the back road at a seventy mile an hour clip.

"Harrison, slow down. You're scaring me."

He took a fast turn and headlights gathered up ahead where cars parked along the distant tree line. He jerked the wheel before they reached the others and slammed on the brakes, driving the car off the shoulder.

"Fuck!" His fist slammed into the steering wheel and she flinched.

Her heart raced as her back pressed into the seat. "Harrison, what happened?"

"Nothing!"

"Clearly, something—"

"I don't want to fucking talk about it!" His voice broke and her fear elevated to concern.

"Hey." Tentatively, she rested a hand on his arm. His skin was burning up. "Everything will work out. Whatever happened, we can fix it."

His lips firmed into a thin line as his cheeks darkened and his jaw locked. He looked down at her hand and frowned, the tension slowly leaving his face. His fingers brushed over hers. "Your hands are so delicate."

Lifting her hand, he traced her fingers with

his. Hers were smooth and his were calloused from sports. One of his knuckles was split, the crack still red with dried blood.

"Did you hurt your hand?" Harrison was an athlete so he always had scrapes and bruises.

"It's nothing."

She touched his fingernails, which were bitten excruciatingly short. "You shouldn't bite your nails."

"Nervous habit." He watched her as she studied his hand. It wasn't unusual for them to explore each other that way. He never tried to pull away or hide from her, at least not in a physical sense. Emotionally, he was more guarded.

Bringing his hand to her lips, she kissed the tips of his ravaged fingernails. Then she kissed his injured knuckle. He dragged the back of his fingers softly along her jaw and she shut her eyes.

His hand glided down her neck, along the slope of her shoulder, until the side of her cardigan lowered. She didn't stop him when he pulled open the buttons of her shirt, nor did she object when he reached between her legs to recline her seat.

"Lie back."

Sometimes it felt like Harrison tried to escape through her. She liked offering him that sort of shelter.

He scooted onto the passenger seat with her, pulling her legs around him and positioning her exactly where he wanted. They shared an explosive chemistry, but then there were the rare moments like this, when he held her close enough to feel his heart beating against her skin.

Sometimes, he couldn't look at her, but she felt the emotions pouring out of him as he buried his face in her neck and hair. He was inside of her, but they were no longer having sex. Sex was just a cover, an excuse for him to find the closeness he so desperately needed.

He didn't shake from passion, but from intense emotion. "It's okay," she whispered as jagged breaths jerked past his lips. He hugged her tighter but didn't say a word.

Tremors shook his shoulders and she wondered if this was how boys like Harrison cried. He never shed a tear, but she felt a strong pull to protect him.

There were several moments like that, never consistent enough to think something was truly wrong, but frequent enough for her to realize Harrison didn't feel as in control of his life as he led everyone else to believe.

She had always hero worshipped him to some degree, but wearing his tears somehow washed away any illusions. Harrison was just as fragile and vulnerable as the rest of them.

Headlights streamed over the house when Mariella's cousin pulled up behind her and she remembered where she was. Shaking off the hold of her memories, she climbed out of the car and greeted her cousin, Braydon, with a wave.

Braydon brushed a hand over his blond curls. Unlike her other dark-haired McCullough cousins, Braydon's hair was full of golden waves, which was partially why the aunts called him the golden child. She and Giovanni inherited their father's Italian coloring, and her Clooney cousins all inherited Aunt Rosemarie's strawberry blonde hair.

"Well, this is weird," her cousin said by way of greeting. "Never thought I'd be walking into Erin Montgomery's house."

She knew most people didn't care for Erin, but she never saw her that way. To her, this would always be Harrison's house, and Erin would always be his little sister.

"Easy, Bray. She's Giovanni's wife now. That makes her your cousin, too."

"That's gonna take some time to process."

Mariella let him inside where the scent of newly painted walls greeted. She searched for a light switch and found one in the hall.

"Where's all their stuff?"

There was a sofa but no tables or lamps. The kitchen had a table and two chairs but no curtains, and the cabinets were mostly empty.

"I think they cleared everything out after Ward died." Giovanni said Erin had planned to sell the house, but changed her mind when they got together.

Braydon got to work measuring the space and jotting numbers in a small notepad. She followed him from room to room, silently taking in the vacant surroundings.

"What kind of addition are they thinking of?"

"Giovanni said she wants to totally transform the house. He wants the master bedroom gutted and completely redone."

Mariella didn't see anything wrong with the master bedroom but supposed everyone had their own taste when it came to decorating. Unlike the rest of the house that had been freshly painted, with newly finished floors, the master bedroom room had been gutted down to the studs.

She left Braydon to his work and drifted down the narrow hall toward the other bedrooms. The first one was clearly Erin's. It had furniture and the bedding was made, clothes still hung in the closets and filled the drawers. A house plant with long tapered leaves hung in the corner, its vines strung from each curtain rod and dangling almost to the floor.

"You look like you could use some water,"

she said to the plant. A quick trip to the kitchen for a glass of water and she returned to the potted vine. "There you go."

Mariella continued exploring, but there really wasn't much to see. At the end of the hall stood a narrow door, different from the others. She knew in an instant it was Harrison's room.

The knob was broken as if someone had bashed in the lock. The paint around the inner moldings was nicked and scuffed, unlike the freshly painted trim throughout the rest of the house.

She didn't see any lamps or light switches, so she flipped on the flashlight of her phone. High school paraphernalia sagged off the walls. Faded pictures and old sports tickets triggered a strong sense of nostalgia.

A layer of dust covered the furniture. Laundry was stuffed in the corner, stiff from time and musty from a leak in the ceiling. She recognized his old football jersey, the blue and gold colors causing a strange ache to bloom in her chest.

The room was a forgotten time capsule full of relics he'd left behind. Each item sad and forgotten. She caught her reflection in the dusty mirror and a chill chased over her skin. Did she belong here with the rest of his discarded past?

The bed was small, too small for a high school boy. And the dresser was missing most of the hardware.

The hollow stretched in her chest as she understood Harrison hadn't abandoned *her* or *his town* all those years ago, he abandoned himself. He left himself behind and become someone else. He hadn't packed a single memento.

She didn't like the feelings the room stirred, but when she turned to leave, her heart stopped. The sheetrock was caved in, exposing the studs, as if something large and heavy had hit the wall. Something the size of a teenage boy.

Beside the door sat a collapsed bookshelf, splintered at the corners and split along the wood as if someone had smashed it with a hammer.

A floorboard creaked and Braydon filled the cavity of the doorway. "Yikes."

"It's Harrison's room." She took in the broken furniture, consumed by the misery of this place. "They just left it like this."

Braydon glanced around the cold room. "Maybe she was waiting for him to come back."

That was never going to happen. Mariella always thought Harrison had run toward something, but seeing his childhood bedroom changed her thinking.

He'd been running away from whatever happened in this house.

She needed to escape the oppressive sight, and she'd only been there for a few minutes. Harrison had been trapped in this house for the first half of his life.

"I'll meet you out front," she said. "I need some air."

CHAPTER 12

Harrison stared at the stack of rock salt along the back wall of the stockroom, his shoulders tense and his ears ringing. A pack of smokes still sat on the wood table in the corner by his father's ashtray.

"What the hell am I doing back here?"

The man had some of the heaviest ashtrays and threw them like he was a shot put champion when he was in a rage. Those fuckers could shatter bones before chipping themselves.

He still had a scar from where he took one to the back of the head. It dropped him like a sack of cement, and he'd had a headache for weeks.

It had been months since the funeral, and

he was still as angry as he'd been the day he left. He told Erin he didn't want the store or anything from the house, but dear old Dad knew just how to push his buttons. The bastard purposely left Erin out of the will and, unbeknownst to Harrison, set up a living trust, which left him solely responsible for the store.

He didn't blame Erin for bailing. It must have crushed her to know, after all she put up with, their father left her nothing but half a house. He had all his assets tied to the business so, until the house sold, she'd get nothing.

What a fucking prick. "You always had to get the last word, didn't you, you son of a bitch?"

Harrison didn't plan to stay long. He'd figure something out with the store and see that his sister got more than her share in the end. Ward would not have the last word.

But being back in Jasper Falls wasn't easy. His life was in New York. His company was in New York. His future was in New York. Nothing had changed.

So why, after three months of being back in the city, did it feel like he left his heart somewhere else?

With practiced discipline, he shoved the thought of Mariella away.

He wouldn't call her. She abandoned him when he needed her most. If he had things his way, he never would have come back, but the property tax on the store was due. He could say fuck it and let the banks foreclose, but that would only deprive Erin of the fair market price she deserved. He wanted to do right by her.

He could remain detached and close up the store. It was business. Nothing personal. In and out.

Once he found a realtor and liquidated what was left on the shelves, he could get the hell out of there and handle the rest by phone. Erin would get a check and maybe forgive him for being such a selfish prick when he last saw her.

She was married now. To Mariella's brother of all people. He hadn't been invited to the wedding or even told about the engagement until after their vows were said.

He should have been there to support her. He could have walked her down the aisle or something.

He sighed, staring at the dimly lit display of garden tools on the back wall. She probably didn't want him there—a hundred other guys she'd likely prefer to give her away.

He wandered around the untouched displays and the dark aisles. A tinge of cigarette smoke still clung to the air. No one had been inside for some time.

Using the light on his phone, he shined it toward the front of the store. He hated this place. Couldn't bear to breathe its stagnant air.

He left the store untouched and locked up. Forgetting his car parked around back, he headed down Main Street on foot, his mind already ordering a shot of something strong as soon as he reached the bar.

The snow was long gone, the garden beds freshly mulched with tiny sprouts just beginning to show as flowers bloomed. The damp air smelled of spring showers and something strangely specific to his childhood. Wisteria, he thought. How strange that one specific smell could trigger so many memories.

"Pardon," he muttered as a group of women bustled past, their arms full of store bags.

Who the hell were all these people? He never knew Jasper Falls to be a hotspot for so many tourists.

Maybe they weren't tourists. Maybe they

were the locals and he was the visitor. He'd been away so long, it made sense that he barely recognized anyone.

He navigated the sidewalk traffic, glancing into store windows and deciding he could probably get a good price for the hardware store if this midafternoon rush was indicative of anything. There were people everywhere.

Crowds didn't usually bother him. Hell, he loved the busy streets of New York. But small towns were supposed to be calm and quiet. This was a madhouse.

He did a double take as a small child with a mossy green head ran past him, followed by a man dressed as some sort of bear. What the hell was that?

An unexpected crowd gathered in the parking lot of O'Malley's. So much for grabbing a quiet drink. There was some sort of festival happening and he wanted no part of it.

More green headed kids in costumes milled about. Their parents also disguised in various rags and—

A gaggle of mini storm troopers came marching through, herding him and many others out of the way as they made it to a makeshift stage set up outside the bar. Was this some sort of comic convention?

"All jedis line up to my right," a voice bellowed from a large speaker at the corner of the stage. "All wookies to my left. And all Sith lords, storm troopers, and other dark side allies line up directly in front of me. The judging is about to begin."

Light sabers glowed and kids scrambled into place. Only then, did he notice the banner strung above the stage that read *MAY THE 4th BE WITH YOU!*

Was that a thing? May fourth was now *Star Wars Day*? He couldn't stay here.

Pivoting away from the throng, he crossed Main Street and looked for a second option, only to stop dead in his tracks at the sight of the café.

His heart beat hard in his chest as he stared at the front window wondering if she was inside. A car beeped at him and he jogged off the street, closer to the café.

Shading his eyes, he looked through the glass, but only spotted an older woman with faded blonde hair. No sign of Mariella.

What if she wasn't in Jasper Falls anymore? It had been months. She could have moved on, gone somewhere else, met someone…

His stomach soured at the thought. He hoped she was happy, but he wasn't altruistic enough to picture her with another man without seeing red.

He really needed that drink. Since O'Malley's was out of the question, he figured he'd head back to his car and find something outside of Jasper Falls. Getting out of there before anyone knew he was back seemed like a wise move.

"How did you find this place?" Mariella unfolded the linen napkin and spread it over her lap.

"My family knows the chef."

The old farmstead house had been stripped down to its original colonial fixtures. Wide windowsills and aged wood floors, authentic to the home, added to its charm. A long, curved bar built by the owners, complimented the timeframe of the house, and the service so far was warm and welcoming.

After enjoying a pre-dinner martini at the bar with Mauricio, they were escorted to a small table in the main room of the house. A fire crackled in the aged stone hearth, further adding to the ambiance.

The waiter delivered a second round of

martinis. Even the stemware looked authentic and old.

"It's beautiful here."

He lifted his cocktail. "Everything's farm to table and served family style. The menu's not very extensive, but the food's outstanding. If the owner's cooking tonight, he'll probably come out and ask how you enjoyed the meal."

She loved when chefs did that. Glancing at the minimal menu, she reviewed the choices. There was a steak, poultry, or pasta option and a few appetizers. "What were you thinking?"

"Your choice."

Everything sounded delicious. "I'm feeling especially carnivorous tonight. How about the steak?"

"Perfect."

The waiter returned and took their order. She and Mauricio usually went to dinner once a week, but she made a point to always go Dutch. She enjoyed their friendship and didn't want to complicate matters with mixed signals.

Her decision to remain single had nothing to do with him. Mauricio was a very handsome man. It came down to her still feeling too fragile to lay her heart on the line and risk being hurt again. But one day she hoped she'd find the courage to try.

"I wanted to run something by you." Mauricio straightened his silverware.

"Okay."

"My brother's getting married in June. It's a destination wedding in Saint Thomas."

She remembered him mentioning it. "I approved your time off."

"Right. Well, I wanted to see if you might want to join me."

Mariella's brows shot up. "In the Caribbean?"

"It's seven days in the Virgin Islands, all inclusive."

"In…the same room?"

"Would that be an issue?" His hand lowered over hers and she understood this was more than a platonic invitation.

It was getting a little warm in there. She glanced at the fireplace but knew that wasn't the culprit. "We work together, Mauricio."

"There's nothing in our contracts prohibiting us from dating a coworker."

He checked? "But we're friends."

"Sometimes friends become more. Many great relationships start out that way."

She sat back and sipped her martini. Her chin quivered and she accidentally dribbled on herself. "Shit." She blotted her mouth with her napkin.

"You don't have to decide right now, but I wanted to make my intentions clear. I like you, Mariella. We've basically been dating for weeks."

Her eyes widened. "We eat dinner together." There had never been a whiff of sexual tension between them that she noticed.

He shrugged and smiled. "I like spending time with you. I'd like us to share more than the occasional meal."

Her face was on fire. She took another sip of her drink and blew out a breath. "This martini's strong."

"Just think about it."

As if she could avoid doing so. Mauricio was inarguably handsome. He dressed well, spoke well, smelled nice, held doors, had terrific taste in donuts, and was one of her favorite coworkers. She should be thrilled he wanted to date her.

So why wasn't she?

"I like our friendship, Mauricio. I'd hate to jeopardize that."

He once again reached for her hand. "No one's threatening our friendship. I'm not shallow like that. Plus, you're technically my boss."

That's right. She was his superior. "If things didn't work out…" Oh, it could get messy.

"We're both professionals, Mariella."

Maybe this was the universe's way of telling her to try something new. She was superstitious enough to believe in signs, but the last time she took a chance she ended up having her heart ripped out and spiraled into an ongoing depression she still hadn't fully recovered from.

Just then, her phone chirped. She welcomed the distraction. "That's probably my brother checking in on how things are going at the house. The inspector was at the house today to review the permits."

He waved a hand. "Go ahead."

She pulled her phone from her purse, but frowned when she didn't recognize the number. She needed to put her number on one of those *Do Not Call* lists. The spam was getting excessive.

She swiped open her text messages, prepared to type STOP when her hands went numb and she dropped her phone.

"Everything okay?"

She quickly picked it up and stared at the screen but couldn't make a sound.

Look up.

HER HEAD LIFTED and she scanned the restaurant. Her heart rate spiking and her pulse pounding.

"Mariella?"

"Oh, my God," she breathed, unblinking.

Harrison watched her from the next room where he sat at the bar. Casually, as if it were completely normal for him to be back in Center County, he lifted a rocks glass and silently toasted her.

Mauricio glanced over his shoulder and back to her. "Something wrong?"

What was he doing there? When had he come back?

"I... I have to use the restroom. Excuse me."

Shoving her phone into her purse, she stood on shaky legs and rushed to the ladies' room. The tiny, simple wash room contained only a toilet and a sink. She didn't lock the door because it would only be a matter of—

The knob turned and he stepped inside.

CHAPTER 14

"Ühat are you doing here?"

Harrison shut the door behind him and flipped the lock. "I had to come back to deal with the hardware store."

So nothing to do with her. "Did you follow me here?"

"No. Pure coincidence." He took a step closer then paused as if changing his mind about touching her. "Who is he?" Distinct disapproval tinged his accusatory tone.

She scoffed. "Are you kidding me? Harrison, it's been months. You haven't called—"

"I was cooling off."

"Cooling off? From what?"

He closed the distance and she backed into the wall. "Who is he?"

"We work together."

"Then why was he touching you?"

She shoved him back, but he didn't budge. "Why do you care?"

His intense blue eyes locked on her and his jaw ticked. "You know why."

"No, I don't."

His height and bulk surrounded her. That approach might intimidate others, but she wasn't afraid of him. "I need to get back."

When she tried to step around him, he curved his hands around her waist, thumbs gently caging her in an extremely intimate hold. He looked into her eyes as his palms glided up her sides, his hold now resting just under her breasts as she tried to slow her breathing.

"Harrison."

"Mariella."

She wanted to sink into his touch. Kiss him. Slap him. "I'm on a date."

Something flashed in his eyes. "How serious is it?"

She couldn't lie to him, but she wanted to protect herself. They needed boundaries. He'd only come back to deal with his dad's store. "How long are you staying?"

"I haven't decided."

He was lying. She sensed it in the way his

gaze shot away. He'd leave as soon as he finished whatever he'd come back to do.

"Let go of me."

He stepped back and pushed his hands into his pockets, facing the door. Her knees weakened and she sagged into the wall.

"Are you in love with him?"

Self-preservation kept her quiet. He watched her through the mirror.

"I have to get back." She slipped past him, but he caught her arm.

"Let me see you tonight."

"Harrison—"

"Please. I just want to talk. You owe me that much."

She balked. "*I* owe you?"

"You didn't come to the funeral."

Shame washed over her, and she lowered her stare. "I couldn't."

"I needed you there."

She shut her eyes. If he needed her, he wouldn't have left. "No, you didn't."

"Well, I wanted you there."

"Harrison, please." Her voice strained around the lump forming in her throat. "Don't make me feel bad for having boundaries."

He lifted her chin and searched her eyes. "Tell me you're not in love with him."

"I don't love him," she whispered. "But I'm here with him, and I have to get back."

"Meet me tonight. Eleven o'clock, in the parking lot of O'Malley's."

"Fine. But I have to go."

He let go of her arm. "Eleven o'clock."

She unlocked the door and left, keeping her head down until she returned to her seat across from Mauricio.

"Everything okay?"

"Oh, everything's fine." She guzzled the remainder of her martini, then decided she shouldn't drink anything else for a while. Her hand trembled as she set down the empty glass.

The food arrived and the steak looked delicious. Unfortunately, her stomach was so unsettled she could barely swallow more than a bite.

Mauricio made no other mention of trips to the Caribbean or his feelings for her, which she appreciated. The conversation safely circled familiar topics having to do with day-to-day life and work.

When the bill arrived, Mariella insisted she pay her half. It was nearly eleven by the time they left the restaurant, and there was no way she'd make it to Harrison on time.

As soon as Mauricio dropped her off at

home, she went inside her house and waited by the front window for him to pull away. The moment his headlights disappeared, she snatched her car keys and headed to her Volvo.

She now had Harrison's phone number but was too impatient to send him a text and let him know she was running late. When she reached the pub, the parking lot was packed.

It was May fourth so the town was doing their big salute to *Star Wars*. Tomorrow, it would be Cinco de Mayo, then Mother's Day, then International Hummus Day, and whatever other holiday the town festival committee decided they should observe next.

The hotel was almost at maximum capacity, which was great for business, but a lot for their limited staff. Had Harrison already checked in?

She didn't see him in the parking lot, so she went inside. The pub looked like the Mos Eisley Cantina, *Star Wars* characters loitering in every corner. The DJ played a Village People remix as C-3PO had a dance off with Chewy center stage.

Someone tugged her arm and she turned, finding Harrison beside her, holding two beers. "Come on."

He led her through the crowd, to the back

of the bar where the pool tables were. Some chick in Princess Leia buns was making out with Darth Vader.

"That's not right," Mariella murmured, as Harrison dragged her toward the back exit. Why was Princess Leia always putting off major *Flowers in the Attic* vibes?

Opening the back door, Harrison waved her outside.

"I'm pretty sure we're not supposed to take drinks outside."

He rolled his eyes and tugged her outside anyway. A set of metal stairs climbed up the back of the building and he sat down. "This town's getting real fucking weird," he finally said.

She laughed. "Don't they celebrate The Fourth in the city?"

"Of July, maybe. When the hell did this become a holiday?"

She sat beside him on the metal steps. "People like Star Wars."

"People are goofy."

She let out a little wookie cry, and he laughed. She smiled up at him. The moment it finally sank in that he was really there, her boundaries melted away. "I missed you."

He looked unsure, then blew out sigh of relief. "I missed you, too. I should've called."

"I didn't expect you to."

"Ouch. I guess I deserve that."

"I know how you work, Harrison. It's fine." It wasn't, but what could she do?

He sipped his beer. "So who was that guy?"

"I work with him."

"Is it serious?"

She looked up at him, debating if she should come clean. "What if I said it is?"

He stared out at the parking lot. "I'd have to accept it."

She let him stew over the possibility for a moment, then confessed, "He's only a co-worker. But tonight he told me he'd like to be more."

"And what about you? What do you want?"

Their hands hung between their knees, beer bottles casually dangling.

"It would be nice if I liked someone in the same town and emotionally available for a change, but that's never been my style."

"Are you attracted to him?"

"He's an attractive man."

He shot her a side glance, and she laughed.

"Not that way. But I do think he's handsome."

They were quiet for several minutes. The music from inside the pub rumbling through the brick walls.

Harrison's head tipped at the machines parked in the distance. "What are they building back there?" Harrison pointed toward the shadowed frame of a bulldozer.

"A winery. Gage King's building it for Perrin and her sister. It'll be part of O'Malley's eventually."

"Did you end up getting the job at the hotel?"

"I did." She chuckled. "Shocked the hell out of me. But Gage is hardly ever there, and Perrin has no involvement."

"I'm staying there."

Her heart raced at the thought of being so close to him while she was at work. She would also have insider information on his reservation and know exactly when he intended to check out.

She thought of the last time they were in the hotel together and all the things they did in that king sized bed. Then she thought about his childhood bed and the state of his old room.

"How are you dealing with everything since the funeral?" She should have been there. She'd honestly tried, but she couldn't do it, not without making a spectacle.

"I'm fine."

"You can talk to me, Harrison. I know you two had a complicated relationship."

"There's nothing to say. I'm just here to wrap up loose ends with the store, then I'm out."

She tried not to take his apathy personally, even if it stung her pride. She changed the subject. "What do you think about our siblings getting married?"

He laughed and took a sip of beer. "That one I never saw coming."

"They seem happy. What does Erin say?"

"I haven't really talked to her."

Surprised, she looked at him. "How come?"

He shrugged. "We're not really close anymore."

She wondered if his sister was another off-limits topic. She didn't want to spoil the night forcing the conversation around subjects he didn't want to discuss, so she kept quiet.

After several minutes of silence, he blurted, "Do you want to get out of here?"

"And go where?"

"We can go back to my room—"

"I don't think that's such a great idea." When he gave her a look of surprise, she said, "Everyone at the hotel knows me."

"Is that really why?"

She dropped her gaze to the dark pavement. "Harrison, every time I let you into my life, you break my heart on the way out."

He didn't deny his actions had hurt her nor did he make a joke of her feelings. But he did take her hand, holding it softly in his. "I'm sorry."

"I forgive you."

He kissed her fingers. "I don't like hurting you."

"I know."

"I don't want to be alone tonight. What if I promised to behave? No sex. Just good conversation between close friends."

Were they close friends? Friends kept in touch.

"What are you thinking?"

She fanned out her hands. "I don't know what to do."

He rubbed a finger over her knee. "What do you *want* to do?"

She wanted to kiss him and hold him. She wanted to feel him inside of her and get lost in his body. She wanted to forget who she was and do something fearless. But she also wanted to avoid getting hurt again.

She was like a chimp in a cage that reached for a reward only to get shocked.

How many times would she hurt herself before finally learning the lesson? Harrison wasn't good for her. But no one else made her feel as good as he could.

"It's not fair when you touch me like that."

"I'm barely touching you."

Yet she felt him everywhere. He was the downbeat of her heart and the skitter of her pulse. The prickle on her skin and the chill dancing on her spine. He was the heat swirling in her belly and—

His lips pressed to hers and she jerked back. "Harrison!"

"I'm sorry," he whispered. "I just… I don't want you to push me away. I don't like it."

She touched her lips, the imprint of his kiss lingering on her mouth. "We have to have boundaries."

"Why? Why can't we just be together? Why can't we just have this escape? I promise—"

She covered his mouth. They would crumble if he put a lie between them. She didn't want him making promises he'd only break.

He pulled away her hand and pressed a kiss to her palm. "I'd never intentionally hurt you, Mariella."

She believed him. But the road to hell was

paved with good intentions. "I think I should go home."

Disappointment stole over his face and he stood. "Can I see you tomorrow?"

"I have work."

"After?"

She couldn't see him in an intimate setting. She didn't trust herself. "How about I come by the hardware store and give you a hand with whatever you're doing there?"

His brow creased. "Why would you want to get involved in that?"

"Because you're my friend, and I know this is a lot for you."

"I don't care about the store."

Maybe not. But he cared about the things it made him feel. "I can meet you there a little after five. That's my best offer."

"You drive a hard bargain, Mosconi."

"You don't make it easy, Montgomery."

He grinned. "Well, I guess I'll see you tomorrow at five."

CHAPTER 15

Harrison shut his laptop and checked the time. Damn. It wasn't even noon yet. The day was dragging. Up at dawn, he put in five hours of hard work, made a few calls, and checked the clock six thousand times.

Groaning, he threw his head back and scrubbed his hands over his face. He should be thinking of the store and coming up with a plan.

He could hire someone to tag and photograph the inventory for liquidation, a one and done simple online auction. He just needed to make a phone call, and he could have someone sent down by the end of the day to get started and find himself back in New York by tonight.

So why wasn't he doing that?

Because he hadn't gone over the plans with Erin. Obviously.

She was away. With Giovanni. Her husband.

Jesus, his little sister was married. He still couldn't picture it. Wondering how long she planned to be out of town, he sent her a text.

How's it going?

WHEN SHE DIDN'T INSTANTLY respond, he checked in on social media. Scrolling down the feed, only half focusing on the images drifting by, he impatiently wondered what could be keeping his sister from replying.

Maybe she was in the shower or at a restaurant. Perhaps she was still sleeping. He didn't know her well enough as an adult to know if she was a morning person or a night owl. He should probably know such things.

He remembered a time when Erin would call him constantly. He was always rushing off the phone to get somewhere, and she'd make him schedule an hour when they could talk again. But he'd been so busy back then, there never seemed enough time. And they soon ran out of things to talk about.

No matter how much he promised to call her back or do better, he never gave her the time she wanted, and eventually, she stopped looking to him for advice, stopped needing him in her life. Her independence made him proud but also sad and incredibly disappointed in himself.

The world moved so fast in New York, it was too much to summarize in a five-minute conversation. And nothing ever seemed to change in Jasper Falls.

His thumb stopped swiping and he glanced out the window overlooking Main Street. Things had changed. Friends grew up and got married. New businesses opened and thrived. There were festivals and crosswalks and tourists for God's sake.

His phone pinged and he opened the text, relieved Erin finally replied.

What's wrong?

HE FROWNED. Why did something have to be wrong? Couldn't he just check in for no reason? Wasn't that what normal families did?

His phone rang and Erin's name popped up on the screen. At least some things hadn't changed. Erin was still impatient when she wanted answers.

He brought the phone to his ear. "Hey."

"Is something wrong?"

"Why would something be wrong? I was just checking in with you."

"Checking—What? Harrison, are you high?"

He scoffed. "No. Why would you ask that?"

"I'm sorry, it's just… In ten years, you've never checked in on me. I don't even know what that means."

"Nothing. It means nothing." Why did he even bother trying? "I'll talk to you later—"

"Wait!"

He hesitated through the uncomfortable silence as it stretched into unbearable. "What?"

"How's…New York?"

"I'm not in New York. I'm in Jasper Falls."

"You are? Since when?"

"The taxes were due at the store and…" And he'd paid them yesterday so why was he still there. "I'm tying up loose ends."

"Oh." That little syllable held the weight

of all their secrets and he hated that she knew him well enough to know this wasn't going to be an easy process for him. "Are you okay? Do you need me to come back and help?"

He didn't deserve her offer, and she'd never know how much he appreciated it, not because he wanted her assistance, but her offer validated that she didn't completely hate him. "No. No, you keep doing what you're doing and enjoy yourself. You've done enough."

"Have you been to the house?"

Last they talked, she was slamming doors in his face and telling him what a coward and shitty brother he was. Part of her anger had to do with his reluctance to set foot in their childhood home.

"No. I'm at the Brick Hotel."

"If you wanted to stay at the house, you're more than—"

"I don't."

She sighed, but he couldn't understand why she would take his decision personally. Hotels just came with more amenities. And Mariella.

"Harrison, it's different now. I've painted and pulled up the carpets. Your room's still—"

"It's your house, Erin." He didn't care what

she did with his ratty old things. "Don't hold onto anything on my account. I've moved on."

Have you? He could almost hear the question drift between them although neither of them said it aloud.

"How long do you plan to stay? I'd like to see you."

Last night he'd been ready to leave. Then he spotted Mariella on a date, and his entire focus did a one-eighty.

Seeing her on a date with another man, smiling and laughing, tilting her head in that thoughtful way she did when she listened… He'd never seen her like that with anyone else. He didn't like it. Those looks were supposed to be for him.

"I'm staying the week," he blurted without considering his schedule or motive.

"Really?" Her voice pitched with excitement. "I'll talk to Giovanni. I can probably get a flight home for a few days."

Shocked she would do that, he grinned. "I'd like that. Would Giovanni come with you?" He supposed he should get to know her husband. Until now he mostly thought of him as Mariella's brother.

"No, he still has performances he's committed to. But that's okay. I'd like to have some time with just you and me."

Again he was shocked by her eagerness and ability to overlook how absent he'd been from her life. "Great. Let me know what you figure out."

"I will. And, Harrison?"

"Yeah?"

"Thanks for checking in."

He ended the call, a strange mix of satisfaction and nervousness churning in his stomach. Sensing he'd done something good and made his sister happy made him happy. But knowing how easily he could mess this up scared the shit out of him. He didn't want to let her down.

With no mom and a fucked-up dad, they didn't have traditions that glued their family together at the seams. No warm memories or holidays that reunited them every season. There was no dependable connection, and maybe it was up to them to create one.

Linked by only their DNA and mutual trauma, he wondered if that was enough. What if the common ground of bad experiences stirred up too many unwanted ghosts of their past? What if the memories never went away, and building a relationship kept them alive?

Disturbed by the possibility, he stood and frantically started tidying his belongings, stuffing his laptop back inside the case and crumpling the scratch paper he used to jot a few notes. Into the trash it went, no trace he was ever there.

Now what?

His body pulsed with a nervous energy he needed to expel, so he threw on a pair of sweats and laced up his sneakers. There had to be a fitness room somewhere in this place.

The hotel was small, only five floors with minimal facilities, but the construction was new and the design achieved a decent balance of small town, historic charm without crossing the line into gothic revival gaudy.

He found the fitness center on the first floor, tucked in the back behind the stairwell. Just a few treadmills, some free weights, two bikes, and a row machine, but it was enough for Harrison to get in a decent workout and blow off some steam.

A damp stain darkened the material of his shirt at his chest and between his shoulder blades by the time he finished. When he left the gym, he got a bit turned around looking for the elevator—or so he told himself—as he wandered into the main lobby.

Pretending to admire the moldings and tour the vestibule, he drifted toward the corridor that likely housed the boardrooms and offices. A soft female voice caught his ear and the side of his mouth kicked up. He'd recognize her voice anywhere.

He spotted a vending machine and checked the selection, listening to the muffled conversation drifting from the door marked MANAGER.

Sliding a buck into the machine, he pressed a button and a bottle of water dropped from the display. He sipped and patiently waited for the conversation to end.

"I'll have a proposal for you by the end of next week. Once you and your fiancé have had a chance to look over the options, we can sit down with our banquet manager and iron out the details."

The door was cracked open, and if he leaned into the wall just so, he could see her working behind a large computer monitor. She clicked a few keys, the soft tick of her finger nails reminding him of all the times she scratched his shoulders and back in a fit of passion. She hadn't noticed him and appeared at ease, unguarded, and natural.

"Great. I look forward to it. Talk to you soon." She hung up the phone and made a note on the large calendar covering her desk.

Her chair pivoted and she stilled, spotting him. He lingered by the wall, caught and unapologetic that he'd been spying. He smirked and she blushed, laughing nervously.

"I didn't know I had an audience."

"I didn't want to disturb your call." He pushed off the wall and entered her office.

Her diploma filled a frame on the wall. *Hospitality Management.* He grinned, finding her choice fitting.

He faced her. "How's your morning going?"

Her gaze dropped to his chest where the damp cotton of his shirt clung to his pecs. "Fitness room?"

"I needed to blow off some steam." He would have preferred to blow it off with her, but that option wasn't on the table at the moment.

"Looks like you succeeded. You're all…" Her stare stroked over his shoulders and arms. "Steamy."

Her fingers pulled softly at the thin pearl necklace around her throat, drawing his gaze to the delicate buttons of her silk blouse. If she opened her blazer, he bet the material was completely transparent.

Slugging down the rest of his water, he chucked the empty bottle in the waste basket by the door. "Lunch?"

She lifted the floral bag beside her computer. "I packed."

"Cute."

"Just trying to be a fiscally responsible adult," she joked.

"Sometimes being responsible is overrated." When he took a step closer to her desk, she drew in a long breath, drawing his attention down to her chest. "We can still eat together."

He'd like to feed her whatever was in that little sack and he could feast on the sweet nectar between her—

"Mariella, did you happen to—Oh."

Harrison glared at the man who so rudely interrupted them by barging into her office and instantly recognized him as the guy from the restaurant.

"Pardon me. I didn't realize you were with someone."

Yeah, me, Harrison almost growled, glaring at the intruder.

Mariella waved off the man's apology. "Mauricio, this is Harrison Montgomery. He's an old friend who used to live in Jasper Falls. Harrison, this is Mauricio Hernandez, our banquet manager."

Old friend? He'd like to think they were a bit more than that.

"How's it going?" Mauricio held out a

hand, and Harrison shook it with a pinch of crippling pressure.

"Good. We were just firming up some plans for tonight."

Mauricio's head cocked and he glanced at Mariella. "I was coming by to see if you wanted to grab lunch."

Mariella lifted her cute little lunch bag again, but before she could say anything, Harrison slipped behind her desk and caressed her shoulders, massaging softly.

She tensed, but didn't shoulder him off. "Thanks, but I'm eating in. Summer's coming and I'm trying to behave."

Fuck behaving. He leveled the other man with a look that made it perfectly clear Mariella was more than a friend to him as he swept the hair away from her shoulder so he could tease the sensitive side spot beneath her ear with his exploring fingers.

Her shoulder lifted, but her effort to nudge him off held little conviction as she also seemed to sink deeper into his touch. Good. He preferred to have her conflicted rather than adamant and distant. They were making progress.

Mauricio chuckled uncomfortably then cleared his throat. "It's always bikini season in the Virgin Islands."

Harrison's hands stilled on her shoulders. Was she planning a trip?

Mariella laughed nervously. "A bikini's a tall order."

Why the hell was she talking to this guy about her body and bikinis? He casually caught the lobe of her ear between his fingers and gave a soft pull, knowing how incredibly sensitive her ears were.

She caught his hand, and blurted, "I'm putting a new proposal together for a December bride. Let's sit down around one today to go over the details."

"Sounds good." The man's glare narrowed on Harrison's hands, then he met his stare with a tight smile. "Nice meeting you, Hudson."

"Yeah, you too, Ralph."

Mariella rolled her eyes and shoved him away the instant Mauricio was gone. "Why didn't you just pee around my desk? Could you have been any more obvious about marking your territory? I'm shocked my ankles aren't soaking wet!"

"What's in the Virgin Islands?"

"Sand." She stood and grabbed her lunch.

He followed her out of the office. "Where are you going?"

"I like to eat outside when it's nice." Her

steps were clipped. That little ear pull definitely pushed her buttons.

He jogged beside her and whispered, "I'd like to eat *you*."

Her steps fumbled and she hissed, "Harrison, I'm at work!"

"That makes it more fun."

Her lips firmed and she glared up at him. An elderly couple exited the elevators, and headed toward the lobby. Grabbing his arm, she tugged him into the elevator. As soon as the doors closed, she poked him in the chest.

"Knock it off. You can't come here and act all territorial when you have no claim to me. You embarrassed me! No massaging my shoulders or touching my ears or—"

His mouth crashed over hers, cutting off her lies. Her lunch bag dropped to the floor as she practically gnawed at his mouth with pent up passion. She was so full of shit with her little unaffected act.

Her fingers raked through his hair as he lifted her off her feet and shoved her into the wall. She moaned into his mouth, grinding her body against his and tugging his hair.

"Embarrassment doesn't make your panties wet," he growled, dragging his kiss along her jaw and sliding his hand under her blazer.

She turned her cheek and stared, panting, at the call buttons. "We're not moving."

He punched out a thumb and hit the button for his floor. "All I want to do is fuck you in that necklace."

She shut her eyes, leaning her head into the wall and groaning as he kissed down her throat. "This isn't what we agreed."

"Tell me it's not what you want, and I'll stop."

The elevator slowed and he waited for her to decide.

"What's it gonna be, Mariella?" He dragged his lips over the pearls draped across the base of her throat and nudged his nose to her ear. "What's going to leave you more satisfied in the end?"

She groaned and dropped her feet to the floor. The doors opened and she shoved past him. "You stink like sweat."

His mouth twitched with a smile. He bent and picked up her lunch, grabbing the bruised apple that rolled out of the bag.

"My room's this way," he called, heading down the hall.

She pivoted and marched past him. "You're evil."

"Am I? Give me five minutes, and I'll show you heaven and have you screaming to God."

She scoffed and shot a paranoid glance over her shoulder. "Hurry. I don't want anyone to see us."

He didn't like hiding. They were adults. "We could just go back down stairs and—"

"Harrison."

He chuckled. "This is me."

Unlocking the door, he waved her in. She checked the hall again, then disappeared inside.

He set her lunch on the dresser and removed his shirt. Mariella closed the curtains, her demeanor tense and paranoid.

"We have to make this quick."

He raised a brow. Was that how she wanted to play it? He toed off his shoes. "Strip."

She shouldered off her jacket and draped it neatly over the back of the chair. He was right. Her blouse was completely see-through underneath and he could see the lace of her undergarments through the thin fabric.

Her fingers trembled as she opened the top button of her blouse, then the next, quickly working down the line. He paused just to savor the show.

"You're not stripping. We only have twenty minutes."

He doubted her lunch break was that

brief.

She slipped out of her skirt and shoes and added her garments to the tidy pile on the chair. When she turned, time stood still and the earth staggered in its orbit. Fuck, she was stunning.

The ivory silk of her camisole matched her panties. Tapered thighs, so lush and tempting. She was a goddess. Such a class act. A vision of heaven on earth. And he was going to fuck that delicate composure right out of her and make her scream until his lips, dick, and tongue all tasted like her come.

He crossed the room in two strides and pulled her into his arms. Her fingers were in his hair, trailing down his shoulders, and scraping along his back. He tumbled her to the bed, urgently needing to get inside of her.

"Wait, wait, wait!" Her hand smacked into his chest. "Condom."

"Don't move."

He raced to the bathroom and rummaged through his toiletry bag, knocking personal items into the sink and onto the floor until he finally found what he was looking for. He bolted back to the bed and staggered to a stop.

Mariella lay in a twist of long limbs and ebony waves, now wearing nothing but the pearl necklace, her body open and waiting for him. She was a goddess.

"Jesus, you're beautiful."

Her blush traveled to her breasts and she smiled. "Beautiful but weak. So much for not having sex."

Her words hurt. "We don't have to." He didn't want to force her into anything she'd regret. "If you want to stop—"

"That's the thing, I don't." Her smile turned rueful. "I want to be with you."

"Then what's wrong?" He tossed the condom aside and sat by her on the bed.

"Nothing. I'm just being stupid."

He frowned and covered her hand with his. "Why would you say that?"

When she looked up at him, her eyes shimmered and his concern doubled. He lowered his body to lay beside her, cradling her close and forcing her to look into his eyes.

"Hey, hey, hey. What's wrong?"

She sniffed and blinked back any sign of tears, but it was too late. He saw the truth in her eyes and knew she was struggling. "Nothing."

"Stop telling me *nothing*. We don't lie to each other, Mariella." Desire took an instant backseat to understanding why she was suddenly upset. "Talk to me."

"That's the thing. We don't lie, but we leave a lot unsaid, don't we?"

He sighed and pressed his forehead to her shoulder. She was afraid he'd disappear again. He had to stop doing that. At least give her the respect of a goodbye. But saying goodbye to Mariella would be…

He'd never been able to do it. It was easier just to leave and try to forget what he was leaving behind—eyes on the future. "What can I do so you're not hurt in the end?"

She cupped the back of his head and pressed a kiss to his hair. "You can't. But I'm a big girl. I can handle it."

Could she? "What do you want me to do?" He didn't want to stop, but he also didn't want to see her upset.

"You could stay."

The air stilled in his lungs. Staying wasn't an option. "Mariella—"

"I'm kidding." She laughed, and he nervously matched the sound.

When she pressed her lips to his, he kissed her, but their heat had cooled under the threat of her tears, and he wondered if they would have been better keeping sex out of it this time around. Unfortunately, they both lacked the necessary self-control to test such a theory.

CHAPTER 16

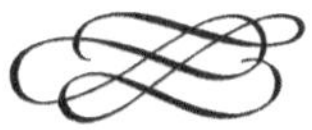

Mariella casually lifted a strand of hair to her nose, breathing in traces of Harrison's scent trapped in the tiny follicles. So much for willpower.

Their afternoon interlude had been incredible, and her body ached with the lingering heat of his possession. So did her heart.

There was seriously something wrong with her. She was an addict who wanted to recover but leapt off the wagon at every opportunity.

She wished she could say she was stronger, but the truth was, he'd always had this effect on her. Even before he knew her name, there was something about him that lured her like a moth to a flame. And that scenario never ended well for the moth.

Her mind drifted back, past this afternoon's interlude, far beyond the last time he'd been in town, before he left home, before all the countless moments they shared, to that first time…

Jennifer Moore threw an epic house party. All four grades were invited, and laws were broken in every room. Mariella arrived with Giovanni but quickly ditched him to find her friends. Guests crowded every room, and while her friends were there, they weren't who she'd come to see.

The house was hotter than a sauna as bodies gyrated to the pounding music. Elbows jostled and red cups sloshed, dousing the carpets and furniture, as she tried to squeeze by, searching for an empty crevice where she could watch the front door and main rooms.

The stench of pungent beer mingled with cheap drugstore perfume. Some couples made out in shadows while others cared nothing about discretion.

"Where're your friends?" Giovanni handed her a red cup, and she chugged down the liquid courage. "Whoa, slow down, Mar."

She caught her breath, and scanned the crowd.

"At ten bucks for a cup, why not get my money's worth." Her attention snagged on the girls lined up along the stairs. They waited like beauty queens trying to impress judges.

"So you're going to get wasted because it's an investment? Didn't realize you were such a capitalist."

She rolled her eyes. "I'm not getting wasted, and I don't need a babysitter." Finishing her beer, she headed toward the steps. "I think I see my friends."

Ditching her brother, she wedged her way through the crowd and moved to the second floor. There was a traffic jam at the landing where the line to the bathroom stretched down the staircase. She didn't want to lose sight of the first floor, so she inched behind a tall blonde and watched the front door.

She'd almost lost hope. The bathroom line snaked down the steps with several new faces and still no sign of him. She needed a refill and—there he was.

Harrison Montgomery. A shiver chased under her clothes as every inch of her body went on sensory overload.

He entered the house alone, his letterman jacket matching his teammates'. He didn't bother with a cup or the keg and looked distracted when *someone greeted him with a high five. In a sea of smiling, flirty faces, he wore the only grimace.*

Skulking past the throng clogging the foyer, he worked his way up the stairs. Mariella sucked in a breath as he passed the landing where she stood with the beauty queens, glad he ignored the other girls as much as he ignored her presence.

She set down her cup and followed him to the second floor.

"The line to the bathroom starts back there," a girl she recognized from her lunch period informed.

Mariella smiled, ignoring her, and looked for Harrison, who was already several steps ahead and swallowed by the crowd. She tugged on the eyelet hem of her tank top and pushed after him, trying her best to avoid the sloshing cups.

That night, she'd carefully chosen her outfit with one intention. Her tight denim miniskirt hugged her thighs as she climbed the last step, the tiny frayed stitching tickling her bare thighs.

A couple stumbled out of the restroom, smirking and giggling, and she lost sight of Harrison. Mariella slipped past them and came face-to-face with the end of the hall, two closed doors and no Harrison.

She bit her lip, a sick thought curdling her stomach. He was definitely behind one of those doors. What if he was with someone? He could have been meeting a girl...

She hadn't come this far to turn back. She tapped the first door and waited, but the music was too loud to hear if anyone answered. Turning the nob, she peeked inside.

"Hello?"

"Get out!" A flash of flesh and blonde hair burned into her retinas. That was definitely not Harrison. Jesus, how did people even bend that way?

Her heart ricocheted in her chest as her gaze shot to the other door.

Two girls stumbled through the crowd in her direction, giggling and falling over each other as they sloshed their beers. "Hey, you're Giovanni's sister, right?"

"Yeah."

"Oh, cool. He's in my chem class. Is your brother here?"

"Downstairs."

"Thanks." The girl asking about Giovanni tugged her friend back toward the staircase.

"Wait," her friend said, staring at the door behind Mariella. "Did you see Harrison Montgomery come up here?"

Mariella reached for the door knob at her back. "He went downstairs. You just missed him."

"*Cool.*" *Arm in arm, they stumbled back the way they came.*

Mariella twisted the knob and slipped through the door, shutting out the party and wondering what the next step of her plan might be.

The music muffled. "You lost?"

A chill raced up her spine. His voice cut through her like a hot knife slices through butter on an August day. Please be alone. *She slowly turned and came face-to-face with the most devastating blue eyes she'd ever seen.*

"No, not lost." She pressed her back into the cool wood of the door, her fingers gliding over the knob and clicking the lock into place.

A large bed and fancy furniture filled the room. This had to be Jennifer's parents' bedroom. Her heart thundered in her chest. No going back now.

"Do I know you?"

It stung. She thought about him every single day, and he didn't have a clue who she was. "I'm Mariella Mosconi."

He cocked his head. "Giovanni's little sister?"

Another sting. "I'm in your Spanish class." She didn't want her younger age to cause an issue.

"Right. I remember you now." He glanced over his shoulder and hitched a thumb to what was most likely the master bath. "Did you have to go?"

She shook her head. *"I wanted to see if you were okay."*

"Me? I'm fine." He laughed. *"Why wouldn't I be?"*

He was lying. Somehow, she knew he wasn't okay, but she had no reason to believe otherwise. Just a strong instinct that his smile and laugh was part of a very heavy mask he never took off. The urge to comfort him drew her deeper into the room. What would he do if she kissed him?

He took a step back. "What are you doing?"

"You came up here without talking to anyone."

"Maybe I wanted to be alone."

"Then why'd you come to a party?"

He might not be in the mood to socialize, but she doubted he wanted to be alone. Something about the hard set of his jaw and the vulnerability in his eyes made her believe he was looking for something. Maybe company. Maybe an escape. She could be both.

His gaze shot to the locked door then back to her. The weight of his stare trailed over her body like a physical caress. "We're not supposed to be up here."

"How do you know?"

"That's the rule at all Jenn's parties."

Yet this was the first place he went when he arrived. "Then why are you in here?"

"Privacy."

"Because you want to be alone?"

"Maybe." His gaze dropped to her chest. "Maybe not. Guess it depends."

"On?"

"The company."

She leaned into the thick post at the foot of the bed and his eyes followed her. They shared a moment where they both acknowledged his inspection and she did nothing to shield his perusing stare. Dropping her head back against the bedpost, she arched her chest and lifted a brow with an inviting smirk.

She'd never done anything like this before. She hadn't planned to throw herself at him, but she wanted no misunderstandings about her feelings.

"I don't feel like talking," he rasped, his stare lingering at the swell of her breasts.

"That's fine." She glanced at the large bed and back to him, making it perfectly clear why she followed him in there.

The side of his mouth quirked in a half grin, and a dimple flashed. "Is this a joke or something? Did someone send you in here?"

She shook her head. "I followed you."

"Why?"

She shrugged. "Because I wanted to."

He took a step closer, his eyes full of dark suspicion. "Why?"

Her breath hitched when he touched the pen-

dant locket hanging from her necklace. This was the closest they'd ever been. She could smell the soap on his skin and see each golden stubble of hair covering his jaw. Her heart beat wildly "I wanted to give you something."

His gaze flicked to hers. "What?"

She swallowed and wet her lips, tasting the sweet flavor of her sugary lip gloss. "A kiss?"

He stilled and the air thinned, making it even more difficult to breathe. She'd never done anything like this before. Bold wasn't necessarily her style, but she was determined.

"A kiss?" he repeated, eyes narrowing as if not fully trusting her intentions.

"Y-yes." She kept her eyes on him, more excited than afraid, but nervous all the same.

He caught her chin and dragged a thumb across her mouth, smearing the sticky cupcake flavored gloss into her lower lip. "Your brother know you came up here?"

His question threw her, and she frowned. "Course not."

He chuckled and glanced down at her cleavage. "This feels a little premeditated, Mariella."

That's because it was. He stared at her mouth and her chin slightly trembled. "No one knows I'm up here."

"I don't want any trouble with your brother or your cousins."

There were at least five of her cousins down-stairs, each one crazy enough to beat the crap out of any guy who might think to take advantage of her, but Harrison wasn't taking anything she didn't freely offer. She wanted this. She wanted him.

"My family won't be a problem. No one knows I'm up here. And I don't kiss and tell."

"Good," he said, abruptly releasing her chin and sifting his fingers into her hair, tugging her head back.

She gasped, his mouth suddenly devouring her, scrambling her thoughts and softening her knees as every feminine piece of her melted into liquid heat. One sweep of his tongue and she was a pool of desire.

The rough pull of his fingers in her hair and the delicious prickle along her scalp proved just how unprepared she was for a guy like him. The second his mouth touched hers, he had the strap of her tank top sliding off her shoulder and her body pressed into the post of the bed.

Harrison Montgomery didn't kiss her. He devoured her.

The mattress hit the back of her thighs and she gasped. The more her mouth opened, the more he took.

He tumbled her to the bed. "Change your mind?"

Heat pooled low in her belly as he held himself over her. She'd imagined a million different scenarios of how this might go, but nothing quite as heated as this.

She toed off her sandals and pulled him down to her, this time prepared for the kiss. A masculine growl hummed from his chest as he stole a taste of her. His fingers tightened in her hair until her scalp tingled and she moaned.

His body melted over her, his weight sinking her deeper into the mattress. She could feel him everywhere. The hard press of his erection at her belly, the heat of his skin burning through his clothes, and the rush of his blood pulsing through his veins as he shoved her skirt to her waist and pulled her legs around him.

She rolled her hips, loving the weight of his body against hers. Liquid heat pooled, and she wanted more. She pushed at his jacket, and he shouldered it off. Her hands fumbled at his belt, trying to find the right angle.

He broke the kiss. "Wait."

They were both panting. She sensed his paper-thin instinct slowing down, but she didn't come up here to find a gentleman. She came up here to get the real him.

"It's okay." Pulling his hand to her mouth, she pressed a kiss to his palm and lowered it to her breast. "I want you to."

He sat back on his knees, a glimpse of uncertainty warring with the desire clear on his face. "We just met."

"So show me the real you. I'm not scared."

Indecision flashed in his eyes. "What is this? Are you drunk?"

She sat up. "I'm not drunk. You aren't taking advantage of me. I know what I'm doing."

His brow creased and he rubbed the back of his neck. "This is...uncommon. Usually girls want to date for a while, get flowers..."

She didn't need any of that fluff. "I'm not that complicated." When he still didn't appear convinced, she took his hand and said, "I just want you."

He stared at her. "Me?"

"You, Harrison. I thought about this a lot. The panties I'm wearing, I chose them for you. They match your eyes." His gaze dropped to her jean skirt which had shifted again to cover her midthigh, and she laughed at his curiosity.

"Can I see?"

She leaned back on her elbows and nodded. His stare fastened to her legs as his hand curved around her thigh, riding slowly up to the denim frayed hem. He glanced at her in question.

"Go ahead."

He pushed the skirt up to her hips and cursed. "Fuck." He smiled at her. "They're blue."

"Like your eyes."

He shook his head in disbelief. "Who are you?"

Hopefully, she was someone he'd never forget. "Tonight, I'm yours."

He laughed as if he'd just won the lottery but never bought a ticket. When his stare met hers again, all uncertainty faded. He was ready to claim his prize.

They never made promises to each other. It was easier to cut away all the false pretenses some girls required. What they shared was raw and honest, deeper than most first encounters, and better than anything she could have imagined.

He knew how to touch her, and when to be gentle, but he was mostly intense. Movies and television couldn't prepare her for the weight of his body pressing into hers or the fullness that came when he entered her. She expected a pinch of pain, but had no idea it could also feel so satisfying. His grip at her hips, his breath beating against the curve of her neck, the pull of his teeth on the lobe of her ear, every second was a euphoric orgy of sensations overwhelming her with incomparable pleasure.

Resting her cheek on his heaving chest, she savored all the new ways her muscles ached. He had been perfect. Gentle at all the right moments and somehow intense at the same time.

"Are you okay?"

"I'm great."

His breathing slowed and she physically felt the ease of his body tightening again. "I have to get up."

He slid out from under her, leaving her alone on the big bed. The bathroom door shut and water ran as a toilet flushed. She supposed it was normal for a guy to clean up afterward.

Should she do something? Her body was too tired at the moment to think.

He emerged from the bathroom but didn't return to the bed. Realizing he was getting dressed, she sat up.

"W-what are you doing?"

"We should go back down stairs."

No one knew they were up there. What was the rush? He set her clothes on the bed and she frowned.

He knelt to tie his shoes, and she worried she'd done something wrong. Maybe it wasn't as good as she thought.

Self-consciously she turned her back to him and dressed.

"Ready?" He wouldn't look at her. More doubt and uncertainty battered her weakening confidence.

"I guess." Her stomach hurt at the thought of leaving things this way.

She should say something. What if they walked

into that hall and never spoke again? She couldn't let that happen.

When he twisted the lock open, she shoved a hand against the door. "Harrison, wait."

He paused but didn't turn to face her.

"Look at me." She could feel walls going up, and she didn't like it.

He met her stare and she swore she glimpsed fear in his eyes.

"I don't need anything from you, but I'd like your respect."

He exhaled and looked away. "Sorry. I... I'm not good at this."

"Good at what? I told you, I don't expect this to change anything, but let's at least be real enough to acknowledge that it happened."

His jaw ticked. "I don't want to disappoint you."

"Then don't."

"I also don't want to lead you on."

She slipped her body between his and the door, forcing his full attention. "Look, I liked what happened tonight. I'd like it if it happened again. The only thing I ask is that we don't lie to each other. Okay?"

"I'm not looking for a relationship."

She nodded, fine with his honesty. "Okay."

"But I'd like to see you again."

She smiled, a bit of her uncertainty fading. "I'd like that, too."

"You're sure you're okay with that?"

She laughed. Did he not realize she enjoyed what they had done as much as him—if not more? "I'm definitely okay with that. But if we're going to make this an ongoing thing, I'd prefer it if you didn't hook up with other girls."

"Deal."

Her smile widened. "This is the part where you kiss me." So he did.

MARIELLA HAD WALKED into that room a girl and left a woman. Being with Harrison was an education in so many things. He changed her, and she liked to think, on some level, she changed him.

They never got around to labeling their relationship, but they continued seeing each other for nearly two years, until the day he disappeared. She spent months wishing she could go back to their last time, thinking of all the things she could have done or said to make him stay.

Now, after so many years, she believed there was nothing anyone could have done, but part of her still wondered. No matter how many times reality crushed her, there was a gullible little girl inside of her who still believed she could persuade him not to leave.

The adult in her felt sorry for that vulnerable girl. She knew reality would return like it always did and crush her. Any foolish dreams once again ripped away. But there was nothing to save the romantic in her from hoping. She simply loved him too much to ever willingly let him go.

CHAPTER 17

Harrison texted Mariella to let her know that he needed to run some errands and would meet her at the hardware store after she finished work. She breathed easier knowing he was no longer at the hotel.

During the meeting with Mauricio, Mariella kept the conversation centered on business, avoided all topics of tropical getaways, and pretended the awkward exchange in her office that morning never happened.

After all collaboration projects were underway, she spent the remainder of the day reviewing the budget. Or so she pretended to as she stared at the computer screen and tried to strategize ways to avoid having her heart ripped out again.

If she was going to help Harrison, she had

to apply some boundaries she could actually honor. Or, at least, apply some strategies so she didn't instantly sabotage herself.

Sleeping with him had been a mistake. A delicious, heart pounding, orgasmic mistake. She had to find some self-control. She really loved butter pecan ice cream, but she'd be the size of a house if she ate it all day every day. Harrison was just a sexier butter pecan. She needed to think about the consequences and protect her future self from the foolish choices of her present self. Too much self-indulgence often ended in regret.

From here on, she was placing herself in a metaphoric chastity belt. She would be stronger. Firmer. No man was her kryptonite.

There should be no easy access skirts or sexy attire whatsoever. She wasn't sure what he was doing at the store, but she was available to *help* him—not sleep with him. Her focus needed to remain glued to the objective. All she had to do was remove any source of sexual tension between them.

In theory, this sounded well and good, but in reality, she knew she didn't stand a chance. And the more times she bent the rules and gave in to temptation where Harrison was concerned, the more she wondered if anything could truly be wrong if it felt so right.

She dashed home and changed into a faded, old pair of leggings with a paint stain on the butt from the time she helped her dad refinish the back deck. Those saggy old pants were the furthest thing from sexy. Then she grabbed a baggy flannel that disguised her figure. Nothing attractive there.

Twisting her hair into a bun and lacing her tattered work boots, she mentally geared up for some manual labor. So long as they didn't touch or flirt or look directly into each other's eyes, she should be safe.

"Where are you going?" Her dad's question stopped her escape out the front door. "You look like you're ready for a shift at the lumberyard."

Mission accomplished. "I'm heading into town to help a friend."

"What friend?"

"Harrison Montgomery."

He frowned. "When the hell did he get back in town?"

"He's taking care of the store." She was surprised her father even remembered Harrison. Maybe Erin had mentioned him. "He's just checking on things while Erin and Giovanni are away."

"Be careful."

His warning gave her pause. Did her father dislike Harrison? Why? To her knowledge, they never shared two words. "I will."

Her father's warning stuck with her all the way to town. Why would he tell her to be careful? She had to be overthinking it. He probably just meant for her to wear her seatbelt and abide the speed limit.

When she parked, she spotted Harrison already inside the Hardware store standing behind the register. She took her time getting to the door, studying how his brow tensed and his lips firmed. This was definitely a challenging place for him to visit.

The front door was locked, so she knocked on the glass. He glanced at the store window, the deeply etched scowl on his face transforming into a smile when he saw her.

Rounding the counter, he tossed some receipts aside and unlocked the door. "You made it."

He bent to kiss her, and she awkwardly dodged his lips and turned her head, laughing nervously when he missed her mouth and kissed her hair.

He chuckled and looked unsure. "You okay?"

"I'm fine." She set her purse on the counter and looked around, keeping her distance. "So, what are we doing?"

He glanced at the aisles and blew out a breath. "I have no idea."

"Well, what's your plan?" She straightened a screwdriver hanging from a display.

"I don't have one yet."

When he sounded overwhelmed, she glanced back and her heart pinched. He stood by the front of the store, the lack of lighting casting him in shadows as his hands shoved into the pockets of his jeans and his shoulders bunched around his ears. If not for the stress lines chiseled around his eyes, he'd look like a young boy, lost and unsure.

Taking pity on him and how over-whelming this must be, she momentarily forgot her rules and walked to him, not stopping until her arms looped around his body and she hugged him close.

"It's okay. We'll get it done. Just tell me what needs to be done and we'll do it. Team work."

His arms closed around her and the tension in his body gradually unraveled. Her heart wavered and his cheek rested on the top of her head.

They fit together perfectly. She rested her ear over the steady pounding of his heart, giving in to the comfortable moment.

"Thanks."

The moment the friendly gesture melted into something more, she broke contact, untangling their bodies and turning back to the aisles. "So what's the end goal?"

"Everything must go."

She glanced at the front door. "You want to sell the store?"

He nodded. "As quickly as possible."

She ignored the selfish outcry in her head that instantly understood, without the store, he'd have one less reason to return. Her gratitude that Erin had decided to keep the house a little longer had never been stronger, but Harrison's sister was rarely in town, due to Giovanni's travel schedule.

It's not about you! She snapped her focus back to Harrison and shoved her worries aside.

"So you need to have a liquidation sale. I can run to the pharmacy and grab some posterboard and markers so we can make some signs for the front window."

"I'll drive you—"

"No, no, you stay here and work on other things."

"Such as?"

She bit her lip and searched the counter, sensing he didn't like being in the store alone.

He needed a distraction—something other than her.

Spotting a legal notepad and pencil, she handed it to him. "Make a list of the inventory by category and write down what the retail price is and what the sale price will be."

He took the notepad and pencil, holding both as if he'd never used such items before. She grabbed her purse and dug out her car keys, guilt prickling that she was already abandoning him.

"I won't be long," she promised. She just needed some air and a moment to regroup and firm up her defenses, because at the moment she only wanted to comfort him and do whatever it took to wash that worried look off his face.

Twenty minutes later, she was back at the hardware store unloading bags of art supplies and spreading out posterboard on the floor.

"There's a table in the back."

"This is fine." She uncapped a thick black marker and wrote SALE in bubble letters. The bright florescent green posterboard was impossible to miss.

Harrison finally turned on the lights, but the store still had the eerie vacancy of a mausoleum. "Can you turn on some music?"

"What kind?"

"Anything. It's too quiet in here."

She outlined her letters in a spiked bubble. When he set his phone on the counter, she pointed to the drug store bags. "There are scissors in that bag. Can you toss them over?"

The slow beat of Ed Sheeran's "Thinking Out Loud" cut the silence and she tensed. Maybe silence was better.

Harrison dug through the bag. "You got a lot of stuff."

The stroke of the marker slowed as the lyrics distracted her. "Well, the goal is to get the town to notice, right? So you can sell the store?"

She didn't care about the store, but she cared about him. Her masochistic heart was basically sawing through the last of his ties to this place.

Throat tight, she said, "I aim to succeed."

"Here." He handed her the scissors.

The love song taunted her and her fingers shook as she cut out the bubble letters. Harrison lowered himself to the dusty floor, folding his feet under his knees as he watched her.

His attention traced over her skin and she tried not to acknowledge his stare, but she felt his focus so deeply she couldn't forget he was there.

Her hand stopped and her head dropped. This was impossible.

"What's wrong?"

Pushing through the emotional turmoil that was gnawing away at her insides, she forced herself to keep making signs. "Nothing."

"What were you painting?"

Her lungs tightened around her breath. "Huh?"

"There's a paint stain on your ass."

That confirmed where his stare had gone. "A deck." His hand trailed the curve of her butt and she tensed. She couldn't focus when he touched her. "Harrison..."

"Hmm?"

"Let's get this done."

The heat of his touch disappeared. "Okay."

For the next hour she designed bold signs and Harrison taped them to the front window. She did most of the writing and cutting, but that was fine. It gave her somewhere to look so she didn't have to face him.

Standing, she brushed the dust off her faded leggings and went outside to get an exterior peek at the display. She came back in and shot him a thumbs up. "It looks great."

James Arthur's voice cut through the store, singing "Say You Won't Let Go" and their eyes met. The instant tangle of their chemistry tied her in knots.

He closed the distance and laced his hand with hers, pulling her close and pressing her palm to his shoulder. She laughed and blushed when he lifted her right hand and started leading her in a slow dance.

Maybe he didn't hear the lyrics, or maybe they didn't mean anything to him and he was just being cute, but as the singer begged someone to *say they won't let go* an ache formed in her chest, rising to her throat, until her eyes prickled with implication.

Harrison never took her to a dance. Tickets were always expensive and they weren't that type of couple. He used to claim he couldn't dance, but he'd obviously learned. A pinch of jealousy nipped as she wondered who taught him.

Their feet shuffled over the dusty floor, and she gave in to the moment, leaning her head to his chest and drawing comfort from the steady beat of his heart. Like the song said, she wanted to live with him until they were gray and old, and she'd probably love him until her lungs gave out. As the thought escaped, so did a tear.

She blinked rapidly, the runaway tear vanishing in the cotton of his shirt, hopefully undetected. Breath tight, she slid her hand from his shoulder and untangled their fingers, pulling away before the song finished.

Facing the door, she showed him her back as she scrambled for composure. The last lyric begged, *say you won't let go,* and something painful tore through her heart, a sort of unspoken promise that she could not lower herself to begging and needed to accept that, like before, he was going to leave.

Enough. That was enough.

With a quick sniffle, she cleared her throat and lifted her chin. "We should make a sign for the door, so people know when the sale starts. You'll have to open for a few days."

She forced her thoughts on simple objectives, keeping all emotion out of it. Having a clear-cut purpose let her amputate the sadness, or at least momentarily anesthetize the pain.

At the prices he'd chosen, it wouldn't take long for the inventory to sell out. And once the store was empty, he'd have no reason to stay. Maybe it was best to get to the inevitable misery, so they could break this cycle once and for all, and she could stop repeating the same old injury.

He taped the last poster to the glass and

stepped back to admire their work. "What are you doing tomorrow?"

She gathered the markers. "I have church and brunch at my aunt's then some family stuff. You're better off waiting to start the sale until Monday. Town's pretty dead on Sundays."

"You don't work tomorrow?"

"No. I'm off on Mondays, so I can help you a little. If you want—"

"Thanks." He accepted her offer before she even got the words out.

She capped the red marker and stood, brushing the dust off her clothes. "You're sure about these prices?" Eighty percent off a riding mower was a steal.

His hands were back in his pockets and he continued to stare out the front window. "I just want it done, so I can get out of here."

A smile reflexively covered her mouth to hide how much his comment hurt. "Right."

He turned, as if realizing what he'd just said. "It has nothing to do with you."

It never does.

"Well," she said with false cheer, turning to gather up the rest of the art supplies.

He caught her arm, but she couldn't bring herself to look at him. "I appreciate this, Mariella."

"We're friends. We help each other."

His thumb dragged over her sleeve. "You're a better friend to me than I've ever been to you."

She couldn't deny it so she wouldn't.

"Let me buy you dinner as a thank you."

She drew in a breath, preparing to exhale an excuse.

"Please. It's the least I can do." He smiled. "It's Cinco de Mayo. There's a place in town advertising bucket margaritas."

That would be Tequila Mockingbird's. And while alcohol was not wise, it seemed to be exactly what she needed at that moment. Releasing the tight hold she'd kept on her resolve, brought an instant relief. It was so much easier not to fight her attraction, but giving in would no doubt prove harder in the long run.

"Okay."

His smile widened and he shut out the lights, dousing the store in shadows. "Let's get out of here."

Tequila Mockingbird's was slammed. There was more than an hour wait and the line snaked out the door. "Sorry, I should have expected this."

"Why should you be sorry?"

"We can go somewhere else."

His mood had completely changed since leaving the hardware store, and he waved away her words. "I don't mind waiting."

At least they were serving drinks to those in line.

Tables and chairs dotted the sidewalk, and servers kept a steady flow of chips and salsa coming out to those waiting to get in. Harrison ordered them each a starter cocktail, and once the alcohol hit her system her anxiety disappeared.

She sipped from the thick straw, her gums jumping at the tart strawberry jalapeño mixture. Her eyes widened when she spotted her cousin.

"Ryan!" She gave him and his wife a quick hug. "Hi, Maggie."

Ryan did a double take. "Harrison?"

Harrison gave a brief nod. "Hey."

"Holy crap. How have you been? *Where* have you been?"

Harrison's demeanor tightened as he uncomfortably explained his decade-long absence. "I've been living in New York." He glanced at Maggie. "I was sorry to hear about Nash."

Maggie was sweet and a little shy, but always nice. Despite everything that happened between Mariella and her sister, Perrin, she never treated Mariella differently.

"It's been a long time," Maggie said by way of acknowledging the inevitable passing of time and the fact that she still grieved the loss of her first husband. "Are you married? Any kids?"

"No," Harrison answered quickly. "I operate better when I'm solo."

Ryan glanced at Mariella. "You guys grabbing some tacos?"

"I'm mainly here for the margaritas." She took a long sip and laughed.

"Careful, cuz. They sneak up on you."

"That's what I'm hoping."

Ryan turned his attention back to Harrison. "We're having a game tomorrow after brunch. You should come."

Mariella did a double take at her cousin's offer. The game was a family tradition, something to kick off the season. Outsiders were rarely included, unless they were someone's significant other. That wasn't a proper label for Harrison.

She expected him to decline, but he surprised her by asking, "What kind of game?"

"Baseball. Up at the field on the mountain. You're going, right, Mar?"

"Of course." It was tradition, something to

celebrate all the younger relatives finally returning home from college.

"You should come, Harrison." Ryan glanced at his phone when it buzzed again. "Well, we're heading in. Our table's ready. See you tomorrow, Mar."

"See ya." Her cousin disappeared, and she turned to Harrison. "You don't have to go if you don't want to."

"I like baseball."

"Oh. Okay. Well, then you're more than welcome to play."

He cocked his head. "Would you rather I didn't go?"

"I don't care what you do."

"Ouch." He laughed, drawing his margarita to his lips.

"I just mean, do what you want. Lots of people will be there." Namely, her entire family. She didn't want anyone getting the wrong impression, which—now that she thought about it—there was a one thousand percent possibility they would misread the situation. "I never bring guys around my family."

His brow lifted. "Are you worried what people might say?"

"No."

He leaned closer and she assumed he was going to whisper something in her ear until his lips closed around her earlobe. When she tried to shoulder him away, he only sucked the sensitive spot harder.

"Harrison!"

Warm breath teased over her throat as he chuckled. "Don't think I haven't noticed you trying to keep your distance." His lips grazed her fluttering pulse. "When you play hard to get, it only makes me want you more."

Her body turned to mush when his hand discreetly slipped into the back of her leggings and squeezed her ass. She leaned into him, shutting her eyes. She was as good as screwed.

"Why the cold shoulder, Mariella? You were a lot warmer this afternoon when your mouth was on my—"

She covered his mouth and cleared her throat, certain no one could hear him, but still very aware that they weren't alone. She pushed his hand away from her butt. "I was making your signs."

"You were making me horny."

She looked at the crowd of people gathered around the door. "Do you think our table's almost ready?"

"Not sure. Do you think your tongue tastes like strawberries? It's bright red."

A jagged breath filled her lungs. He was

really pushing her buttons. "How are the chips?"

"Fuck the chips. What's going on with you?"

"Nothing."

"Liar."

"We're at dinner—"

"That's not why you're pushing me away. I thought we already established—"

"Harrison," she cut him off before he could say more. "I just think it's better for everyone if we try to keep things platonic."

"We've never been platonic."

"Then we should start."

"No."

She scoffed. "No?"

"Yeah, no. I'm not doing that."

"Well, you don't really have a choice."

"There's always a choice. If you're single and I'm single, and we have incredible sex whenever we're together, why make a problem when there isn't one?"

Of course he wouldn't see the problem. It usually presented itself after he was gone.

She folded her arms over her chest, her brain fuzzy from the tequila. "Let's not have this discussion here."

"Why not?"

"Because we're in public and it's complicated."

"So let's uncomplicate it. Explain it to me."

"There's nothing to explain. You're here, and in a matter of days, you'll be gone."

"All the more reason to make the most of our time."

He was breaking her down and it had already been a losing battle. "I can't go through this again. I can't do this only to have you disappear and never even pick up the phone to call and ask how I am."

"This time I'll call. I swear."

He might call, but he'd never promise not to disappear on her. "Let's drop it."

"Mariella, I never—" Thankfully his phone buzzed, cutting off any more meaningless speeches about his good intentions. He glanced at the screen. "Our table's ready."

"Great." She pushed through the crowd. This time leaving him behind.

CHAPTER 18

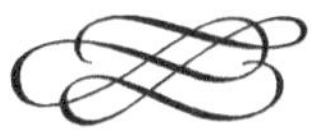

Sunday afternoon, Harrison traveled up the mountain, fueled by sheer curiosity and a need to fix the awkwardness that somehow interrupted his and Mariella's chemistry. Several cars parked around the field, surrounded by dense evergreens that covered the mountain. The baseball diamond was as nice as the ones at the high school, complete with custom dugouts and long metal bleachers.

Harrison parked beside an old Jeep Cherokee and twisted his cap backward, searching the benches for Mariella's dark hair in a sea of men and red-headed women. Young children raced around the sandy lot, while adults sorted equipment and carried coolers to the folding table set up between the dugouts.

He recognized several McCulloughs and Clooneys before anyone noticed him. Mariella had a huge extended family, even though she and Giovanni were basically it for the Mosconi line.

Two siblings, just like him and Erin, yet that was where the family similarities ended. Even in her brother's absence, Mariella had an endless reserve of people in her life that cared for her. That brought him comfort.

Last night hadn't gone quite the way he'd planned. After dinner, she declined his invitation to come back to the hotel and somehow managed to say goodnight without getting close enough for him to even kiss her.

"Harrison," Ryan called from the cluster of cars and jogged over. "Glad you could make it."

"No problem." He once again searched for Mariella, but didn't see her in the cluster of McCulloughs and Clooneys. "Have you seen Mariella?"

"She, uh, left early."

He frowned, more confused than ever. "Did she say why?"

"My Uncle Paulie was having some indigestion at breakfast, so my brother suggested he sit this one out and take it easy. She drove him home."

"Paulie is Mariella's dad?"

"Yeah." He waved a hand as another car door slammed. "Luke, over here!" Ryan yelled. "Anyway, gloves and bats are over there. Help yourself to whatever you need."

He needed Mariella. Without her, there was no point in him being there.

"Holy shit, Harrison Montgomery." Luke clapped a heavy hand on his shoulder. "Where the hell did you come from?"

A beautiful little girl hung on his hand as if his arm were a rope swing. "Daddy, I wanna go play with Addison."

Luke glanced at the kids racing around the outfield. "Find out where Daddy put the sunblock, first, and have him put some on your cheeks."

"I will." The little girl bolted toward the bleachers.

Remnants of their old rivalry fizzled at the realization that they had all moved on and grown up. Luke would never know how much his success had cost Harrison, and he never should.

Harrison smiled. "Good to see you, Luke."

"Same."

A man appeared at his side and Luke

frowned. "I just sent Alexis to find you. Did you bring the sunblock?"

"Alec and Sheilagh have it." The man glanced at Harrison and cleared his throat.

Luke made the introduction. "This is my husband, Tristan. Tristan, this is Harrison, Erin's brother."

"I didn't know Erin had a brother."

"I've been away, living in New York."

"Nice. You playing, today?"

Rather than regurgitate the same old bull-shit—Where had he been? How long was he back? What was he doing with his life? —the guys seemed mostly focused on the game. It was a welcomed reprieve and one he hadn't anticipated.

When Pat Clooney arrived, the conversation shifted to the status of Paulie's indigestion. Apparently, Ryan's younger brother, Pat, was now a doctor and married to Julie Cook.

Harrison once again felt like he'd been through a time warp. He debated texting Mariella but didn't want to bother her if she was with her parents.

"Luke, be a dear and get the cooler out of the truck for me." Mrs. McCullough shuffled over, dabbing the sweat off her brow with a crumpled paper towel. "It's hotter than Satan's arsehole out here."

"Nice, Mum."

She ignored her son. "Harrison, it's good to see you again."

"Hi, Mrs. McCullough."

She turned back to Luke. "Are you waitin' for a written invitation? The cooler. The kids will want the ice pops."

"I'm going. I'm going."

Luke and Tristan disappeared and she shook her head, blotting away more sweat. "Carried him and his brother for nine painful months. The least he could do is haul a damn cooler full of ice pops for me."

"Can I, uh, help with anything?" Harrison didn't know if he should stay or go, but he didn't want to come off as a freeloader who crashed the game.

"Aren't you sweet?" She stuffed the damp paper towel into her ample bosom. "There's a beach towel on the front seat of my truck. It's that old Jeep over there. Could you grab that for me so I don't singe my arse on the bleachers? The sun's beatin' down hard enough to give me two dozen new freckles today. We can't have both ends cooked."

He ran off to fetch the towel before Mrs. McCullough made any further mention of her ass.

Once everyone was there, they divided

into teams. Harrison hung back in the dugout, keeping his eye on the game, but his thoughts continuously returned to Mariella.

After an hour, he casually approached Pat to get some more details about Mariella's dad's condition. "So your uncle's okay?"

Pat's hands gripped the fence of the dugout as one of his cousins cracked the ball into the outfield, his focus clearly on the game. "He'll be fine. My Aunt Col was bitching at him all morning. She could give anyone chest pains."

If the family doctor wasn't worried, he shouldn't be. But Mariella's continued absence concerned him. He decided to shoot her a text, just to check in.

Hope everything's okay with your dad. You're missing a good game.

THE GAME CARRIED on for seven innings before the kids in the stands grew rambunctious, and several of the wives started packing up for the day. All in all, it was a great game, even if Harrison's team didn't win.

He lingered on the field, hoping that Mariella might make a last-minute appearance, but she never showed or responded to his text.

Uneasiness stirred in his gut on the drive back to the hotel. Maybe her absence wasn't about her dad but about them. It had been Ryan who invited him to the game, after all. Maybe she didn't want him there.

He couldn't escape the sense that he'd left something unfinished. He should have pushed the conversation last night and figured out why she was sending so many mixed signals.

One minute she was tearing his clothes off, and the next minute she was putting up walls. They'd always been up front with each other, but it was obvious she was keeping something from him.

Maybe this was about her coworker. Harrison might have interfered in something that he shouldn't have. However, he wasn't a decent enough person to actually feel sorry about that. If that guy wanted to sleep with Mariella, tough shit. Harrison got there first.

But the other guy would eventually outlast him, and Harrison wouldn't be able to stop him from going after her. He didn't want to think about that.

Once back at the hotel, he showered and texted Mariella again, asking if she had plans for the rest of the day, but she still didn't respond. Her silence was starting to piss him off.

Antsy, and bored, he grabbed his keys and went for a drive. Twenty minutes later he was parked outside of his childhood home, unsure what he was doing there.

No one was home, and no one would know if he went inside. It seemed like a safe time to look around. For what, he didn't know.

He didn't have a key, but he knew where one was hidden. Shimmying loose the corner brick of the back step, he found the hidden key and let himself inside.

He'd been prepared for the pungent stench of his father's cigarette smoke but was surprised by the fresh scent of paint and wood polish. The carpets were gone and there was hardly any furniture.

What the hell did Erin do with everything?

The house looked completely different, yet strangely the same. His hand traced over the newly painted moldings, the sheen of high gloss latex highlighting the architectural detail he'd never noticed before.

Had Erin done all this herself?

Guilt churned in his stomach. He should have helped her—sent her some money. At least she would have been able to take whatever she needed from the store.

The sun faded behind the mountains on the horizon, leaving the hall dim. He slowly walked the narrow path as he'd done a thousand times before.

Echoes of childhood memories teased the silence, and a chill of unease set his teeth on edge as he staired at the unpainted door at the end of the hall.

He stared at the corner, where his father used to make him stand. Divots carved into the sheetrock where the clasp of his dad's belt had missed him and hit the wall. Those little nicks matched some of the scars that spattered his skin.

There used to be a table at the end of the hall. His fingers traced the scar on his temple as he recalled Ward throwing him into it when he was no more than nine.

He pushed open Erin's door and found a room that belonged to a woman he didn't know. Perfume bottles and books and several other signs of her maturity filled him with a sadness he couldn't square away.

A picture of her and Giovanni sat on the nightstand. He picked it up and smiled at her happy expression, something he hadn't seen in a long time. In just a glimpse, he made up his mind that Erin's husband was good for her. He wanted to know the man, perhaps buy him a beer.

Staring at her smile, he tried to imagine her laugh but couldn't remember the sound. He needed to work on that.

Leaving her room as he found it, he faced the chipped door to his childhood bedroom. Images from that final day flooded his mind unbidden. He remembered Erin's panic as he shoved whatever he could fit into a bag and rushed through the house, needing to get out before his father got home.

When he told Ward about the scholarship falling through, his father pelted him with a laundry list of disappointments, calling him a failure who would never amount to anything. For most of Harrison's life, his indignant anger and determination to prove his father wrong provoked a strong work ethic.

But over time, there seemed a primal wound that wouldn't heal, a scar that forever reminded him the two people who should have loved him most in this world never loved him at all. And when his father died, he'd expected that lifelong vendetta to die, too, but it hadn't.

All the unresolved battles, and missing explanations, stung on a daily basis, a swarm of yellow jackets that never tired and couldn't be outrun. He'd swipe away the memories and barrel toward some other challenge, anything that demanded enough of his focus that the peripheral of his past might fade.

The floor creaked as his weight settled forward into another step. His muscles locked as he stared at the battered wood and chipped paint of the door.

Before he left Jasper Falls, Harrison told his father that *he* was the failure and blamed him for all their problems. Ward got ahold of him then, cursing him for being an ungrateful son and bellowing about what a burden both he and Erin had been.

For a moment, Harrison stopped fighting him, thinking it might be easier to simply let go. But as his father's thumbs crushed into his windpipe, something came over him, demanding he get out of there.

He swung, needing only one good hit to knock his dad off of him. Harrison scrambled to his feet, every inhalation burning like fire as the air scraped down his ravaged throat.

He looked down at his dad with such hate, he feared if he stayed one of them would eventually kill the other. If he ended up killing Ward, he'd only prove his father right and end up living a wasted life. With no college future and no place to go, maybe prison wouldn't be that bad. Thoughts like that spurred him to leave, and he frantically packed what he could before allowing himself the chance to change his mind.

He'd backed out of the hardware store that afternoon and never looked back. Erin didn't understand and he didn't have time to explain it to her. One more night in that house would have killed him—one way or another.

Ward was rough on Erin, too, but never to the brutal degree he hurt Harrison. His father despised him to a point no amount of therapy could fix. He didn't know why, and that sort of cruelty would always be one of life's mysteries. There had been no grace, no mercy, under that roof while he'd lived there.

At least for Erin, there had been moments of peace. Moments when their father would simply gripe and throw things rather than raise his fists.

He pushed open the door to his childhood bedroom and his stomach dropped. His gaze swept over the marks on the wall. Just like his scars, they hadn't healed.

Why didn't she paint it? He'd been gone for ten years. She emptied the whole damn house. Why the hell wouldn't she gut this room first?

Because you're not her mess to clean up...

He backed out of the room, careful to not touch anything or disturb more ghosts of his past. When he left the house, he was empty.

He sat in his car, staring at the garage door as pressure built in his skull. His jaw locked and his breathing turned unsteady as a burning fury of rage boiled inside of him.

"Fuck!" he shouted and punched the steering wheel.

He fished his phone out of his pocket and stamped out a text.

Could really use some company...

HE STARED AT THE SCREEN, waiting for any movement, but got nothing.

He should just go. Fuck the store. Fuck the sale. Fuck this place.

He glanced at his bag in the back seat. Screw his clothes. He had his laptop and could have the hotel ship whatever was left.

Backing out of the driveway, he sped through the back roads on auto-pilot, not stopping when he passed the hotel or hesitating when he reached the outskirts of town.

His car idled at the exit for the interstate. If he shut his eyes, he could already smell the exhaust of city traffic and feel the stampede of New Yorkers bustling by. His foot lifted off the brake and his phone buzzed.

Mariella's contact flashed on the screen, and he debated if he should even open the text. What the hell were they doing anyway? He had no business disrupting her life when he knew he couldn't promise her any sort of a future here.

He thought of the suitcase still sitting in his hotel room. Mariella would know he left in a frantic rush if he asked the hotel to ship his belongings.

"Shit." He snatched the phone off the seat and opened the text, unable to leave without giving her a proper goodbye.

My dad had a heart attack. We're at the hospital.

ALL THOUGHTS of leaving vanished as he backed down the exit and whipped his car around, heading directly toward the hospital, back to Mariella.

CHAPTER 19

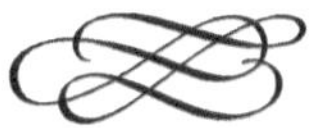

$\mathscr{H}$arrison shoved through the double doors leading to the ICU and spotted Mariella sitting alone on a chair pushed up against a wall. She didn't notice him at first, and his heart broke at the sight of tear tracks on her cheeks and the notable exhaustion weighing down her shoulders.

His steps slowed and she looked up, her expression lost in a sea of disbelief. Something painful shot through him, a poignant need to hold and protect her, followed by the logic of knowing life sometimes took unfair tragic turns, and he might not be able to save her from this. In that split second, all his hopes and dreams turned to just one—let her dad be okay. He desperately wanted to be her anchor, but at the same time, he feared drowning under so many palpable emotions.

Before uttering a word, he dropped to his knees and hugged her close. She sucked in an audible breath, and he heard her body shake as much as he felt it. A withered tissue twisted through her fingers as she worried her hands.

"How is he?"

"He just got out of surgery. My mom's with him now, but we don't know anything yet."

Pushing her hair away from her face, he pressed a kiss to her worried brow. "Everything will be all right. I'll stay with you."

She sniffled and wiped at her red-rimmed eyes. "He was fine. Patrick checked him over and said it was probably nothing. Then we got home, and he was standing in the den talking when he suddenly collapsed."

He moved to the seat beside her and held her hands in his, the crumpled tissue fisted in her palm. "I'm sure the doctors are doing everything they can to help him."

"I can't reach Giovanni. He has a show tonight, and he's not answering his phone. I left him five messages but I don't want to freak him out and—"

"It's okay. I can call Erin."

Her mouth pinched tight and her chin quivered. "Thank you."

There were signs posted everywhere asking people not to use cellphones. "How about I find you a soda and make that call? I'll be back in five minutes."

She nodded, and he pressed another kiss to her hand, reluctantly letting her go. Assuming space might loosen the tension in his chest, he moved through the double doors to the adjacent hall, but distance didn't help the worry to subside.

The muscles of his neck flexed and knotted. His heart pounded. The scent of antiseptic filled every tight breath, and his ears twitched at the quiet shuffle of hospital staff nearby. This place was all function and no comfort, and he wanted to get her out of there but knew that wasn't an option. Unlike him, Mariella loved her father.

Once away from the patient rooms, he dialed his sister.

"Hello?"

"Erin, hey. I, um...Are you with Giovanni?"

"Sort of. He's on stage. Why? What's up?"

"Okay, don't freak out. I'm at the hospital with his sister."

"Mariella? What happened?" Her voice sharpened with panic.

"She's fine, but his father had a heart attack. He just got out of surgery and that's all I know. Mariella's been trying to reach him."

"Oh, my God. What…What should I do?"

"I don't know. Can you come home?"

"Of course we'll come home. But should I pull him off the stage?"

He wasn't the right person to make that decision. He didn't know how normal families operated in situations like this. "Is he close to his dad?"

"I mean, they argue but—compared to our family—Wait. What am I saying? *Yes,* they're extremely close. Shit, Harrison, I don't know what to do."

"Okay, calm down. Just take a breath. How much longer is his act?"

"I don't know. Where's my phone?"

"You're on it."

"Fuck." He could hear her frantically moving about. "He's been *on* for about a half hour. He won't be done for at least another twenty minutes. I should get him, shouldn't I? What if something else goes wrong, and we don't get there fast enough?"

"Erin, breathe. Here's what you're going to do. You're going to call a driver to take you back to the hotel so you can get your stuff together. On the ride there, book two flights home. Get your luggage and go back to the show. By then Giovanni will be finished and you two can head directly to the airport. I'll pick you up when your flight gets in."

"Okay. I can do that." She exhaled. "Is it bad, Harrison? Is he going to be okay?"

"I don't know. Don't think too far ahead. Just focus on getting out of there and getting home."

"Okay."

He ended the call and found a vending machine with sodas. When he returned to Mariella, she was speaking to a nurse. As soon as she saw him, she rushed to his side.

"The surgery went well, and he's just waking up. They're going to move him soon."

"Good." He handed her the soda. "I talked to my sister. She and Giovanni are flying home tonight."

Her lower lip quivered. "I can't believe this is happening."

He never saw her so worried. Every little tremble spiked his anxiety. Once again, he wanted to get her out of there, but this was where she wanted to be, close to her family.

"I'll stay with you."

She hugged him, her body momentarily

sinking into his, as if the weight of so many new worries made it a struggle to stand. "Thank you."

Over the next few hours they situated Mr. Mosconi in a room and several more relatives came to check on him. The nurses were adamant that no more than two people go into the room at a time, and Mrs. Mosconi refused to leave her husband's side.

When Mariella finally got to see her father, Harrison waited in the hall with Frank and Maureen McCullough, and the rail thin, tiny Italian relic that was Mariella's grandmother.

"Does she always stare like that?" he asked, whispering to Mrs. McCullough.

"Oh, just ignore her, love. She's just takin' your measure."

He glanced back at the little old woman who watched him with twin beady eyes. "Measuring me for what?"

Mrs. McCullough patted his knee. "It's good you were here with Mariella. She doesn't have anyone, and with Giovanni away, well, it's just nice of you to be there for her."

He glanced at Frank McCullough who hadn't taken his eyes off the door to Paulie's room.

Mrs. McCullough lowered her voice and whispered, "Paulie's his best friend. Frank was very upset when we got the news. Not too long ago I was in my sister's position, waitin' on my husband to come around so I could give him an earful of shite for scarin' me so. Paulie was there the whole time, waitin' with me for Frank to come out of it."

Harrison looked back at Mr. McCullough, noticing the balls of his fists and the hard set of his jaw. The whites of his eyes weren't very clear, and he wished he knew the words to offer some sort of comfort, but he had no clue what to say to a man in such situations. The mere idea that a family could care this much for each other shocked him.

Frank McCullough had always been a rugged, intimidating man. Yet he'd never once made Harrison uneasy. Funny how some men just put off different vibes. He wondered what sort of man he was.

His gaze dropped to Mrs. McCullough's hand, noting the way she rubbed Mr. McCul-lough's arm. Had he done that to Mariella? He'd been so worried about simply getting to her, he couldn't remember how he acted when he first arrived.

Harrison had no one in his life who might show such concern if he were in an accident. No one who would hold his hand the way Mrs. McCullough held her husband's.

He glanced back to his left, toward Mr. Mosconi's room and flinched, remembering the little Italian granny still glaring up at him.

"Hi," he said, uncomfortably.

Her fixed dark eyes narrowed on him. "Who are you?" Her thick accent rolled through the air with heavy accusation.

"I'm Harrison."

"I do not know Harrison. You know my son?"

"He's Mariella's friend," Mrs. McCullough explained, speaking louder than he thought necessary. "He's here with Mariella."

Loud or not, that did the trick. The little Italian woman's expression instantly changed and she pressed a gnarled hand to her chest. "Mariella *mia nipote*—my granddaughter." She lifted the pendant hanging from her neck and kissed the gold face of the Virgin Mary. "Paulie's my son."

At a loss for words, he said, "I heard the surgery went well."

She nodded. "My boy *è molto forte*." She made a fist and pounded it on over her heart. "Strong."

He suspected he had good genes as well,

because this woman looked about a decade past one hundred.

"I wonder if Colleen's had anything to eat," Mrs. McCullough whispered to her husband. "She hardly touched her breakfast, and I doubt she's had anything since."

"I can run down to the cafeteria," Harrison offered, happy to be of some service while Mariella was away with her mom and dad.

"Oh, that would be lovely, Harrison. Thank you. Maybe just some cookies and a cup of soup. Perhaps some crackers, too, if they have them. And maybe something chocolate. My sister's a snacker, especially when she's emotional. She probably hasn't had anything to drink all day, either. Her sugar gets low, so some juice might be good…"

"I'll get a bunch of stuff."

"Thank you." She squeezed his arm, the gesture full of affection and somehow filling him with warm satisfaction. "Such a sweet boy, you are."

Before heading to the cafeteria, he drifted past Mariella's father's room. She and her mother sat at his bedside, quietly talking, while Mr. Mosconi slept. Machines chirped and several wires surrounded the bed.

Colleen looked up, spotting him, and

tapped Mariella's knee. Mariella's breath noticeably caught the moment she saw him and she came to the door. "Are you leaving?"

"No, just running to the cafeteria. I'm taking special requests."

She turned to her mother. "Mom, did you want something from the cafeteria?"

"I couldn't eat if I tried, but thank you anyway."

No way he was coming back empty handed and disappointing Mrs. McCullough. He'd get a variety and see if Mariella's mom changed her mind when food was in front of her.

Mariella met his eyes and whispered, "Can you try to find me some aspirin?"

"In a hospital? I'm sure I can figure something out."

She smiled, but the expression was tired, and her eyes reflected the stress of the day. "Thank you."

He spent a small fortune at the visitor station and cafeteria. When he returned upstairs, the Italian grandmother was in with her son and Mariella was waiting in the hall with the McCulloughs.

Harrison filled an entire chair with snacks and tore open the aspirin for Mariella. "Do you have a drink?" He dropped two pills in her hand and opened a bottle of water for her.

"Thank you." She swallowed the pills then leaned into his side, resting her eyes.

He didn't pester her with questions or try to make small talk. He simply rubbed a hand over her arm, trying to bring her a touch of comfort.

The McCulloughs eventually left with Mariella's grandmother. Mrs. Mosconi stayed by her husband's side, and Mariella slept, leaning into the curve of Harrison's arm.

The sun was coming up when Erin finally called, the ring of his phone startling Mariella awake.

"Hey."

"We're here."

"Did you get your luggage yet? I can leave now—"

"Don't worry about it. Giovanni didn't want to waste any time, so he called an Uber. I'll have to catch up with you after we visit the hospital."

"I'm still at the hospital."

"You're... What?"

"I'm still here. I never left."

"Wait..." Behind Erin's confusion he could hear Giovanni speaking to the Uber driver. "Harrison, why are you there?"

"I…" He was suddenly self-conscious about his presence. "I just am. I'll see you when you get here."

"O-okay. Do you have any news about Paulie?"

"He's sleeping. Everything seems calm."

She let out a relieved breath and whispered, "Thank God. They're not like us, you know? Giovanni would be devastated if anything happened to a member of his family."

She was tired and not thinking about her words, but her comment left him staggered. *They* were family.

"Drive safe, Erin. I'll see you when you get here."

CHAPTER 20

When Mariella saw her brother walk through the doors of the ICU, a wave of relief washed over her, and she was up and running to greet him. For hours, her energy had been sapped dry from endless apprehension, but Giovanni's presence delivered a reserve of much needed strength.

He hugged her hard, his worry clapping like thunder against hers, but somehow she knew, now that their whole family was there everything would be okay.

"How is he?"

"He woke up for a moment but went back to sleep. He's on a lot of meds, and the doctor said sleep is good for him."

"Where's Mom?"

"She's with him."

With a nod, Giovanni went into the room, leaving Mariella, Erin, and Harrison in the hall. Harrison and Erin had yet to hug, and she wasn't sure if they'd said hello.

Mariella turned to her sister-in-law and smiled. "Hi, Erin."

"Hi." Erin's stare followed Giovanni then hung on the door of her father's room.

Mariella had been confused but happy for her brother when he told her he eloped, but now she realized there would be an awkward adjustment period. They all grew up in the same small town, but Erin was never what Mariella would call congenial, which was why so many people were shocked by her and Giovanni's connection.

She wanted to get to know her sister-in-law and form a relationship with her. "Thank you so much for getting him here. I'm sorry this interrupted the tour."

Erin's brows lifted. "We wanted to be here. Giovanni loves his father. He would've never been able to focus on work if we stayed out of town. He needed to be with family."

Her words sent a misty rush to Mariella's eyes and she hugged her. "I know we're not there yet, but I just… It's been a really emotional day and we *are* family, so…" Mariella's arms cinched tighter, and the startled stiffness of Erin's body gradually softened.

Looking over Erin's shoulder, she stared at Harrison. His brow pinched as he watched his sister.

"He's stable now?" Erin asked, taking a step back.

"They think so."

Giovanni's wife pushed a hand through her blonde hair and, once again, stared at the door to his father's room. "Giovanni's been a nervous wreck."

"Uh…How was your flight?" Harrison asked, his expression no longer unguarded and a mask of composure sliding into place.

"Long." Erin drifted closer to the room, subtly peeking inside to spy on Giovanni.

Mariella glanced at Harrison, wondering why he was acting so stiff. "Are you okay?"

He did a double take, his attention drawn to his sister as she lingered outside of the hospital room. "I'm fine."

"You look…I don't know. Confused."

He glanced back to his sister. "I've never seen her like this." He frowned. "She's so worried… So concerned…" He looked at her and asked, "Is she close to your dad?"

"Not really, but I don't think my dad is who she's worried about."

Just then, Giovanni came out of the room and hugged Erin. The moment was tender and intimate. They both watched the sweet exchange, Mariella's heart warming at the sight despite the nip of envy she suffered.

"She loves him," Harrison whispered, as if finally deciphering a confusing equation he couldn't solve.

That much was obvious. "Of course she does." People didn't usually get married unless they were in love.

Mariella stared at the couple, happy for her brother. She wondered what it might feel like to have someone who worried over her and hugged her like that, someone who would drop everything and fly across the country for her, even if there was nothing that person could actually do to improve the situation.

Mariella wasn't sure anyone had ever loved her in such a way. But it was clear Erin loved Giovanni that much.

She glanced at Harrison. The difference had never been made more clear. She had to stop pretending things existed that weren't actually there. "You don't have to stay."

A divot formed between his brows. "I don't mind."

"You have your sale at the store today, and you haven't slept. My brother's here now. The rest of the family will probably visit throughout the day…"

She didn't feel like fielding questions or explaining why Harrison was there. Honestly, she hadn't expected him to show let alone stay the night with her.

She appreciated his presence, but she didn't want to misread the situation. He was just being a friend. And while her sense of self-preservation had never been strong when it came to Harrison, enough remained that she knew it wasn't healthy to lean on him in times of trouble.

An unreadable mask blanked his expression. "You want me to go?"

It wasn't what she wanted, but it was probably for the best. If she was doomed to stay single, she at least wanted to be the strong sort of independent woman who didn't need a man to hold her—even though it was nice to let her guard down for a few hours and pretend the man she loved actually loved her back.

But his support wasn't real. It was temporary. A momentary solution that would disappear.

It was selfish to ask him to sit around in a hospital all day just so she didn't feel so alone. Her family was there for her. Plenty of shoulders to lean on.

It wasn't wise to depend on him that way. She knew better. "Go home, Harrison. I appreciate you coming, but my family's here now. I'll be okay."

He hesitated, glancing at his sister who held Giovanni's hand as they spoke quietly to a nurse.

His brow pinched and his lips firmed. Glancing at her and then the doors, he finally nodded. Of course he didn't argue that he should stay. "Call me if you need anything. I don't mind running back."

"Thanks. I will." She wouldn't, but she was too tired to explain the complicated truth.

Yesterday had been a nightmare of uncertainty. She'd thought to call him a hundred times but always changed her mind, knowing she and Harrison did not share that sort of relationship.

Seeing him walk through that door yesterday…

For a split second, she lived the future she'd fantasized about as a girl, the one where he loved her more than anything else in this world and would always come running whenever she needed a hero or someone to hold her hand. But that wasn't reality.

Now that things were more stable with

her dad, she could breathe a little easier. Erin was still in a conversation with Giovanni and the nurse, so Harrison didn't bother saying goodbye to them.

When the doors swished shut behind him, and she was by herself once more, the sense of loneliness hit harder than usual. Used to handling things alone, she didn't need a shoulder to lean on or someone to bring her sodas and aspirin. She could do those things for herself.

But it was nice pretending she didn't have to for a few hours.

Shortly after the day shift nurses arrived, the doctor returned to check on her father. Aunt Rosemarie and Uncle Liam visited and urged Mariella's mother to go home and get some rest, but her mother refused to leave her father's side.

Mariella napped on and off between visitors, but never slept for more than twenty minutes at a time.

"Hey." Her brother nudged her shoulder. "You want a coffee?"

Mariella sat up and checked the time, her body jittery and her nerves frayed. "No, I've already had too much. Where's Erin?"

"Bathroom. You need sleep."

She took in the dark circles under his eyes

and the lines of worry bracketing his con-cerned stare. "So do you."

"I napped on the plane."

"Liar."

They stared down the hall, where twin glass doors blocked another hallway that T-boned into a different area of the hospital. A tall vending machine faced the doors and Erin appeared, searching the options for food.

"She's different with you," Mariella commented.

Giovanni's eyes never left his wife when she came within view. "She's always been who she is. People just never had the guts to get close to her."

"Well, that worked out for you."

He chuckled. "Yeah, it did." He sat back and sighed. "What was Harrison doing here?"

"He's handling stuff with the hardware store."

Her brother shot her a skeptical glance. "And that led him to the hospital, how?"

She shouldn't feel guilty or responsible for Harrison's actions in any way, but she under-stood what her brother was getting at. Looking up at him, she shrugged. "We've been hanging out."

"Seriously, Mar? *Harrison*? Why would you put yourself through that again?"

She bristled at his disapproving tone. "I'm not *putting* myself through anything. We're friends."

"Just be careful."

Her father had given her the same warning. "Do you have a problem with him?"

They all knew each other, but Giovanni never expressed any dislike for Harrison before. And now, being that they were brothers-in-law, he had more reason to like him. But that didn't seem the case.

"He's always making the women in my life cry."

There had been a few unfortunate incidences in the past when Giovanni had tried to cheer her up. The worst was just after Harrison had left Jasper Falls the first time. But that was ten years ago. They were kids, and it had been her first broken heart.

Everything had been hard to comprehend back then. The fact that Harrison had left everything in his locker and not even warned his team that he wasn't coming back, felt surreal at the time, utterly unfathomable that anyone could so completely ghost an entire town and never return to explain why.

Her brother had been around for that aftermath. Harrison's disappearance destroyed her, and there was nothing her friends or family could do to cheer her up during that time.

But her brother's dislike no longer stemmed for Harrison's treatment of Mariella alone. He said Harrison made the *women* in his life cry—plural.

She looked at Erin. It was difficult to imagine someone so tough crying, but she supposed anything was possible. "He doesn't mean to hurt anyone."

"Don't defend him. He's a grown man."

"And I'm a grown woman. This isn't like before. I'm completely aware of his baggage."

"Are you?"

He studied her as if she couldn't possibly know Harrison that well and the familiar pinch of loneliness returned. Her brother probably knew details about the Montgomerys she did not.

"I know he's not staying here." She didn't need all the details to realize Harrison's father had been a toxic person in his children's lives and his death had stirred some confusing and difficult emotions. "Trauma doesn't have a shelf life. Ward's death doesn't make the pain go away."

"He told you?" Giovanni shot her a skeptical look then glanced at his wife as she casually paced on the other side of the glass doors while nibbling from a bag of chips, obviously giving them some time to talk.

Mariella shook her head, wishing Harrison trusted her enough to share his deepest secrets, but he didn't communicate that way. "He didn't have to."

Mariella didn't need words or stories to piece together the source of Harrison's pent-up rage. She'd been to enough of his games to guess which injuries came from the field and which did not. She also knew, beneath that rigid exterior hid a very vulnerable and compassionate heart, which explained why he was so guarded.

But she trusted him on a level others couldn't possibly understand. "Harrison would never hurt me. Not intentionally."

"Sometimes unintentional wounds are the hardest to heal, Mariella. Just be careful."

That night, with Giovanni at Erin's, her mother still at the hospital, and Nona at Aunt Maureen's, the house was eerily silent. Mariella was exhausted, but too wired to sleep.

She showered and made herself some chamomile tea, but her brain wouldn't shut off long enough for her to rest. After tossing and turning for hours and trying to find something boring enough to sleep through on TV, she gave up and pulled out her phone.

But social media didn't fix her craving. She wanted meaningful human conversation, something real that made her feel connected.

She couldn't call him. It was late and she already decided it wasn't right for her to lean on him for that sort of comfort.

Clicking off her phone, she shoved it aside. She needed sleep. Just a few hours, then she could go back to the hospital and sit with her mom.

The weight of the silent house pressed down on her, constricting her lungs and tuning up every little follicle in her ears until she could hear the click of the clock in the den and the soft sputter of air pushing through the vents in the hall. When her phone buzzed, it might as well have been a gong by her ear.

She sprang upward and knocked the phone off the covers then scrambled to grab it off the floor, nearly falling completely out of bed in an inelegant swan dive. She expected it to be her mother with an update about her father or a request that she grab something for her while at the house, but it wasn't.

The sight of Harrison's text sank in like a

drug finds the vein of an addict. Instant relief and comfort blanketed her.

How's it going?

SHE SMILED at the mere sight of his name on her phone.

Okay. I'm home now. Too exhausted to sleep. How was the sale?

SO MUCH FOR helping him with the store. Her only two days off were gone, and if the sale went well, he'd be gone before she had another one.

Want some company?

SHE GLANCED at her old pajama pants and mismatched socks. Her hair was still wet from the shower. Her mind volleyed between healthy and indulgent options, wondering if there was any real harm in seeing him if his presence might calm her down. She needed sleep—

The doorbell rang before she could decide what to tell him.

Thinking it was another cousin dropping off food or picking up something for her mother, she went to let them in. But as she opened the door, Harrison's dark blue stare shot through her, and her foolish heart sighed in absolute relief.

"I was in the neighborhood."

She lifted the phone in her hand. "I was just about to text you back."

He shook a box of Fruity Pebbles. "I remembered you had a thing for Fred Flintstone. Hungry?"

She loved that cereal and hadn't had it in years. "Are you offering to cook for me?"

A quart of milk hung off the index finger of his other hand. "You provide the dishes and I'll do the rest."

He followed her inside, and she pulled down two bowls and grabbed spoons. He unpackaged the cereal and poured. The sweet smell of sugar brought her back in time.

He drizzled some milk over the colorful flakes. "How's your dad?"

"The same but improving. They said it'll be a few days before he's back to himself." Curling her legs underneath of her knees, she lifted her spoon. "Cheers."

Harrison tapped his spoon to hers. "Cheers."

They each tasted the cereal and laughed.

"Oh, my God."

"Why is this so good?" He chuckled over a rainbow bite of crispy mush. "Adult food's never this delicious."

"I'm sure you've enjoyed some incredible cuisine in New York."

He shoveled in another bite. "Sophisticated food isn't as fun."

"I don't remember this being *this* good."

Funny how they gave certain pleasures up as they aged. She couldn't remember ever deciding to stop eating Fruity Pebbles, but one day her preferences just changed and healthier options appeared.

"We're going to have a sugar rush. No way this is good for us."

"Maybe that's why it's so addicting." He refilled his bowl, dumping twice as much cereal as he had before.

She watched him eat, enjoying the boyish

way he gripped his spoon. "You never told me how the sale went."

"How are you holding up?" he said at the same time.

Her cereal was getting soggy. "I'm okay."

She took a bite, but it wasn't as good as it had been a few minutes ago. Some good things just didn't last as long as she hoped.

He pushed his bowl back, folding his hands on the table. "I didn't open the store today."

"Why?"

He shrugged. "I don't know. It didn't feel like the right time."

"So what did you do all day?"

"Worked from my laptop. Thought about you."

She smiled, her heart spiking the slightest bit out of beat. "That's sweet."

He sat back and rubbed a hand over his hair. "I can't stop thinking about Erin and your brother. It's weird seeing her married."

She laughed. "It is weird, but they look really happy together."

He shook his head not in denial but a sort of disbelief. "Do you think they'll have kids?"

"Probably. Eventually."

His brow furrowed. "I can't imagine Erin

as a mother. Mostly because I can barely remember my own mother."

"Maybe your parents have nothing to do with it."

"Or they could have everything to do with it." By the worried look in his eyes, she suspected he wasn't worried about Erin resembling their mother as much as he was worried he might one day take after his dad.

She brushed a hand over his arm. "Sometimes we learn from our parents' mistakes, Harrison, and each generation becomes a little bit better."

"My mom left. That's what she showed us. What if Erin leaves too?"

"Your sister doesn't strike me as the sort who runs away." That was him. "She's happy, Harrison. People change when they're happy. They grow and learn to trust others."

Was he worried for Giovanni? That struck her as odd, being that her brother didn't hold much compassion for Harrison.

He twisted his spoon over the rim of the bowl, the metal softly clicking against the ceramic. "Who are you like?"

She cocked her head. "What do you mean?"

"Are you more like your mom or your dad?"

"I guess I'm more like my dad. We both sort of go with the flow, and I have his olive skin and dark hair."

"What about their flaws?"

"I get my competitiveness from my mom." She laughed. "She's stubborn."

"So you didn't just inherit the good stuff."

Realizing something was bothering him, she frowned. "What's wrong, Harrison?"

Uncertainty danced in his stare, as his fingers flexed into a fist then relaxed. "My greatest fear is that I'll turn into him one day."

Her hand closed over his fist and he instantly laced his fingers through hers. "You won't. Maybe you two butted heads so much because you were already too different."

"Or maybe it was because we were too alike." He chewed back the thumbnail on his free hand. "We look like them. Every time I see Erin, she looks more and more like our mom. And I look like my dad."

"That's only on the outside. On the inside you can be whoever you want."

Realizing he was biting his nails, he stopped. "Do you really believe that?"

"We aren't solely designed by our parent's influences. And even if we are, we can choose to behave differently."

Unlike Harrison, Erin chose not to run

away. Mariella wondered if Harrison ran because at the time it seemed like his only option. Maybe after watching his mother leave, he thought that was what people did.

He scrubbed his face with his palms and groaned. "I don't know why I'm even thinking about this crap."

"Because you're home, and there are a lot of memories in this town for you." She gave his hand a gentle squeeze. "Some good and some not so good."

He sent her an appreciative smile and his gaze dropped to her pajama pants. "Can I stay with you tonight? Before you say no, I realize you're exhausted and under a lot of stress. I'm not after anything but your company. I swear. I'll be a saint."

As much as she loved the idea of sleeping in his arms, she might not love the feelings it stirred come morning. She lifted the spoon in her mushy cereal, the color no longer as vibrant and the appeal gone. "I don't know."

She needed something that would last more than one night. It wasn't fair to tease her heart with such comforts when they'd ultimately go away.

"We aren't kids anymore, Harrison. There are certain things I need."

"Tell me what you want."

"Trust me, you aren't offering."

"How do you know?"

"Because I know."

It didn't escape her that he flipped her words, subtly calling her *needs* wants. She *wanted* lots of things, but what she *needed* was some sort of stability in her life. She needed a man she could depend on.

"I want you, Harrison, there's no denying that. But I need more. I need someone who will see me as a life raft on their worst day, not as an anchor that might hold them back."

"That's not fair."

"That's the truth. You told me you never said goodbye because you were afraid I'd hold you here."

"I meant you'd make it harder to go."

"Exactly. I don't want to make anyone's life harder, Harrison. I want the opposite. And I think we both need to accept the reality of us. We don't work, at least not long term." She forced her hands back into her lap. "We just want different things."

"Is this about that guy?"

"No. This is about me." She wanted someone to watch over her the way Erin and Giovanni watched over each other, the way her mom watched over her dad.

He brushed a finger over her knee, his

nails bitten even shorter than before. "I would have stayed with you at the hospital."

"And I appreciate that, but you're eventually going to leave. The reality is, you're not staying in Jasper Falls and I'm not moving to New York."

"Why can't we just live in the moment?"

It was time to tell him the truth. For years, she'd danced around the heavy topics, too afraid her feelings might scare him away, but he'd left anyway. She couldn't keep repeating the same painful patterns. It was time to break the cycle.

"Because I'm in love with you."

He stared at her, his face a mix of confusion and regret. The unmistakable meaning of his silence gutted her, but she heard his truth loud and clear.

"Those feelings last longer than a fleeting moment, Harrison. You don't take them with you when you leave."

A tear rolled past her lashes but she was too exhausted to wipe it away. His gaze turned toward the table, as if the sight of her sadness was too much for him to bear.

She sensed him pulling away from her. As always, the moment things got too real, his instinct was to disappear.

"I can't keep pretending our connection is

casual when it's always been the exact opposite for me. I can't be something meaningless to you."

His head shot up and he glared at her. "You're not meaningless to me. How could you think that?"

"I guess, what I'm trying to say, is that I need to mean something more to the person who holds me through the night. I want your arms physically around me, Harrison, but I need someone who won't emotionally let go."

His head lowered, his voice dropping to a rasp, "It would mean something."

"But it wouldn't change anything."

CHAPTER 21

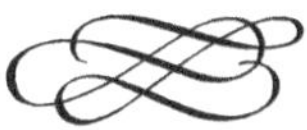

The bell at the front of the store jingled, and Harrison tossed another cardboard box he'd constructed into the pile on the floor of the back room.

"Hello?" a voice sung from the front. "Anyone here? Are you open?"

Harrison exited the back room and found Maureen McCullough perusing a display of masking tape options. "Mrs. McCullough."

"Harrison, love, I wondered if you were here. Are you open? I saw the lights on and the door was unlocked—"

"We're open." He cut her off, knowing she'd keep talking if he didn't stop her.

"This is quite a sale you're having. Is it eighty percent off everything or is it just some items?"

"Everything's on sale."

It all had to go. The sooner the better.

"Well then..." She tossed six rolls of duct tape into the basket looped over her arm. "Have my sisters been here yet?"

"No one's been here." He hadn't opened since the news about Mariella's father, but after last night…

He couldn't believe she finally ended things. When he hugged her goodbye, it was clear neither of them wanted to let go, but she was right. It wasn't fair for him to keep hurting her. She deserved more. He'd always known that, but since returning to Jasper Falls, he thought…

He didn't know what he thought. Nothing had changed. She was still too good for him, and he would only wind up hurting her again.

She had every right to turn him away. It was unfortunate that it had to happen now, when he could really use a friend, and she was also going through a tough time. But it was for the best.

It just sucked.

He'd opened the store out of sheer desperation. He couldn't do another day trapped in his hotel room thinking about Mariella.

Mrs. McCullough perused caulk guns in

aisle two. "Were you looking for something in particular?"

She laughed. "My youth, but I'm sure I won't find that here." She curiously edged past him and he followed her toward the back. "Are the mowers marked down as well?"

"Everything's on sale."

"Oh, my." She dug in her purse and withdrew a dated flip phone, bringing it to her ear. "Rosemarie, you better get down here. The hardware store, love. They've got everything marked down to *eighty percent off*! I'm looking at a four-hundred-dollar grill, and I'm about to buy for—Harrison, what's the sale price of this?"

"Eighty dollars."

"It's eighty dollars, Rose! No, Frank already has a grill. But I have five sons with birthdays and it's gettin' damn expensive to find gifts they can actually use." She covered the edge of the phone. "How many grills do you have in stock?"

"Six."

"He has six. That leaves one for you. You'll have to play favorites between Ryan and Patrick. Maybe a riding mower for the other. Or maybe we should save the last grill for Colleen. She only has Giovanni to think of—"

Her words cut off as her sister's voice

squawked through the phone. The dusting of cinnamon freckles covering Mrs. McCullough's complexion darkened to a deep ruby and she frowned at the prattling phone.

"Well, then get your arse down here and get it! Christ, I'm the one who called you." She snapped the phone shut and shoved it into the deep abyss that was her handbag. "Some thanks I get for trying to do her a favor."

Within an hour, Mrs. McCullough made twenty-some calls and packed the store with frantic bargain hunters. She was louder than a siren and more effective than an ad in the *Penny Saver*.

As he rung up her order at the register, additional customers continued to walk through the door. Word of the sale traveled and there seemed a mad rush to get there before all the coveted items were gone.

Despite the great discounts, Mrs. McCullough spent well over two thousand dollars.

She swiped her credit card then tucked it neatly back into her bulging wallet and adjusted the battered leather bag over her shoulder. "Now I'll need you to hold these items for me."

Harrison's attention jerked from the long receipt spewing out of the register. "Uh, we don't typically—"

"Just for a day or two, dearie, until I figure out how to deliver them. You don't deliver, do you?"

"No, ma'am."

She took the long printout of her order and wadded it around her fingers, stuffing it deep into her purse. "Well then, I guess we'll both live in suspense until a solution comes to me. Toodle-loo."

"But…" Harrison stared after her, wondering how he just became a storage unit when his only goal had been to empty the store.

"Is this eighty percent off?" An older man asked, holding up a bottle of weed killer.

"Yes."

"And this?" He lifted a packet of seeds.

"Yes."

"And what about the shovels and spades."

"It's all eighty percent off." Were the signs not bright enough?

He massaged his temples as more customers flooded in, each one pelting him with redundant questions. He tried to field each one with a smile, and even hung signs displaying the simple math of eighty percent off various ticket prices, but the questions kept coming.

"Is it cash only?"

"Do you have any more grills?"

"What's your return policy?"

And then there were the rumors. "I heard he'll store whatever you can't transport."

"We don't hold items!" Harrison hadn't meant to lose his temper, but how could he make it any clearer? He wanted everything gone so he could leave!

"Oh." The woman with the gray curls looked back at her companion. "Well then, we'll just have to pay for delivery, Ruth."

"We don't deliver," he grumbled into his palms, giving up.

At the end of the day, the shelves were ransacked and—despite his consistent protests—large purchased items that needed to still be picked up—or *delivered*—congested the front half of the store.

He locked the door at five on the dot and closed out the register. Then he spent the next hour consolidating the inventory from four aisles into two.

Seeing the notable progress filled him with mixed emotions. He was closer to getting out of there, but he was also running out of reasons to stay.

He stared down at the stack of Ready Mix Spackle. There had been twenty buckets of the stuff that morning. Now, there were only three left.

Snatching one off the stack, he grabbed a putty knife, hit the lights and left through the back. Ten minutes later he was parking in front of his sister's house.

Thinking of the house as Erin's helped diffuse some of the anger linked to his childhood home, but nothing protected him from the surge of unwanted recollections. Too many memories survived his dad, and he hated that something as simple as the sight of their mailbox could trigger unwanted thoughts of his past.

He pounded on the front door and Erin opened it, eyes startled. "Harrison, what's wrong?"

"I brought you this."

"What is it?" She frowned at the bucket. "Spackle?"

"Can I come in?"

"Um, sure. We were just about to eat."

His footsteps halted at the scent of food and the sound of soft music streaming from the kitchen. The image seemed all too wholesome for this house. "You cook?"

Her eyes narrowed as she shut the front door. "Yes, I cook."

They mostly ate canned Spaghetti-O's

growing up. Erin did a lot of the cooking back then, too, but it never smelled the way the house smelled now. He shot her a suspicious glance. It smelled a little too good.

"Fine," she hissed. "I heated up a casserole Giovanni's grandmother sent over. But I made the damn salad, jerk."

He laughed. Strange how he found comfort in the fact that some things didn't change. He followed her into the kitchen. "Where's Giovanni?"

"Showering. He should be out soon." She opened the fridge and offered him a beer.

Not thinking, he cracked the cap off the top of the fridge like their father used to do.

"*Harrison!* Do you mind?"

"Sorry." It wasn't the battered old fridge that had been there months ago. As a matter of fact, all the appliances were new. He scanned the kitchen, admiring the fresh flowers on the window sill and the bowl of fruit on the counter.

"Are you staying here?"

"For now. Giovanni postponed his shows so he could stick around and help out his dad." She checked on the casserole in the oven and joined him at the table with a glass of iced tea.

A bowl of mixed salad sat on the counter

beside dishes he didn't recognize. "You look different." It wasn't just Erin. The whole place seemed changed, yet also exactly the same.

"Good different?"

He took in her loose blonde hair and faded cotton of her shirt. It wasn't even a good shirt. It was the kind people gave away as swag. He didn't recognize the company logo. "Yeah. You look…natural."

"Well, if I'd known anyone was coming over, I might have thrown on some makeup."

"No, I meant you look…happy." And it bugged him that she categorized him as company.

Her defensiveness faded. "Thanks." She sipped her tea.

"I thought I heard you talking to someone." Giovanni entered the kitchen and shook Harrison's hand. "How's it going? Erin didn't tell me we were having company."

Erin shrugged. "I didn't know."

Again with the company…

Giovanni paused, taking the pulse of the room. "Everything okay?"

"Everything's great." Harrison stood, grabbing the bucket of spackle. "I have to take care of something. Call me when dinner's ready."

"I guess he's eating over?" Erin teased with mock imposition.

He glanced back over his shoulder. "As long as you didn't cook it, I'm in."

It was a nice byplay, sort of normal, but there was no missing the protective way Giovanni watched Erin, as if not trusting Harrison's presence in their home, which massively pissed him off, being that it was Harrison's home long before it ever belonged to Giovanni.

As he left the kitchen and headed down the hall, he couldn't shake the sense that they viewed him as an intruder in his own house. Last time he'd visited, Erin begged him to stay a while. He was finally there, willing to stay for more than a few minutes and working through his bullshit, but his sister's welcome wasn't quite as warm.

Ignoring their soft chatter, he focused on the purpose of his visit. Unsealing the spackle, he mixed the putty and slathered it over the nicks carved into the plaster wall at the back corner of the hall. There were a lot of divots to fill, and his mind wandered as he worked.

He tried to focus on anything but the necessity of his task. Most homes didn't have belt-marks in the plaster. His back knotted with tension and his jaw clenched the longer he stared at the offensive little slashes.

Each time the putty smoothed over a chip in the wall, covering traces of deep grooves put there in a fit of rage, the ache of old injuries burned like a scab being ripped away. Abuse was sometimes worn on the surface, but the real scars hid deep within a person's soul.

Like an arthritic ache that spontaneously acted up, environment sometimes played a part. Certain surroundings simply brought about more pain than others.

The longer he stood in that hall, staring at the corner he'd faced so many times before, manually repairing the surface damage of his past, the less the marks unnerved him. He didn't try to avoid the memories as he worked, but his mind eventually grew bored with the old images and moved onto more interesting things, like Mariella and the progress he'd made at the store.

"What are you doing?"

Startled by his sister's accusatory voice, he dropped a glob of spackle on the trim and used a finger to quickly scoop it back onto the putty knife. "This wall was all banged up."

"We just painted that wall!"

"So? I'll paint it again. You can't leave those marks on the wall. They look terrible."

She shook her head. "Dinner's ready."

Sitting at a kitchen table with his sister and her new husband was a lot more intimate than he imagined it would be. It had been years since he ate a home cooked meal like this, with potholders under the Pyrex and paper napkins in a wicker basket beside his plate.

It reminded him of childhood suppers, sort of like the ones he watched on television. Unlike the memories of their past childhood dinners, this food looked edible, and there was no sense of impending doom.

Giovanni passed him a basket and Harrison stared down at the steaming garlic bread swaddled in a checkered dish towel, strangely quaint and unsettling. Who were these people? He selected a warm piece and set it on his plate then passed the basket to Erin.

Her husband had already put a piece of bread on her plate so she set the basket down. Harrison stared as Giovanni also filled her plate with salad. His mother and father never interacted that way at a table. It seemed strange but also incredibly caring.

"So how long are you staying in Jasper Falls?" Giovanni passed him the salad tongs, his easygoing manners shifting to shrewd observation.

Harrison caught the change right away, the contrast so drastic, there was no mistaking the sentiment that went unsaid. Giovanni didn't like him.

Harrison wasn't sure he'd interacted with the man enough to warrant his dislike, but he supposed it had something to do with Erin. "Not sure. I guess as long as it takes."

"It?"

"The store."

"Well, I'm sure you have pressing business back in New York that requires your presence."

"Nothing quite as *pressing* as a comedy show."

"Harrison." Erin shot him a warning glance.

Giovanni rested a hand over her hand where she gripped her fork. "It's okay, babe."

Harrison popped a cucumber slice in his mouth, disliking the sense that he was being pushed out of his own home. "Maybe I'll stick around for a while."

Giovanni chuckled, the sound dry and mocking. "No need to break tradition and let grass grow under your feet."

"What the hell does that mean?"

"If you ever stuck around long enough to find out, you'd know."

His fork clattered to the table. "I'd rather just cut to the point. What's your fucking problem, Mosconi?"

"That's it." Erin shot to her feet and snatched Harrison's plate, dumping it right in the sink. "Get out."

Now it was starting to feel like a family dinner. "He started it!"

"What are you, twelve? This is our home, Harrison."

"Last I checked, it was my home too."

"You left. Twice. Don't even try to rewrite history to suit your mood swings. You can't burst in here, start changing things without even asking if it's all right, and disrespect my husband. This might have been your house, but it's our home."

"I didn't know I needed a written invitation to visit my sister." He tossed his paper napkin on the table and stood. "So much for trying to be a normal family."

"Shut up!" Despite the hard set of Erin's jaw and the jut of her chin, a wall of unshed tears trembled in her eyes. "I don't want that negativity anymore. Go dump your baggage somewhere else."

Her words stung. He thought they were just communicating, acting like family and arguing as families do. He hadn't meant to make her cry.

He looked away, his stare falling on the tidy countertops and the matching hand towels hanging off the front of the oven. Little touches to add a homey sense of comfort that never existed in this place before.

He envied how healthy and normal it all appeared and wanted to prove it was fake, because how could Erin have come so far after so much when he still felt so incredibly broken? What was wrong with him?

He needed to get as far away from them as possible. "You're right. I'm sorry."

"Why are you even here?" she snapped.

"I don't know."

He had to go. His presence only fueled the ugliness they shared. That was their common ground. His absence had broken any sibling bonds, and too much time had passed to bridge the gap.

He pushed in his chair and left, thinking she might try to stop him but not at all surprised when she didn't.

He tried it Erin's way, tried to bury the bad memories, but they kept resurfacing like weeds that spoiled a garden when pretty flowers attempted to grow. No matter what he did, he couldn't stop his crap from resurfacing.

Covering up the resulting damage didn't erase the experience that left an injury. He absolutely hated that his father still had this much impact on him.

Erin was different. Stronger, maybe. She lived through things he could never tolerate, somehow faced those battered walls every day, passing those marks until they stopped bothering her. She saw Harrison's attempt to hide the scars more disturbing than the physical reminders of their brutal past.

How did she do that? How had she processed their past so completely and moved on?

Waiting at the traffic light, he stared at the road out of town. His inability to cope with his past urged him to keep driving. This place made him think about shit he didn't like to contemplate.

There was no point to these confusing emotions. The marks would always be there, scars and emotional damage poorly disguised under fancy hand towels and fresh paint.

If he returned to New York, the commotion in his head would fade, drowned out by the unignorable rush of life. He longed for such metropolitan distractions, missing the sense of urgency and steady force of motion.

Of course his head was a mess. There was nothing to do but think in a town as quiet as Jasper Falls, but his thoughts were starting to piss him off. Inconsequential bullshit that wouldn't matter the second he returned to the city, so why the hell did he care about such things now?

That was it. He did care. He cared about Erin, and he cared about Mariella. He even cared about chatty old Mrs. McCullough enough that he'd probably arrange to have her items delivered to her eight-hundred kids. But, damn it, caring was a pain in the ass, and he didn't recall signing up for this.

He could just bail. Cut out and let everyone else smooth out the loose ends. But then he'd do exactly what they expected— leave before any grass could grow beneath his feet.

That Giovanni was a real asshole. Who did he think he was, psychoanalyzing him?

He knew nothing about Harrison's life outside of this town. If not for Erin, he might have said something to put the guy in his place, but he didn't want to upset his sister more than he already had.

And there was the crux of it. As mad as he

was at her husband for calling him out, he respected the guy for protecting Erin in such an unflinching way. Without actually saying the words, Giovanni made it loud and clear that Harrison had no business getting involved in Erin's life if he only planned to take off again.

And he wasn't the only Mosconi sending such warnings his way.

CHAPTER 22

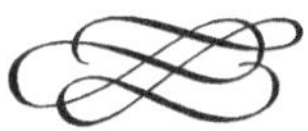

$\mathscr{I}$t wasn't even seven-thirty when the bell above the door rang, announcing the first customer of the day. "We're not open yet," Harrison yelled from the back.

"Wow, you're even starting to sound like him."

"Erin?" He staggered out of the back with a stack of invoices and order slips in his hands, unsure if he'd imagined her voice.

His sister admired the vacant racks and empty displays. "Are you *giving* stuff away."

"Pretty much." He set the paperwork on the front counter. "What are you doing here?"

After the miserable way he behaved at dinner, she was the last person he expected to see.

"I couldn't sleep last night. I didn't like the

way we left things, and you being you, I was worried you'd skip out of town before we had a chance to make things right."

He rolled his eyes and waved a hand at the endless aisles of inventory. "Does it look like I'm taking off anytime soon? Someone has to stick around and deal with all this crap."

"See, right there. That's a tried-and-true Montgomery trait—bitch and moan about your personal obstacles and somehow blame others for the challenging stuff. I've done my share, Harrison. I handled everything after he died. He left the store to you."

"Yeah, one final way for him to say fuck you."

"Or maybe it was the only way he could think to keep us together as a family."

"Don't." He grabbed a box of drill bits and pushed past her. "Let's not pretend he did this for any reason other than to insult you and interfere with my life in New York."

She followed. "I'm not letting you go until we fix this."

"Fix what?" he snapped. "There's nothing to f—"

His words cut off as his gaze fell on the casserole dish sitting on the front table beside a bag of coffee grounds. "What the hell is that doing here?"

She didn't need to follow his stare. "We don't have a lot of traditions, but that crumb cake kept customers coming to this store for decades, and those customers kept food on our table and a roof over our heads."

"Now who sounds like him?" He shook his head and turned away. "You can't rewrite history, Erin. That cake caused more problems than it solved. And he loved this store more than he ever loved us."

"He's dead, Harrison. Dead." She didn't raise her voice or yell, but he sensed her frustration all the same. "We grew up in an abusive house with a cruel father, but our home was not absent of love."

Her words sharpened and poked at something tender in his chest, causing his eyes to prickle. He firmed his lips and shoved the sensation of guilt away. "I won't glorify his memory."

"No one expects you to. But could you at least stop lumping the rest of us in with those miserable parts of your past. I loved you. You're still my big brother. We used to play together and laugh and help each other whenever things got bad."

"I know I'm still your brother." His voice strained around whatever was clogging his throat. And what the hell did she think he was doing here if not helping her?

She removed the foil covering from the crumb cake and pulled a stack of napkins out of her bag.

"We get to choose, Harrison. We get to choose what parts of our past we keep alive and which parts die with him."

She was delusional if she thought to mend their family with a crumb cake. How many casserole dishes had he seen shatter over the years?

"Get that cake out of here."

She opened the bag of coffee grounds and spooned out a heaping scoop, filling the trap of the coffee pot where she fit a ruffled filter. "The cake will be gone in a matter of hours, because the people love it. They love us, Harrison."

He shook his head. The residents of Jasper Falls didn't give two shits about them. They loved Ward.

"You wouldn't believe how kind they've been to me since he's passed away." She lifted the glass pot, carrying it toward the back sink. "I was terrible to them because defensiveness was my default setting. But then I realized they weren't out to hurt me and a sort of trust formed. That urge to get away faded, and I actually like it here now. Believe it or not, I was homesick while we were on tour."

"I'm happy for you."

Her lips formed a thin line. "Don't be a prick. I'm trying to help you."

"I don't need any help."

"Right. You don't need anything or any-one. You're doing just fine on your own. That must be why you're so damn pleasant to be around."

His stare dropped to the floor, his gaze tripping over a magic marker that had rolled under the lip of the bottom shelf. An image of Mariella making the signs for the front window flooded his memory. He missed her.

"You're literally scowling."

"Huh?" He cleared his expression. "I wasn't scowling."

"You were. You always are. Don't you get tired of being pissed off all the time?"

Yes! He wanted to scream but couldn't seem to work the word through his fury. "What do you want me to say, Erin?"

"I don't want you to *say* anything. But I want you to try. We're it, Harrison. As far as family goes, we're all we've got. I'm sick of watching you leave, and I'm tired of hoping you'll call. And it's not okay that you and Gio-vanni don't get along."

"Hey, that's on him. I don't know what his problem is with me—"

"His problem is that you hurt me, Harrison!"

She shoved past him, the echo of her words ringing through the air like cannon fire. He staggered as a sharp ache formed in his chest. If her target was to hit his heart, she nailed it.

The faucet ran and she took her time filling the coffee pot. Her anger emanated from the back, but he somehow could sense her tears.

He followed her into the storeroom. "Erin…"

The water shut off, and she shook her head. "I just don't get it. Don't you love me, Harrison?"

Pressure rushed through him, painful and too big for his bones to hold. "Yes, I love you," he rasped, the words awkward and clumsy in his mouth.

She turned to face him, the sight of her tears triggering his own. "Then act like you do. Otherwise, you're no better than him."

That was his greatest fear. What if he wasn't any better than Ward? What if all he ever did was hurt the people he was meant to protect?

"I don't know how to be better."

"You start by simply being present, and from there we'll figure the rest out."

It sounded simple yet grueling. He wasn't good with open ended expectations. He liked clear cut objectives and goals. Deadlines and end dates.

It had been so long since he acted like any sort of brother, he didn't have a clue what she might expect. They were kids when he left, and he was pretty sure she wasn't looking for a *ManHunt* buddy at this age.

He thought about Mariella and Giovanni. She'd been so relieved when her brother arrived at the hospital. Harrison wanted to be that sort of comfort for Erin, but he wasn't sure he had it in him.

He could close a million-dollar deal, even sell a ketchup popsicle to a woman in white gloves, but he only ever disappointed his family. He doubted his integrity to such a degree, he truly believed he'd only let his sister down if she depended on him for too much.

"I'm not good at this."

"Neither am I."

His gaze shot to hers, and he had to laugh at the snarky smirk on her face. They really were awkward when it came to sticky emotions. But within that awkwardness they found common ground.

He wasn't sure if the moment called for a hug or some other sort of sentiment, but nothing about her posture welcomed human contact and he rather not go there.

He laughed. "You're tougher to navigate than Normandy Beach."

"There have been a few times when Giovanni almost lost a hand."

"I bet."

She chuckled, but quickly sobered. "We need to do better, Harrison. Both of us."

They couldn't possibly get any worse at this. "Tell me what you expect from me as your brother. I can do better, but I need to know your priorities."

She rolled her eyes. "My priority is to become a less dysfunctional family."

"Okay. So what does that look like?" When she gaped at him, he held out his hands. "I'm not trying to be obtuse or offend you, Erin. I honestly don't know. If you tell me what you want, I'll work on it. I'm trying to be real with you. This is how my brain works."

"Okay." She nodded. "Well, I want a brother who loves my husband like a best friend. I'm talking full-on bromance. I want casual traditions, like loud football on Sundays with dip and chips. I want family vacations in the summer and busy holidays with shared recipes in the fall and winter. I want egg hunts for our children and pool parties with water guns and hose fights. I want cutthroat chili cookoffs and wholesome chaos and pop-ins. I want to see you more often—at least a couple times a month. And maybe one day we can get dogs from the same litter or put our kids in the same sports league. I just want to be normal and boring, but I want you to be a part of my world."

"Is that all?" His ears rung in the resounding silence that followed her long list of impossible expectations.

"And I'd like you to find someone who wipes that grimace off your face, because I swear to God, Harrison, I will not stand by and watch you turn into Dad."

She breezed past him and poured the water into the coffee machine. Once again, her words left him staggered.

He followed her to the front of the store. "And what about you?"

"What about me?"

"Don't you think you have a role in all this?"

"Duh. I plan to make the dip."

"Let's forget for a second that you think I

can just mail order the perfect woman, but have you considered the fact that I live in a different state?"

"Yes, and I'm done letting you use that as an excuse. It's a short drive from New York, and there are plenty of places for you to stay when you visit. You could stay with us. We could fix up your old room."

Acid burned his stomach. "I can't stay in that room."

"It's just four walls, a ceiling, and a floor. We can renovate."

He swallowed back the bile rising in his throat. "I'm a hotel guy."

A beat of silence passed where she studied him, both of them acknowledging that his love for hotel amenities wasn't the reason he wouldn't stay in his old room, but neither of them uttering the truth.

"Fine." She sighed and nodded, respecting his limitations. "I think coming here more often will help with your…other issues."

He frowned. "What other issues?"

She flicked on the coffee machine setting it to percolate. "Well, you're sort of a dick."

Breathing in a calming breath, he silently counted to ten and exhaled slowly. If she'd been pulling her punches before, she was done holding back now.

However, he couldn't argue with her, because she was right. He was a miserable bastard on most days. He didn't want to be that way, it just sort of came out of him.

Erin crossed her arms and leaned a hip against the front counter. "Thank you for spackling the wall."

He did a double take. "I thought you were mad about that."

"At first I was. I mean, you never visit and then, all of a sudden, you show up and ruin my beautiful new paint job. But this morning, I looked at the marks you covered and I realized… it felt really good not to see them anymore." She moved behind the counter and pulled a red apron off the hook on the wall, tying it around her waist.

"What are you doing?"

"Helping you."

"Why?"

"Because that's what normal families do." She crossed the store and flipped the sign on the front door to OPEN. "And you're repainting my hallway tonight."

Ignoring the instinct to refuse any commitment that obligated him to stay there, he kept his mouth shut and slipped into the back so that he could catch his breath, unsure if he felt relief or panic. It was all sort of jumbled at the moment.

He could have handled the store on his own. Hell, he could have even delegated the closing to someone else and gone back to New York, but it felt right to see it through and even more right to have his sister by his side. Yet something inside of him warned that he shouldn't get too comfortable with this close arrangement.

His dad always kept files in the back, alphabetized by each resident's last name. He searched the cabinet for Montgomery, but all the notes were in his dad's handwriting and the yellowed papers were more than a decade old. Then he spotted a freshly labeled file under MOSCONI.

Removing the folder, he opened it and grinned at his sister's handwriting. His finger traced down the various materials that listed the finish she used on her floors and the width of moldings she'd ordered to update the doors.

His stare dragged down the page, the short nail of his index finger stopping just beneath the word HALLWAY. He jotted down the code for the paint color and closed the file, happy to finish the job he'd started last night.

The bell over the front door rang and the

morning rush began. As the inventory thinned, a sense of urgency expanded, leaving him hyperaware that his time was running out. He wasn't sure if he'd been counting down the days until he could return to New York or the dwindling moments he had left to make things right with Mariella.

Did he want to make things right? Maybe this was as good as things could get. She wanted more and he wanted her to have everything she needed. The right thing to do, if he had no plans of sticking around, meant getting out of her way.

So why the hell did his chest hurt like a heart attack every time he thought about letting her go? Rather than try to figure out the problems in his life he couldn't seem to solve, he busied himself with quick fixes that masked his misery with productivity.

The people of Jasper Falls loved a good sale. Every purchase brought him closer to an end, but the longer he interacted with the townspeople and hung out with his sister, the more confusing the future appeared.

Every customer that came in raved about the crumb cake. Ward had always insisted that cake could make or break a sale, and as much as Harrison hated the man, in the case of the cake he was right.

During the midafternoon lull, Harrison watched Erin clean the front window. He didn't know how she could put so much pride into something they mutually hated.

"Why are you doing that?"

She sprayed the glass of the front door. "Doing what?"

"You're cleaning like we're keeping this place."

Her hand paused but she didn't look at him. Then she continued wiping the glass. "This store's a part of us. Throwing it away feels like we're giving up."

The unusual warmth he felt after their talk that morning shifted to cold dread. "Erin, we're selling the store."

"I know that's the plan, but it isn't the only solution."

What the hell was she talking about? "Yes, it is." She wasn't thinking clearly. "Are you going to run it? How about Giovanni? What happens when he goes on tour again?"

She crumpled the dirty paper towel between her fingers. "We don't have to run it and it doesn't have to stay a hardware store. It's prime storefront on Main Street. We could rent it."

"Is that what you want?" He had no issue

signing over the deed to her so she could generate some passive income.

"No, I..." Her mouth pursed. "I just don't see the rush to sell it."

They let the topic drop when another customer arrived, but her words echoed in his head. Was it really about owning a rental property, or was this about her fear that he'd disappear once the store sold? Maybe she feared he'd have no reason to come back.

He wanted to assure her that wouldn't happen, but he didn't fully trust himself. Truth be told, the only reason he returned at all was because the taxes were due, and he wanted to get the sale over with so he'd never have to pay taxes or return to Jasper Falls again.

When he got to his sister's house that night, he checked the spackle and set the paint and sand paper in the hall. Giovanni watched television in the den and paid him no mind while Erin chopped vegetables in the kitchen.

"I'm making tacos," she announced as Harrison stared into the skillet on the stove. "Do you want chicken or beef?"

This strange, new side of his sister amused him. Who knew she could be so...domestic? "Beef."

"Lay a tarp down before you sand. I don't want that dust getting in the cracks on my floor."

Her floor… He liked that she'd become so territorial about the house. Thinking of it as Erin's home somehow made it easier to visit.

When dinner was ready, she laid out an assembly line of toppings. Giovanni ignored his presence as he spooned diced tomatoes, shredded lettuce, and cheese into his taco. They sat at the table and ate in awkward, crunchy silence.

"I think you should take down the sale signs," Erin announced.

"Why? We've liquidated more than fifty percent of the inventory. The signs are working."

"Eighty percent off is ridiculous. We're losing money."

"We're trying to empty the store, Erin. Profit isn't a part of it."

"Maybe it should be."

He glared at her. "Did you talk to your husband about this?"

Giovanni looked at her. "About what?"

She shrugged. "About possibly keeping the store or maybe turning it into something else."

Her husband frowned, appearing to find

the idea as ridiculous as Harrison had. "Like what?"

"Maybe an office."

"What kind of office?"

She carefully relocated some tomato cubes that had fallen off her taco. "What do you do, Harrison?"

"I—" Understanding dawned. "Forget it. I work in New York."

"But you don't need to be in New York to do what you do. You said it yourself, you could work anywhere."

"Yes, but I don't want to be here."

The room chilled. Erin's eyes flushed with pink, and she stood from the table before Harrison could retract his words.

"Erin, wait."

She left the kitchen and the door at the end of the hall slammed.

Giovanni glared at him. "Well done."

How was this his fault?

"The plan has always been to sell the store. If she wants the building, fine, but none of us are going into the hardware business so where's the confusion?"

"Did you ever think it's not about the fucking store, Harrison?" He shoved back his chair and left the kitchen.

"What's it about?" Harrison yelled, but the only answer was another door slamming.

He thrust away his plate, no longer hungry.

He could work on the hall, but they were in the bedroom and he wanted to give them privacy, so he cleared the table and wrapped up the leftovers. Then he washed the dishes.

When the front door opened and shut, he turned off the water and heard a car backing out of the driveway. Worried Erin had left, he turned to go after her only to find her standing in the doorway of the kitchen watching him.

"He's going to visit his dad."

Her eyes were rimmed with red, and he could tell she'd been crying. "Erin, I…"

"It's okay. I don't know what I was think-ing. I know neither of us want to run the store." She picked at her fingernail. "Today was just nice, and I thought…it might be nice if we had more days like that in the future."

Today had been long and filled with mo-ments of back-locking tension. But they did laugh a few times over dumb stuff. That was nice.

"I'm sorry I made you cry." This was be-coming another bad habit of his.

"It's not your fault. I've been overly emotional lately." She drew in a long breath and released it with a huff. "I don't know how to convince you to stay, so I'm just going to ask. What would it take for you to stick around for a while?"

He frowned and shook his head, hating to continuously disappoint her, but certain there was nothing she could do to change his mind. "Erin, my life's in—"

"I'm pregnant."

His head lifted and the excuses in his head vanished. "What?"

Her smile was tentative and packed with fear. "I'm having a baby. She'll be here by Christmas."

"She?"

Erin nodded. "We haven't told anyone yet. Obviously, this wasn't planned."

"Are you happy?" She looked terrified.

The fear in her eyes morphed to a kind of uncertain joy. "Scared shitless." She laughed. "But we're excited."

He thought to hug her, but they didn't hug. "Do you need anything?"

"I need my brother."

Her words, once again, left him staggered. Did she truly need him, or was she trying to cast some role of modern family she thought they needed to play?

"You're going to be an uncle, Harrison. Think about that. Think about how jealous we used to be of the McCulloughs' big family. You could spoil her rotten and teach her how to skip rocks and throw a curve ball."

A giddy bubble ticked up his chest. "What about Giovanni?"

"His curve ball sucks."

He laughed. "Uncle. Uncle Harrison." He liked the sound of that. "Do you have a name picked out?"

"We mostly call her Bean."

"Bean." He laughed again. "Holy crap, Erin, you're going to be a mother."

"Whatever that means," she joked then her eyes turned serious. "I just really want her to be happy. I never want her to feel afraid or unloved. I'm trying to make sure this house always feels safe to her, a place she feels perfectly at home to grow and become exactly who she's meant to be, whatever that is."

A tight ache formed in his chest and his words strained past the lump in his throat, "I want that for her too."

"Harrison, I know how this place can feel. But a lot of that negativity's in our heads. We keep it alive, and we don't have to. It doesn't have to be so hard I've realized."

"It's not that easy to shut off. Not for me."

"I know." She crossed the kitchen and mimicked his position, hips leaning into the counter so they stood side by side. "But what if it's our turn at simple? What if, for once, we worked together so we didn't have to fight as hard?"

"Erin, I don't want to own a hardware store."

"Then make it an office or something else. The mayor had another tower installed and our Wi-Fi's up to three bars now. The whole world's going virtual. You can commute on days that you absolutely need to be in the city for work and stay here the rest of the time. Honestly, Harrison, what can New York offer you that Jasper Falls can't?"

"Ambiguity."

After their talk, Erin disappeared to take a bath. Harrison tarped the hall and started sanding the spackle and prepping the paint. While alone, he once more ventured toward his room, but the moment he opened the door a sort of crippling paralysis set in. He couldn't do it.

Shutting the door, he set his mind to finishing the wall. Maybe in time those memories would fade. But, for now, they seemed preserved in a time capsule—too many sensory triggers to process while sober.

It pissed him off that a vacant room could fill him with such boyish fears. But not enough for him to face down those fears. And that was another thing he didn't want to examine too closely.

CHAPTER 23

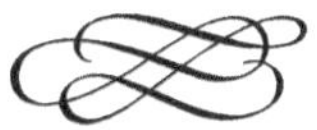

"What's up your ass?" Mariella asked as her brother glared at the cutting board where she chopped cucumbers.

"Nothing. Erin's brother's on my nerves."

At the mention of Harrison her hand trembled. "Is he still here?"

Every morning she checked the hotel logs to see if he checked out, but today she'd called out of work again to help her mother get her father back home and settled, so she hadn't been able to look.

Giovanni stole a slice of cucumber and popped it in his mouth. Then he went to the fridge and rummaged around. "Where the hell's the salami?"

"Mom threw it out. Daddy's on a strict diet."

"So we all have to suffer?" He shut the fridge and stole another slice of cucumber.

"Yes, Giovanni, it's all about you and how we can make you suffer." She tossed the cucumber slices into a bowl and moved onto quartering cherry tomatoes. "What did Harrison do?"

"Nothing. As usual. The guy just shows up, sends a bunch of mixed signals, then takes off. I'd be surprised if he sticks around to the end of the week. I just know he's going to screw Erin over and dump her with the sale of the store."

Her hand trembled, making it difficult to slice the tomatoes. "You think he'll leave this week?"

He studied her. "I told you to be careful with him, Mar. I don't know why you let him do this to you."

"I didn't *let him* do anything. As a matter of fact, I told him the other night that it was over."

"You broke up with him?"

"We were never together."

"You know what I mean."

She switched to cutting onions so she had an excuse for her burning eyes. "I'll never be enough to make him stay."

"Bullshit. Don't blame yourself for his inadequacies."

"Harrison's too good of a guy to spend his life alone. Eventually he'll meet the right woman, and he'll settle down, but I'm certain I'm not that woman."

"I can't listen to this." He went back to the fridge and continued rummaging through the shelves, searching for something to munch on. "Why do girls always think the issue is with them? Did you ever stop to think *you* might be too good for *him*? And are you telling me we don't have any cheese, either?"

"Didn't you eat dinner?"

"No. Erin got upset, and I barely ate half a taco. I'm starving."

She shoved him aside and moved the jar of pickled eggs, revealing a bag from the deli. "Put it back when you're done."

He laughed, unwrapping the prosciutto and shoveling a piece in his mouth. "I knew Nona would have something hidden."

"Just don't tell Dad."

He returned to his seat. "You need a normal guy who doesn't have any baggage."

She arched a brow, watching her brother moan over the cold cuts as if the meat were a beautiful woman falling onto his tongue. "A normal guy? Hmm. What's that like?"

He stilled, realizing he was making a spectacle. "What?"

She rolled her eyes. "You're making sex noises over meat."

"So? I like food. That's not baggage."

"Harrison's baggage is the same as Erin's."

"Harrison *is* Erin's baggage. At least she tries to deal with it. He just runs."

She didn't know the extent of their upbringing, but she attributed a great deal of Harrison's issues to his past. Their mom abandoned them when they were both very young. She couldn't imagine growing up without a mother, but also growing up knowing the one woman meant to love them unconditionally had left and never tried to contact them again.

It made sense that Harrison feared abandonment as much as he mimicked his mother's behavior and ran away from family. But despite all his mommy issues, she believed most of Harrison's self-doubt stemmed from his father.

"Sometimes sons have it worse than daughters."

As soon as the words left her mouth, her

mother and grandmother entered the kitchen.

"Giovanni! When did you get here?" Both women pelted her brother with kisses, asking if he needed anything. "Did you get a haircut? It looks so nice. Look at those beautiful eyes."

They praised him for simply existing, telling him how handsome he was more than twelve times in the span of a minute.

Mariella rolled her eyes. "Sons certainly don't have it harder in Italian families, however."

When their mom and grandmother left them alone again, Giovanni leveled her with a serious look. "That's the thing, Mariella. There's a lot you don't know. Ward Montgomery was a mean old bastard, despite what the town saw. That's why their mom left."

"I figured as much."

"Well, that sort of thing gets passed down. You need to be careful."

Realizing he was warning her away from more than general heartache, she frowned. "Harrison would never intentionally hurt anyone."

"He hurt you."

"Not intentionally."

"Right. It was an accident. I wonder how

many abusers tell their victims the same thing."

"Giovanni." Her defenses shot up. "Harrison's far from perfect, but he isn't cruel. I know him better than you. I know what he's capable of and what he's incapable of. He would never put me in any sort of physical danger, if that's what you're implying. Especially me."

"How can you say that?"

"Because I know."

It wasn't her place to tell her brother how terrified Harrison seemed at times, how overwhelmed and fragile. Everyone remembered him from his football days, a big guy who could take a hit. But she knew the real him. He was vulnerable, caring, gentle when he needed to be, and he had fears like everyone else.

"He's got a whole city of people back in New York. Let him find someone there."

She scowled at his suggestion that everyone just wash their hands of him.

"He doesn't need a whole city. He needs someone who sees the best in him and can teach him how to trust again. Whether he finds that in a good woman or through reconciling with his family, I hope he finds it either way. Even if his future doesn't concern me, I wish the best for him. And as his brother-in-law, you should too. At least for Erin's sake."

"So long as he keeps upsetting my wife and sister, I don't owe him anything."

"Did you ever think you could actually help the situation by being a friend?"

"He's not my friend. Harrison only thinks of himself. Until that changes, I doubt he'll have any friends."

"I'm his friend."

Giovanni crumbled up the deli wrapper. "I'm telling you, it's not healthy the way you are with him."

"You want to lecture me about healthy? You just downed half a pound of processed meat in one sitting."

"Just be careful." He stood and kissed her on the cheek. "You have a good heart, and I don't want anyone to take advantage of you."

As soon as he left the kitchen and she was alone, she put down the knife and flattened her palms on the table, blowing out an unsteady breath. Maybe Giovanni was right. Maybe Harrison was dangerous.

But deep down she couldn't believe that. Yes, he had some issues to work through, but he wasn't broken. He was a good man, and no matter how much it crushed her to think of him with someone else, she loved him enough to want to see him happy.

They both deserved happiness, which was why she decided to move on. Maybe, over time, they could actually try being friends again, but for now, distance was necessary.

And soon the distance wouldn't be an issue at all because Harrison would be gone.

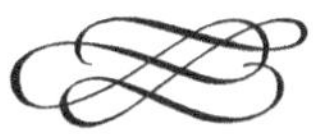

"**W**as this how you pictured yourself when you were a kid?"

Harrison frowned at Erin's question as they restocked the last of the paint brushes from storage. "No."

"How did you see yourself?"

She hoisted a can of paint, and he took it from her. "You shouldn't be lifting heavy stuff."

She rolled her eyes. "What did you want to be when you grew up?"

Her questions were silly but challenging—and endless. Pregnancy had put her on some sort of philosophical quest to unpack the last of their family's baggage. She didn't seem to understand that Harrison liked to travel light and she wasn't getting past his carryon.

"I don't know, Erin. I think I wanted to be a fireman at one point or a cop. I didn't put much thought beyond wanting to drive something with a loud siren."

"So you wanted to be a hero."

"Not necessarily. Hand me those mixers."

She passed him the stack of wooden paint stirrers, and he stuffed them into a yellow bucket on the counter.

"Did you picture yourself married?"

"Yes."

"With kids?"

He sighed. "I guess."

"You know, you're getting up there."

"Jesus, Erin." He grabbed the dust mop and swept his way to the other side of the store, away from her and her endless questions.

She followed. "What's the deal with you and Mariella?"

His spine stiffened. It had been eight days since he heard from or saw Mariella. He was doing his best to respect her wishes, but he thought about her constantly. Erin had actually proved a pretty good distraction in that department, until now.

"I don't know what you're talking about."

"Bullshit. I saw you at the hospital with her. You don't hold a woman like that without feeling something for her."

"Her father just had a heart attack."

"Exactly."

"There's nothing going on between me and Mariella." That much was true.

"Did you two have a fling?"

He shrugged and kept his head down, pushing the broom down the aisle. What they had went much deeper than a fling. "I wouldn't call it that."

"Giovanni said she was in love with you."

He pivoted and faced her. *"What?"* He was well aware of Mariella's feelings but surprised she'd shared those feelings with others. That meant she'd been talking about him. He needed a timeframe. "When did she say this to him?"

She grinned at his response. "He said you two had a relationship in high school, and you broke her heart. Is that true?"

He scowled, his jaw locking at the accusation that he'd broken her heart and was disappointed these assumptions stemmed from decade old news. "We never put a label on it, and we both knew what it was at the time." And what it wasn't.

"Did you love her?"

He quit sweeping and walked the dust mop to the back. "We're not discussing this."

"Why?"

"Because it's irrelevant. And none of your business."

"Oh. Okay." She lingered in the doorway of the storeroom as he straightened up the cleaning tools. "I just thought you might want to know we're going on a double date with her and some guy this weekend."

He shoved the mop and bucket into the wall and barked, "I'm going to get a coffee."

"I just made a fresh pot!" she yelled, but he was already out the back door.

The scorching day matched his temper and the last thing he needed was a hot cup of coffee, so he went for a walk up Main Street to calm down. He wasn't thinking about where he walked or the fact that he was heading back to his hotel. He wasn't really thinking at all. But when he reached the lobby, he strode right past the elevators and into Mariella's office.

"You're going on a double date with my sister?"

Mariella and three other women startled at his outburst. Then Mariella scowled. "Will you excuse me?"

She rose from her chair, looking especially decadent in a tailored pencil skirt that hugged her ass and a sleeveless blouse that might as well have been lingerie for how delicate the fabric appeared.

She grabbed him by the elbow and dragged him into the hall. "Have you lost your mind?" she hissed. "I'm in a meeting with clients."

He mirrored her scowl. "Why are you going on a double date with my sister?"

"Because my brother set it up. It has nothing to do with your family."

"My family's married to your family so it sort of does."

"You're acting like a child, and I'm in the middle of a meeting."

"Who is he? Some lumberjack? Or—"

"It's Mauricio."

His mind flashed to the man he saw her on a date with at the restaurant, the man she worked with every day. Somehow that was worse.

When she said Giovanni set it up, Harrison assumed it was a blind date. This guy was a repeat offender.

"Are you dating him?"

How serious were they at this point? Had he put his hands on her? Did they have sex? He couldn't catch his breath.

"I can't do this here, Harrison. If you want to talk, call me after work."

"Maybe I'll join you this weekend and bring a date of my own." He was being a child, but he didn't care. She could have at least waited until he left town.

Her chin jutted upward and her expression blanked. "You do whatever you want. I have to get back to work."

Finding himself staring at the solid oak door to her office, he cursed and left the hotel. His temper only heated on the way back to the store.

Erin seemed to recognize he was in no mood to talk, so her inquisition took a rest. At five o'clock she said goodbye but invited him to join them for dinner again.

Harrison sorted through the various papers covering the desk in the back and grumbled a reply, neither accepting or declining her invitation.

Being that they were operating as a store, they would have to keep things organized for tax season next year, and he wanted to make sure they kept impeccable records so there was no confusion when that time came. It was a flimsy excuse to skip dinner and work late, and they both knew it was bullshit.

The bell at the front of the store rung, and he looked up. Maybe it was Mariella coming to talk to him and tell him that she didn't care about this other guy and she was through avoiding him.

He set down the papers and left the storeroom. "Hello?" The lights were out and the sign on the door had been flipped to CLOSED. The bell hadn't been someone coming in. It had been his sister walking out.

He was alone. Utterly alone.

Normally, being by himself didn't bother him, but he'd grown so used to his sister's company the silence didn't sit right.

He'd finished painting Erin's hallway several nights ago, but noticed an old electrical socket that needed updating when he'd been touching up the trim. Grabbing a new outlet cover and some tools, he locked up the store and headed to his sister's.

Erin's back was hurting from being on her feet all day, so she was resting on the couch with her legs up when he arrived. Giovanni was in the kitchen cooking.

Harrison took the opportunity to grab a beer out of the fridge and get to know his brother-in-law a little better. "Erin tells me you guys are going out this weekend."

Giovanni scrambled ground sausage in a hot pan. "That's right."

"She said Mariella's joining you."

He gave Harrison a shrewd, measuring

glance over his shoulder then continued turning the ground meat. "You don't miss a thing."

He definitely didn't miss the way Giovanni disliked the thought of him with his sister. He had some nerve, considering Giovanni never once checked in with him regarding his intentions to marry Erin.

Still, Harrison wanted information. "You think this guy's right for Mariella?"

Giovanni sprinkled the pan with fennel seeds. "Being that he lives here and has no intentions of ghosting her for a decade, I'd say he's scoring better than the last loser."

Harrison took a quick step forward and caught himself. Keeping his voice low, he growled, "The last loser was Bran Dawson."

"Another guy I'd like to knock out."

That was it. He slammed his beer down on the counter and looked him dead in the eye. "You wanna knock me out, Mosconi? Go for it. I dare you. Take your best shot."

He'd taken enough hits in his life not to worry about whatever Erin's little husband might be able to dish out.

Giovanni shut off the stove and pushed the cast iron pan back. "You think you intimidate me? I know exactly who you are. You're the guy who takes what he wants and runs away whenever anyone needs anything real in return. Don't over exert yourself with the act."

Harrison's jaw locked. "I didn't take anything."

"You took plenty."

"Did you ever stop to think that it might have been your sister who threw herself at me?" The shove caught him off guard and when he caught himself against the sink, an empty can of crushed tomatoes rattled into the basin.

"She did not!" Giovanni snarled. "She was a kid. You were a senior. You took advantage of her innocence and got exactly what you wanted."

"Ha! If you think there was anything innocent about your sister the night she and I hooked up, you don't know your sister at all. She might have been inexperienced, but she was in complete control. Mariella doesn't do anything she doesn't want to do."

"You used her."

"I never used her!"

"You abandoned her! Just like you did your sister! And it's just a matter of time before you do it again!"

Something snapped inside of Harrison and his fist shot out connecting with Giovanni's nose. His brother-in-law's head whipped back, a stunned look on his face, then he hurled himself at Harrison, piledriving him into the fridge and ramming his knee into his side.

Harrison plowed forward, shoving Giovanni out the back door and they went tumbling down the steps. Pain exploded in Harrison's back as Giovanni rolled over him in the lawn.

This wasn't like his high school days when he could fall without hardly batting an eye. His shoulder hurt from how he'd landed, and he couldn't remember punches stinging so badly.

"Stop this right now!" Erin's piercing voice cut through the night and both he and Giovanni stilled.

A clump of grass and dirt clung to his mouth so he sat up and spit it away.

Giovanni wheezed and brushed at a streak of mud marking his jeans. "These are brand new pants."

Harrison blinked and squinted. "You knocked my contact out."

"What the hell is wrong with the two of you?" Erin shrilled.

Giovanni stood and pointed at Harrison. "Your brother—"

"I don't want to hear it! We have neighbors. Is it too much to ask that we not be the hillbillies on the street for once? Could we at least *pretend* to be civilized? Both of you, get in the damn house!"

As Harrison stood, his knees protested and his joints popped. He hadn't had Giovanni pegged as a fighter, but the guy actually had a pretty decent right hook.

They marched through the door, heads down, as Erin barked out orders. "Both of you park your butts on the couch and don't say a word. I have to pee."

As they waited for her to return from the bathroom, they stayed silent.

The tension Harrison had felt earlier had lessened, but his body shook uncomfortably, likely from the jolt of adrenaline. It had been more than a decade since he'd had a physical altercation, and he didn't like the way it made him feel.

It was as if Giovanni had been purposely bating him and pushing his buttons. Accusing him of using Mariella had struck a nerve.

Then he realized this wasn't just about him. This was Giovanni's way of protecting those he cared about. Harrison respected that, because he cared about Erin and Mariella too.

He hated the fact that Giovanni thought they needed protection from Harrison. And he despised the fact that his brother-in-law might be right, and he'd likely hurt all of them in the end.

Erin returned and paced the living room. "What started this?"

Neither of them said a word.

"One of you better start talking."

"He brought up Mariella."

Harrison's temper sparked anew, and he glared at Giovanni. "I never used her."

"Don't even talk about her."

"I'll do more than talk about her—"

"Hey!" Erin snapped. "Giovanni, sit. Harrison, shut the hell up." She continued to pace. "I am so over the two of you not getting along. You don't even know each other!"

"I wasn't the one with a problem," Harrison reminded everyone.

Giovanni scoffed. "You *are* the problem!"

Erin jumped to her brother's defense. "Giovanni stop—"

"Everyone needs to stop defending him! I know you want everything to be copacetic when the baby comes, but this is causing you more stress than you need right now."

Harrison swallowed back any rebuttal and looked at Erin's stomach. Her health was a top priority for all of them. At least he and Giovanni had that in common.

Was she stressed? She seemed rather calm compared to how he remembered her.

"He's my brother, Giovanni. He's the only family I have left. I know I might be fighting a losing battle, but you have to let me fight it."

Harrison looked at both of them, wondering when he became invisible.

Giovanni stood and cupped Erin's face in his hands, pressing his forehead to hers. "When he starts treating you like family, I'll respect him as such. But until then, I reserve the right to protect my wife."

Now it was Harrison's turn to wish he could disappear. "Look, maybe I should go."

Erin's glistening stare snapped to him. "Seriously? That's what you got from all this? That you should go?" She flung her hands out at her sides, and her voice grew incredibly high pitched. "I just don't know how to get through to you!"

Certain this had as much to do with pregnancy hormones as it did with his words, he tried to calm her down. "Erin, I was just offering you two a little privacy."

"I don't need privacy! I need my brother and husband to get along." She burst into tears and rushed down the hall, once again slamming the door.

Harrison looked helplessly to his brother-in-law. "That was pregnancy hormones, right?"

"Oh yeah. But some of it was you." Giovanni swiped the remote control off the coffee table and sat back, making himself comfortable. "She'll be out in a little while and everything will be fine."

It didn't feel fine. Rather than watch TV and wait, Harrison went to the kitchen searching for something to do. He didn't want Erin stressing over him, but he also couldn't rearrange his life simply because he was getting a niece, could he? He knew some families were close, but he wasn't sure how they got that way. He never imagined it took work. He just assumed they started close and all the pieces fell into place.

There was nothing for him to do in the kitchen so he returned to the living room. "Are you really just going to sit there while she's upset?"

"I'm letting her cool off. When she's ready to hear my apology, I'll make it up to her. I suggest you do the same."

Oddly, the fight seemed to have removed the hostility between them. But Harrison still didn't want to watch television with the guy.

He returned to the kitchen, thinking about how he might word his apology. He hadn't meant to wrestle her husband on the lawn. Nor had he meant to upset her. He really was terrible at this big brother thing.

Thinking back to when they were kids, he remembered how she would look up to him. She would often wait for him to come home, and sometimes she'd beg him to miss practice just so she had someone to talk to.

In all the years since he'd left Jasper Falls, she never asked him for money or help. She only ever asked for his time. And, somehow, he'd let her down.

He stared at the canisters lined up along the backsplash. The casserole dish rested on the dishrack by the sink. Erin had forced that damn crumb cake back into their lives every day since she started helping at the store. He hated it, but for whatever reason, it was important to her.

Gathering a bowl and the measuring cups, he got to work, mixing the batter and preheating the oven. He'd seen it made enough to know the recipe by heart.

As he poured the batter into the casserole dish, he had a flashback of Erin trying to make the cake when they were little. Neither of them knew how to bake, and she needed to get it done or their dad would flip out.

Harrison chuckled, recalling the sludgy

mess she'd tried to pass off as cake. Back then she'd been afraid of getting in trouble, but now the memory only struck him as charming and innocent.

He tried to imagine Erin's blue eyes and blonde hair on a smaller version of herself, tried to picture what his niece might look like.

Once the cake was baking, he returned to the den. Giovanni was lost in some nature show about hippos.

Harrison replaced the outlet cover in the hall then drifted toward his sister's room and knocked on the door. "Erin?"

"What?"

He chuckled at her unwelcoming tone. "I'm coming in."

She lay on her side on the bed, scrolling through her phone as songs of TikTok softly played in short clips.

He sat by her feet. "I'm sorry."

"No, you're not."

"Yes, I am. I shouldn't have lost my temper."

"Why did you?"

"He accused me of using Mariella."

She rolled over on the bed and faced him, no longer interested in her phone. "Every time her name comes up you get this possessive look in your eye and start acting nuts. If you like her that much, why aren't you with her?"

"It's complicated."

"Does it have to be?"

"She doesn't want to be with me."

"That's not the impression I get from everything Giovanni tells me."

And what was Mariella telling Giovanni? He remembered what Mariella had said about what they want not always being what they need.

"Sometimes we want the wrong things. She needs someone dependable."

"Oh, give me a break. You act like you have a disease. You're dependable when you need to be, Harrison."

"My track record—"

"Sucks. I know. But when you were notified that the property taxes were overdue, you showed up. When I called to tell you dad died, you got here that same night. You're dependable when it matters. The question is, does she matter to you?"

There were only two people who mattered to him in this world, and Mariella was one of them. The other was sitting by his side.

"I don't want to hurt her."

"Then don't. Have a little self-control and

make the difficult choice once in a while. It might actually make your life easier in the long run."

He believed he could go to Mariella and apologize for all his past mistakes. Hell, she probably didn't even need that, but he'd do it anyway. Then they could talk about an actual future. But then the expectations would come, and mount, and sooner or later he'd let her down.

His stomach rolled over countless uncertainties and doubts. "We've never labeled it. She's always been more of a..."

"Booty call?"

"No." He glared at the idea of referring to his relationship with Mariella as anything so crass. "More like a side squeeze."

Erin rolled her eyes. "Oh, that's much better. God, men are so stupid. It's the same thing!"

"No, it's not." But maybe it was. "Fine. We're friends. Good friends. But we don't do long distance."

"Why not?"

"Too many complications. She's too good for that. Eventually she'll meet someone else and..." Maybe she'd already met him.

"You're afraid she'd leave you for someone more available?"

Maybe that was it. Physically, they lived in different places, but he also wasn't the most emotionally available guy. She deserved better. Eventually she'd realize that.

No one liked rejection, but after his mom walked out on them, he never wanted to feel anything like that again. He never wanted to disappoint Mariella to the point that she left him.

The twisted irony was that he'd been the one to leave her. It didn't take a genius to realize part of his motivation came from the fear that she'd eventually abandon him.

"She deserves someone incredible."

"Oh my God." Erin sat up. "You *do* love her."

His brows drew together. "No."

"Yes, you do. You love her, Harrison. Oh my God, I had no idea it was anything this serious!"

"Erin, stop." He glanced at the door, paranoid Giovanni might overhear. "What I have with Mariella is just—"

"What you have…" She laughed. "What you have is *love*. You're totally in love with her."

"Will you lower your voice!" he hissed. "We never even dated."

"Exactly! You want her but you won't let

yourself have her, because you only want her to have the best. That's the classic struggle. You know, the whole if you love something, truly love it, then you let it go? You love her so much you're worried you're not good enough for her, but you are. We just have to smooth out a few of your dings and dents."

"Am I an old Cadillac in this scenario?"

"You're definitely a fixer-upper." She sat up straighter. "Don't you see? This can be our thing!"

"What are you talking about?"

"Our brother-sister bonding thing! A point of commonality and connection." She grabbed his hand and squeezed, startling him, because Erin didn't usually touch others, and he wasn't someone who enjoyed being touched. "You're lost, Harrison. But I'm going to be your compass. I'm going to help you find your way home."

Dread and the unwanted pressure of expectation had his shoulders tightening.

Erin sniffled and wiped her nose on her knuckle then stilled. "What's that smell?"

His cheeks flushed. Now his little peace offering felt foolish. "I, uh, made the crumb cake."

"You..." Tears flooded her eyes. "You made the crumb cake?"

"Jesus, don't cry again." He glanced back at the door then shoved the tissues sitting on the nightstand at her. "Here. Blow your nose." Was there an off valve on women's tears?

"I can't believe this." She sucked in a jagged breath and stuttered, "S-s-s-see? You're growing. This is huge."

"Erin, what's the matter?"

Harrison winced at the sound of Giovanni's voice. He slowly turned and came face to face with his brother-in-law's scowl. Suspicion, concern, and accusation burning from his dark pupils.

The man's eye's narrowed on him. "What did he do now?"

"He…" Erin lost her words as a sob slipped out. "He baked the crumb cake."

Giovanni took a menacing step forward then stilled, processing Erin's words. "He… Wait. What? Why are you crying?"

"Because I'm pregnant!" she bellowed, an unladylike snot bubble flashing from her nose. "My body just leaks non-stop now. I'm either peeing or crying!"

Harrison laughed and handed her some more tissues. "If this is going to become a habit, you might want to practice a more graceful facial expression."

She laughed and whaled out another sob,

her nose blaring like a trumpet as she blew it into the crumpled tissues. "You're such an asshole."

He patted her shoulder. "It's okay. You can get away with an ugly cry, because you're usually pretty. You're just not real pretty right now."

"Jerk." She threw her snotty tissues at him and laughed.

As he bent to pick the trash up off the floor, he caught his brother-in-law watching them, a look of approval on his face and what might be the hint of a smile in the corner of his mouth.

Harrison stilled, holding the other man's stare long enough to send the message that he would try to do better. Not just by Erin, but by everyone, including Mariella. He didn't like being the villain, and he wanted to change that.

Giovanni, appearing to read his intentions loud and clear, gave a short nod of approval and backed out of the room—leaving them to their brother and sister moment.

CHAPTER 25

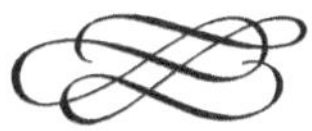

An email notification flashed across Harrison's phone as he closed in on the last mile of his morning run. The fitness center was empty, as usual, and his ears rattled with the upbeat encouraging words of Redbone's "Come And Get Your Love."

Another email notification appeared. Then another. His sister was blowing up his phone with relationship articles and goofy Pinterest content about winning over an ex.

Basically driving him crazy, but he sort of loved her determination.

He cranked up the volume and increased his speed. But there was no outrunning his sister's persistently annoying devotion to fix him.

When he hit six miles, he killed the treadmill and chugged his water. A text cut through his music with a shrill ping. Glancing at the screen of his phone, he rolled his eyes.

You can't ignore a pregnant woman. It's bad luck. God will punish you with a stye.

IT WASN'T EVEN seven a.m. and she'd already used the pregnancy card twice. Once, to beg him to grab a bagel on his way into the store that morning, and now to threaten him with a bacterial infection brought on by an old wives' tale.

He jammed his thumb into the elevator call button and texted her back as soon as he stepped inside.

Who dis?

Ha. Ha. Very funny. Did you read the email I just sent you?

The one about extending my car warranty?

You're hilarious. If you want, I can print it out and bring it to work.

HE IGNORED the fact that she started calling the hardware store *work*. It wasn't work. She had a job managing Giovanni's touring schedule. And Harrison's job was back in New York.

Speaking of which, he opened his laptop and scrolled through his email, deleting the junk and marking off the stuff that needed his attention. He scanned the articles Erin had sent and texted her the moment his homework was done.

Read them all. No need to kill a tree printing them out.

EACH DAY she sent more and more articles about understanding female needs, communicating openly, and overcoming commitment phobias. He drew the line, however, when she attempted to send him advice about satisfying a woman in bed.

He and Mariella definitely didn't struggle in that department. And there was no way he was discussing his sex life with his sister.

He did, however, stop denying that Mariella was someone important to him. He wouldn't label his feelings, though, because that would lead to more expectations on his sister's part. And Giovanni's, because he had no doubt Erin told her husband everything.

Harrison wasn't sure if he loved Mariella. He'd never cared about a woman as deeply as he cared about her, but he had very limited experience with love.

He loved Erin, but that was different.

His feelings for Mariella were complicated and layered. Their story was more than a decade long and full of unspoken moments that seemed to carry more implication than any four-letter word possibly could. She was sweet and sexy as hell. She made him laugh, and he rarely had to pretend around her. Despite all of the ways they didn't work as a couple, there were a lot of ways they did.

They had a policy that they never lie to each

other. That might explain why he avoided her at times, because when the truth would inevitably hurt her, he couldn't bear to see it through.

Most of all, Mariella didn't put up with his bullshit. She accepted him, but also called him out on his crap. She held strong to her boundaries, and even though that put unwanted distance between them, he respected her all the more for having such high standards for herself.

Was that love? Was love letting someone go so they could find something better, as Erin had said? A selfish part of him didn't want to give Mariella space. His greedy side wanted to force her to see and talk to him and tell him exactly how he could fix this. But a fearful part of him feared there was no fix for them and any pressure would only destroy what little connection they had left.

After responding to a few clients that required instant feedback, he closed his laptop and took a quick shower. He was out the door and heading toward the elevators by eight thirty for another day of selling discounted tools on Happy Fucking Lane.

The elevator doors parted on the ground floor, and he came up short when he came face-to-face with Mariella and the son of a bitch who worked with her now touching her ear.

"Harrison." She noticeably tensed, the man's hands touching her hair and ear as his head tipped close to hers.

Harrison's jaw locked. What the hell was this? Those were *his* ears.

"That should do it," the man said, getting his fingers off her lobes before Harrison snapped his hands at the wrists.

Mariella flushed and touched the side of her head. "I lost the back of my earring."

So she let this clown touch her? How was that the solution?

Harrison pushed past them, not looking back as he left the hotel. When he got to the store, Erin already had the coffee made and music playing. He threw the bag with her bagel inside onto the counter.

"You're in a mood. Did something happen?"

"Why are you texting me at six in the morning? Shouldn't you be sleeping in your condition?"

"I've been up since four." She held out her hands and shrugged. "Bean's a morning person."

"Well, I'm not." He opened the register and counted the cash. They needed to make another deposit. "Where can I get a pair of earrings around here?"

Erin bit into her bagel and grinned. "Earrings for a girl?"

"No, earrings for my cat. Yes, for a girl. Nice ones. The kind with good backs that won't fall off."

He couldn't get the image of that man putting his hands all over Mariella's ears, breathing in her hair, his breath exhaling on her skin. He slammed the register and Erin flinched.

"There's a jeweler that just opened up by Town Hall."

He stuffed a stack of bills into the leather bank envelope and zipped it shut. "I'm going to the bank."

He was still steaming when he made the deposit, his temper only mildly cooling when he found the jeweler. He glared at the display of glittering engagement rings, his attention tied to an emerald cut ring he thought might look nice—

What the hell was he doing? He was there for earrings. He could guarantee one thing though. If they were married, no one else would lay a finger on Mariella's sexy ears again. They were his.

"Where are your earrings?" he barked, forcing his eyes away from the rings.

A woman in a red suit directed his attention to the back wall. "This is our signature collection, and there's a seasonal display in the front. Are you looking for something in particular?"

"Strong backs."

The woman frowned. "All of our jewelry's made of fine metals. We also offer insurance if you want additional protection."

He just wanted a reinforced back so other men kept their grubby paws off of her. "What about these?"

"Oh, those are lovely. The pearls are moored from a little town in Ireland. The setting is platinum and the stones are cushion diamonds, two karats total weight. Would you like me to take them out?"

He nodded and she removed the velvet tray from the glass case. The studs were simple but exquisite. A square cut diamond glittered from the platinum post and a dainty saltwater pearl dangled below.

"You'll notice these have a lever back closure. *Very* secure."

"I'll take them."

Startled by his abrupt decision, she smiled. "O-oh, wonderful. I'll get a box." She carefully secured the earrings on a black velvet cush-ion. "Would you like them wrapped?"

"Sure."

She tore a strip of black paper from the roll under the counter. "All of our jewelry is certified and comes with a lifetime guarantee against regular wear and tear. She can come back and have them polished and steamed at any time for free."

Three thousand dollars later, he was on his way back to the hotel.

Mariella was at the front desk when he arrived. As soon as she saw him, her expression froze and her smile turned guarded. He hated that he made her nervous in such a way.

"Can I speak to you in your office?"

She glanced at the desk clerk and excused herself. "Sure."

He followed her into the little office as she held the door. She gently closed it, but made sure it didn't shut all the way, as if she wanted privacy but didn't want to be alone with him.

"What did you need, Harrison?"

He reached in his pocket and set the small wrapped box on her desk.

She looked at the gift then back to him. "What is it?"

"It's for you. Open it."

She hesitated, but her curiosity overruled

and she slowly reached for the box. She gave it a little shake. "I don't understand."

"Just open it."

A brief smile teased her lips as she peeled back the paper and removed the velvet box. The hinges creaked as she snapped the lid open and she gasped. "Oh my God." She looked at him in question. "Harrison, what is this?"

He crossed the office and reached for her ears, gently removing the knockoff studs. "The woman said they have strong backs, so they shouldn't fall off."

Her old earrings were flimsy and cheap, lacking the weight and sparkle of the new ones. He set them aside and took the box from her. Swiping her hair behind her shoulder, he carefully slipped the earring post through her lobe.

The diamonds glinted under the florescent lights. "Beautiful." He attached the other one and snapped the box shut. "They should hold."

She looked up at him, their mouths only a few inches away. "You bought me diamond earrings?" she asked, brow kinked with confusion.

"I also got you the insurance in case anything happens to them." He gave the pearl a little tap. "The pearls are from Ireland." He withdrew the paperwork from his pocket and handed it to her. "Everything's certified."

The divot between her brows deepened as she shook her head. "Why?"

His jaw locked as he met her stare. "I didn't like seeing his hands on you."

There were a hundred other less possessive excuses he could have given. He'd missed her last ten birthdays. He thought they'd bring out her eyes. She deserved more than knockoff gems and paste. But he didn't want lies between them, and the simple truth was, he never wanted that man to touch her ears again.

"He was trying to fix the post. There was nothing sexual—"

"I didn't like it."

The air grew heavy, and he found himself breathing with her as he held her stare. One of the articles Erin had sent him advised a *no contact* rule. The article suggested keeping his hands to himself to hike up the other person's desire for his touch.

It wasn't easy. He sensed the moment Mariella would have let him touch her and fought the urge to drag his hand up the inside of her skirt.

He cleared his throat and stepped back. "I'll let you get back to work."

Her posture shifted as if his abrupt dismissal knocked her off balance. Maybe there was something to be said for those silly blog articles. Because as he walked out the side doors, he could see Mariella's reflection in the glass.

Sure enough, she watched him leave, her fingers delicately caressing the diamond earring in her ear.

CHAPTER 26

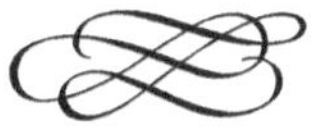

"Mariella, take the bread out of the oven and put it in the basket on the table."

Her Nona stirred a large vat of sauce as her mother carried a stack of plates to the dining room. It was the first family dinner since her father came home from the hospital, and Giovanni and Erin were joining them so everyone was in a celebratory mood.

"No butter." Her mother took the dish out of Mariella's hand and replaced it with a bottle of olive oil. "The doctor says olive oil's better. Throw some pepper flakes and garlic in it. But no salt."

Her father had an appointment that morning, and the doctor cleared him for *regular* food. "When the doctor said Daddy could go back to regular foods, I don't think he meant pasta with meat sauce."

Her father swiped a finger across the sauce spoon and sighed as he tasted Nona's carbonara. "Look at my mother. She cooks with love and doesn't look a day over sixty."

"The woman's older than dirt," Mariella's mother mumbled under her breath. "He might have a point."

Mariella adored her grandmother, but she looked more and more like Yoda every year. "Sure, Dad."

Nona grabbed her son's face in a hard grip and kissed his cheek. "I make'a you strong again, Paulie. *La cucina è medicina.*"

He smiled. "I love you, Ma."

Mariella's mother rolled her eyes. "Get a room."

"Where we at?" Giovanni called, as he and Erin came into the kitchen.

No better than Nona, Mariella's mother rushed over to greet her son, showering him with kisses and similar unearned praise. Her Irish heritage overrun by Italian culture.

Her father chuckled as he shook his head at the inflated display. "Talk about needing a room."

Mariella laughed. His heart might be weak, but his hearing was just fine.

Erin placed a box from the bakery on the table. "How are you feeling, Paulie?"

"Good as new. In fact, I could go for a glass of Pisano."

"Not a chance," their mother snapped, finally releasing Giovanni. She grabbed the bakery box and peeked inside. "These look wonderful. Mar, prep the coffee for after dinner."

Mariella brewed a pot of decaf and stuck the dessert by the mugs. As soon as the pasta was ready, Giovanni helped Nona transfer it to a serving dish and carried it to the dining room.

"They're nice earrings, Mariella." Erin smiled as if she had a secret. "Are they new?"

Mariella's hands subconsciously went to her ears. "Um, yeah. I just got them."

"Oh, my," her mother said, just noticing her jewelry. "Are they… They're not real, are they?"

Mariella's stomach pinched at the thought of what such stones must cost and her cheeks heated. "They are."

Erin continued to grin as her mother scowled. "Mariella, why would you spend your money on such things when you still have school loans to pay?"

"I didn't buy them."

Everything stilled, her family's expectant eyes locking on her as Erin nearly bounced with glee. Yeah, her sister-in-law knew who gave them to her.

"Who bought them?" her father finally asked.

She glanced at each suspicious face. "Harrison Montgomery."

Giovanni scoffed. "You should pawn them and pay off some of your loans."

Erin smacked him in the shoulder. "You, shut up. I think they're stunning."

"I honestly don't know what he was thinking. We've barely said a word to each other in the last two weeks."

Her mother frowned. "Well, they have to mean something. A man doesn't buy a woman diamonds and pearls without good reason."

"That's what I was thinking," her father growled.

"I swear, I didn't do anything to provoke this." She felt like a suspect who had done nothing wrong.

They settled in at the dining room table, a brief truce taking place as they dished out the food.

"If you didn't do anything to earn them, then I'm sure he expects something in return. You should give them back." Her father fished out a slice of Italian bread from the basket. "Col, where the hell's the butter?"

"We're using oil now."

"I don't want oil. I like my Italian bread with butter."

"It's how they eat it in the Mediterranean. And when a man gives a woman good jewelry, she keeps it. End of story."

Her father gave up trying to persuade her mother and turned to his own mother. "Ma, will you get me some butter?"

Nona rose, her instinct to serve her son's every whim ingrained after years of service.

Mariella's mother stopped her. "Mary, ignore him. Paulie, so help me God, if you mention butter one more time, I'm dumping your plate and making you a salad."

Giovanni chuckled, and Mariella rolled her eyes. These restrictions would never last. Her father lived off red wine, fats, and processed meat.

Giovanni popped a bite of meatball into his mouth. "I thought you two were avoiding each other."

"Who's avoiding who?" her mother asked, ladling more sauce onto the pasta.

"He's talking about Harrison," Mariella answered. "And, of course, we see each other. He's staying at the hotel."

"He was very nice to sit with Mariella at the hospital," her mother commented. "He waited with her all night, Paulie. You would have been proud."

"We're just friends."

"Friends don't buy each other diamonds, Mariella. A mother knows these things. Those earrings mean something."

"The earrings probably just mean that he's in love with her," Erin said then pointed across the table. "Can someone pass the salad?"

Mariella gawked at her. "What?"

Giovanni scowled and passed the salad, grumbling, "So much for not getting involved."

Erin shrugged. "I don't know why we can't talk about it. I think it's great."

Her mother wiped her mouth and took a sip of water. "Mariella, is this true?"

"No." She shook her head. "Harrison and I… We… I don't…"

"You're in love with each other. There's nothing to be ashamed of."

She was going to murder her sister-in-law. "Your brother is not in love with me!"

"Oh, I beg to differ. By the way, he's joining us this weekend."

"*What?*" What the hell was happening? She

gaped at Giovanni. "Why would you invite him?"

"Don't look at me. This is all Erin."

She looked at Erin who grinned and took a big bite of lettuce. "I love a good cucumber."

"Excuse me. I've lost my appetite." Mariella pushed away from the dining room table and escaped to the kitchen.

Still holding a piece of bread, she ripped it in half and swiped it over the butter sitting on the counter and shoved it into her mouth.

Giovanni followed her into the kitchen and she mumbled over a mouthful of dough, "Whad duh hell is wrong wiff yer wife?"

He reached for the bottle of wine on top of the fridge but it wasn't there. "She has this crazy idea that you're in love with her brother."

She swallowed the clump of bread. *"You told her?"*

"We're married. We talk about stuff. Where the hell is the jug of Pisano?"

"Mom hid it from dad." She opened the cabinet under the sink and pulled out the bottle. "Don't let him see it. I don't feel like listening to them fight."

He rolled his eyes. "Like Mom's not dousing her coffee with whiskey."

"Whatever Erin's doing, she needs to stop. Harrison's not in love with me."

He poured wine into a small jelly jar and took a sip. "How do you know?"

"Because…" She frowned, wondering how he was so calm. Typically, whenever the topic of Harrison came up, her brother had nothing but nasty things to say. "Because I know."

Giovanni shrugged. "I wouldn't be so sure."

"What the hell are you talking about? And what's going on? You hate Harrison."

"Hate's a strong word. The man's my brother-in-law."

"Two weeks ago you were totally opposed to the idea of me even being his friend."

"No, I got pissed because you act like you're not good enough for him. I still think you're out of his league. I probably always will. But you need to stop acting like he doesn't love you, like the idea's impossible. Mariella, you're easy to love."

His words were sweet and kind but still inaccurate. "Giovanni, he doesn't love me. What are you telling Erin?"

"Nothing. But her and Harrison talk a lot. They're in the store together every day, and he eats dinner at our house on most nights."

"So…" She frowned. "You like him now?"

"He's okay. I still think he's got problems."

"Everyone has problems. And you're crazy if you think I'm out of his league. Harrison's done very well for himself."

Giovanni waved away her praise. "He's emotionally handicapped."

"He had a hard life."

"That's not an excuse, and stop defending his behavior when he's a grown ass man perfectly capable of making better choices."

She swept another piece of bread through the butter. "I'm not defending him. You are! You're the one saying he might be in love with me."

"And I stand by that."

She shoved the bread into her mouth. "He doth not lug me."

Her brother shrugged, finishing his glass of wine and setting the cup in the sink. "Maybe he loves you the best way he knows how to love someone."

By leaving? She shook her head. "You guys have to stop."

"He's been at the house a lot. He's honestly not as bad as I first thought—when he's around, that is. When he pulls that avoidance bullshit, I can't stand him."

Because Giovanni was left with her and Erin and all their tears.

Mariella then understood Erin's motive to get them together. Her sister-in-law believed if Mariella and Harrison fell in love, he wouldn't leave. But he'd left her twice before. Because he absolutely did not love her.

She couldn't be the linchpin responsible for keeping their family together.

With trembling hands, she tried to remove an earring, but the damn clasp wouldn't budge. "I can't get these off."

"Leave them." Her brother pulled her shaking hands away from her face. "They bring out your eyes."

She had no doubt he could see the tears she was fighting. "He'll leave again. You can't let Erin think I have some sort of hold over him, Giovanni. I never did."

He gave her a sad smile but whatever he was about to say was interrupted when Erin came into the kitchen. "Are you mad at me?"

"Erin, I can't go this weekend, not if Harrison's going."

"What? No! You have to come."

Mariella shook her head. "It's too much. I'm sorry."

"I promise it won't be that bad. Trust me."

How could she say that? "I already invited Mauricio. It'll be totally awkward if you're brother's there and—"

"I'm pregnant."

Mariella's brain jerked to a stop. "What?"

"I'm pregnant. And you can't disappoint a pregnant woman or you'll get a stye."

She looked, wide-eyed, at her brother. "Is she messing with me?"

"About the stye? I'm not sure."

"No, you idiot. Is she really pregnant?"

He grinned and looped his arm over Erin's shoulders. "Yup. I'm a stallion."

"Pregnant," Mariella whispered, and they both nodded. *"Pregnant?"* They nodded again, then she jumped up and down and screamed, "You're having a baby!"

"What the hell is going on in here?" Their mother came rushing into the kitchen. "Are you trying to give your father another heart attack?"

"They're having a baby!" Mariella shrilled. "I'm going to be an aunty!"

Her mother squealed, bouncing up and down with her and wildly hugging Erin and Giovanni. Their grandmother rushed into the kitchen, their panic morphing to euphoria as soon as Erin yelled, "I'm pregnant!"

Tears of joy dampened their laughter as more wine was passed around and calls were made.

"Yes, Maureen, that's right," their mother

shouted into the phone. "I'm going to be a grandmother! Don't you dare say a word until I tell Rosemarie."

Mariella couldn't believe it. Her brother was going to be a father. She linked her arm through his and lifted her glass in a toast. "Ten bucks says you're bald by forty."

He gasped and ran a protective hand over his thick dark hair. "That's a terrible thing to say!"

"Dad's hair started to go as soon as you were born."

"That's because boys are stressful." He shot her a sidelong glance. "We're having a girl."

Her heart swelled as another thrill of anticipation bloomed in her chest. A sweet little girl. She could hardly wait.

"I guess this means you won't be traveling as much."

"We're going back on the road for two months but then that's it until after the baby's born. But there are no rules that say you can't travel with an infant."

She laughed. "True. But there is common sense. If you think you'll be able to take Mom's first grandchild away from her, you're out of your mind." She snorted. "You'd have better luck bringing Mom with you, and you know how that ends."

They both looked at their grandmother who moved in with their parents the day they got married and never left.

"You make a good point."

The euphoric mood lingered long after they left, and Mariella couldn't stop wondering how things might change in the year ahead. She tried to picture their next holiday and a thought occurred.

If Harrison planned to be a part of his niece's life, he might be around for Christmas and other important dates. They'd continue to see each other year after year. Over time, he might start a family of his own, and bring a wife to such holiday events.

Her happy mood withered into cold dread. What if he married some metropolitan bombshell? What if Mariella remained single? A dinner double date was nothing compared to a lifetime of holidays spent watching the man she loved build a happily-ever-after with someone else.

CHAPTER 27

Headlights streamed across the house as Harrison carried the last bag of trash down to the curb. Erin's car pulled into the garage and the engine turned off. He'd hoped to be gone before they returned from dinner at Giovanni's parents', but his task had taken longer than expected.

"Harrison? What are you doing here? I told you we were having dinner with the Mosconis." His sister's gaze shifted to the contractor bags lined up along the curb.

"I know. I, uh, had some things to take care of."

Her expression faltered. "Are you leaving?"

"No. I'll show you."

He led her into the house and down the hall. Erin paused when he reached the door to his old bedroom. The molding around the doorframe was gone, exposing some studs and tufts of insulation inside the wall.

"We have some nice trim left at the store. I'll have this replaced in a day or two."

She hesitated, her uncertain stare studying him as much as she studied the glimpse of demolition.

Shoving down the urge to chew his fingernails, he led her into the room. "Bulk pickup is Saturday, so I'll drag the bed out tonight."

She stood in the center of the empty room, turning and taking in the stripped space, frowning when she saw where he'd removed the sheetrock behind the door.

"The hole was too big to spackle. I'll replace it."

The longer she stayed silent, the more nervous he felt. Gripping the back of his neck, he walked to the corner by the window.

"I was thinking you could put one of those diaper stations over here and the crib could go in the center of that wall. New carpet, because babies crawl, and we don't want her knees getting splinters from the hardwood floors, and you could hang one of those mobile things here."

Her chin quivered and he panicked.

"Please don't cry."

She blinked hard, trying to honor his request, but it wasn't easy for her. "You... Everything's gone."

"Not everything." He glanced on the bed where an old shoebox held a few random items.

She lifted the box and stared inside. "A can tab and a key? This is all you're keeping?"

He crossed the room, reaching into his pocket and removing the magic marker he'd been carrying around for weeks. He dropped it in the box. "I lost my key to the house. I've been using the one under the bricks out back."

She looked up at him, her eyes pink and full. "You could have made a copy. We have a key maker at the store."

"This one was mine."

"And the can tab?"

"A keepsake—from one of Jenn Miller's parties."

She frowned. "Did you and Jenn—"

"No. But that's where I met Mariella. It's from the first night we..."

"Aww, Harrison, you're killing me." She sniffled. "What about the marker?"

"That's a recent one. Let's call it the day I realized I couldn't let her go."

Her face crumpled and she covered her mouth. "Look away, I'm hideous."

He laughed as she lost the battle against her tears, a snotty sob ripping out of her. "It's okay." He hesitated, then wondered what the hell he was waiting for. He wrapped his arms around his little sister and held her tight.

A jagged sob belted out of her as her arms banded around him, cinching tight at his waist. His hand rubbed up and down her back as she cried into his chest.

"I'm sorry it took me so long to do my part."

Her tears soaked the front of his shirt as she whimpered and shook, her arms only tightening.

A lump lodged in his throat. "I promise to do better from now on."

She howled and bellowed into him, her response no doubt amplified by the pregnancy. "I love you, Harrison."

"I love you too." His vision blurred. This moment was the first of many good memories he hoped to come from this room. He kissed the top of her head. "I'm glad we're family."

Wiping at her eyes, she pulled back, her face a blotchy mess of hives and tears. "God, I can't take all these hormones." She wiped her nose on the collar of her shirt. "I'm a hot mess."

He laughed, thinking how normal this sort of turmoil actually was. "You're perfect."

Her stare met his and she smiled. "This is big, Harrison." Pressing her hand to her chest, she scanned the room. "I think this room is going to be a happy place from now on."

He glanced at the empty space, no longer seeing the past, but able to finally picture the future. "I think so too."

CHAPTER 28

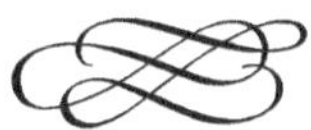

"Can I take your wrap?" Mauricio peeled the chiffon scarf off Mariella's shoulders after they entered the restaurant.

"Thanks." She looked for her brother, and spotted him and Erin in a large rounded booth in the corner, relieved to see no sign of Harrison. "There they are."

She'd begged Erin not to press the issue between herself and Harrison, assuring that while her sister-in-law's intentions were good, the outcome would not be.

"You made it," Erin scooted over, making room for them to sit.

Mariella counted place settings, noting two extras. Giovanni introduced himself to Mauricio with a handshake and seemed quite relaxed about the dinner, which made her think Harrison might have bailed. She wouldn't be surprised.

The waiter arrived and provided a cocktail menu. "Should I remove the other settings?"

"Sorry I'm late." Harrison appeared behind the waiter and lowered into the booth, ignoring the extra place settings and settling in so his thigh rested snug against Mariella's. "Main Street was a madhouse."

Mauricio frowned, now sandwiched between Mariella and Erin.

Harrison traced a finger over Mariella's knee. "You look beautiful."

She jerked her knees together and glared at him. "Harrison, you remember Mauricio."

"Right. The work friend."

Mariella drew in a calming breath. "Mauricio, you remember Harrison."

"I'm afraid I don't."

Giovanni chuckled at the obvious slight, and Harrison's eyes narrowed.

"How are the specials tonight? I'm feeling rather voracious." His hand slipped behind Mariella, and he pinched her ass.

Her spine stiffened and she dug her nails into his thigh, warning him to keep his hands to himself. "When's the waiter coming back for our drink order?"

"Thirsty?" Harrison teased.

"God, I miss alcohol," Erin whined. "Maybe I'll order a mocktail."

Harrison continued to stare at Mariella, rudely ignoring the fact that she was on a date. "What are you in the mood for? Something wet and strong, I bet."

The waiter returned, and Mariella ignored Harrison's inappropriate comment. "I'll have a martini, please."

"She likes it extra dirty," Harrison commented. "I'll have the same." He handed the drink menu off to the waiter.

Giovanni glared at him, equally unimpressed by Harrison's innuendos, as Erin ordered a virgin cosmopolitan.

"I guess I'll be the designated driver," Mauricio said. "I'll just have a club soda."

When the waiter left, the awkwardness draped the table like a second set of linens. Erin's pregnancy seemed a safe topic, so Mariella kept asking baby questions. But in the process of trying to ignore Harrison, she unintentionally ignored her date as well.

By the time dinner was served, she was nice and tipsy and desperately in need of sustenance. She twirled her pasta between her fork and spoon and sighed as the rich sauce hit her tastebuds.

Sucking the spaghetti through her lips, she

moaned, laughing as she realized she had an audience.

"Good?" Mauricio asked, staring intently at her mouth.

"Mm-hmm. Want to taste?" She twirled more pasta onto her fork and lifted it to Mauricio's mouth only to still when Harrison's firm hand closed over her thigh.

Mauricio didn't notice and leaned in to accept the bite, humming with appreciation. "Wow, that's delicious."

"Did you attend culinary school?" Erin asked, oblivious or blatantly ignoring the tension on the other side of the table.

"I did for a short time, but then my focus shifted toward event planning."

The touch on Mariella's thigh dragged higher, teasing bare skin and hiking up the hem of her dress. She turned the fork around and fisted the handle, stabbing it directly into the back of Harrison's wandering hand.

He cleared his throat, pulling his hand away, then leaned close and whispered, "I remember your hand jobs being much gentler."

She elbowed him in the ribs. "Have you had any morning sickness, Erin?"

"Not much. But I don't like the smell of raw chicken since being pregnant. Giovanni was making soup the other day and it chased me right out of the house."

"I didn't know raw chicken had a smell."

"It definitely does."

Harrison's hand returned to her thigh and she stiffened. "Nothing's worse than being around something that makes you want to puke." She gave Harrison a pointed look, but he only chuckled.

If she pushed him away, she'd draw the attention of the others, and she definitely wanted to avoid that. Clamping her thighs together, she held his hand captive before it could travel any closer to her panties.

He smirked and sipped his water using his free hand to hold the glass. Setting the glass down, he touched his lips, clearing his throat with a cough and transferring an ice cube from his mouth to his free hand. The wet cube landed in her lap and she squeaked, parting her thighs.

"Did you say something?" Mauricio asked, just as Harrison's fingers brushed the silk of her panties.

"I, uh, have to use the restroom. Excuse me." She kicked Harrison in the shin and shoved her way out of the booth.

When she got to the bathroom, her body

was in a full sweat. Irritated, she dug out her phone and texted him.

What is wrong with you?

Did you want me to join you?

No! And can you please not feel me up while I'm sitting next to MY DATE?

No. I can't make that promise.

HARRISON!

That's what you'll be screaming tonight, when I have my mouth where my hand just was. I'm done staying away, Mariella. Game on.

Game on? Game on? What did that even mean?

This isn't a game to me!
Nor to me.

That wasn't fair! She was trying to move on, and he wasn't letting her. Pissed, she washed her hands and returned to the table, only this time she planned to make her position unmistakably clear.

Harrison stood and she scooted into the booth, sitting extra close to Mauricio.

"Did you want dessert?"

She smiled at her date. "Yes, let's split something."

When the waiter returned, Mauricio ordered the chocolate mousse. Giovanni and Harrison ordered coffees and Erin ordered a side of mashed potatoes.

"Don't judge me. The bean wants potatoes."

Giovanni laughed. "The bean gets what the bean wants or everyone gets a stye according to Erin."

Mariella laughed. "Where did that even come from?"

"Your Nona told me if anyone denies a pregnant woman a craving, they get *merda occhi*—shit in the eye."

"That can't be right." She looked at her brother in question.

Giovanni shrugged. "I'm not messing with it."

The dessert, coffee, and mashed potatoes arrived, and Mariella cuddled closer to Mauricio, which prompted him to spoon feed her a bite of the whipped chocolate.

She moaned almost sexually as the satin

texture melted over her tongue. "Mmm, so good."

Her brother looked appalled every time she keened, but she couldn't let that deter her from making a point. Harrison deserved a spectacle. It was the only way to get through to him that she was moving on.

But as Mauricio fed her half the dessert, Harrison suddenly stood, throwing several large bills on the table. "Dinner's on me. I have to run."

"You're leaving?" Erin's expression filled with disappointment.

"I forgot about a call I need to make. It's for work, so don't put any pink eye pregnancy voodoo on me. I'll catch you later."

Erin looked accusingly at Mariella when she didn't intervene or beg him to stay. They all knew Harrison didn't have to make a call. But Mariella was on a date. What did they expect her to do?

"More?" Mauricio asked, holding out the spoon.

She shook her head, her stomach now turning with guilt. "No, thank you."

Mauricio excused himself to use the restroom and Mariella's behavior seemed to slide under a microscope. "Don't look at me like that."

"Even I feel bad for the guy," Giovanni said as the three of them looked to the front of the restaurant, but Harrison was already gone. "That was mean, Mariella."

"I'm mean? He was taunting me all through dinner."

"When?" Erin frowned. "I didn't see anything."

That was because Harrison had a gift for putting everything out in the open and somehow remaining the most ambiguous person in any room. "Trust me, he did more than earn what he got tonight."

"Here comes your date," her brother murmured into his coffee cup.

Mauricio slid back into the booth and pulled her close, taking liberties he'd never taken before. Her eyes widened as she realized what she'd done. By taunting Harrison, she'd unintentionally led Mauricio on.

Great.

On the ride home, Mauricio offered to take her out for another drink, but she declined. When he pulled up in front of her house, she sensed he intended to kiss her. He put the car in park and leaned close, but she pressed a hand into his chest.

"I think we have to talk."

He sat back, clearly confused by her mixed

signals. Then he sighed. "Does this have to do with us or the guy who crashed our date tonight?"

She winced. "I'm sorry, Mauricio. I really am. But I think we're better off as coworkers and friends."

He didn't hide his disappointment, but he also didn't give her a hard time. "Who is he to you?"

She wanted to say he was no one, but that would be a lie. She could have explained him as a friend from high school or simply Erin's brother, but he was asking for the truth this time.

The truth was, Harrison had always been someone important to her. More than a high school fling. He had been her everything.

He was the reason she started wearing mascara and the hidden meaning behind every love song. He was the only man who could awaken the passion in her. No one else could give her such butterflies or make her feel so alive, but at the same time, she never allowed herself to be that vulnerable with anyone else, and no one else had the power to hurt her as deeply as Harrison could.

"Honestly, I think he's my soulmate."

Mauricio blew out a breath. "Wow." Then he frowned. "Can I ask you something?"

"Sure."

"If he's your soulmate, why aren't you with him?"

She dropped her gaze. "It's complicated."

"Mariella, it's none of my business, but if a guy doesn't jump at the opportunity to be with you, he's an idiot and doesn't deserve you."

Her mouth formed a sad smile. "I tell myself that every single day."

He sat back and stared out the windshield. "I guess this means I'm going to my sister's wedding alone."

"I'm sorry. It sounds like an incredible trip, but I think it's best that I pass. Besides, you might meet someone there. If I go, it'll send the wrong impression."

"It would be nice to meet someone available."

His words burrowed into her like a bullet. She was single, but she was emotionally unavailable.

How long was she going to let this go on? She needed to close this chapter of her life once and for all, but wasn't sure how to find closure when her stubborn heart refused to move on.

"Goodnight, Mauricio."

His smile was an unspoken truce. "I'll see you at work on Tuesday."

She waved as her date drove away, then drooped her shoulders the second his headlights disappeared, emotionally and mentally exhausted. She walked slowly up the path to her front steps, digging her house key out of her clutch.

"Long night?"

"Jesus, fuck!" Her heart jolted out of her chest as her bag fell onto the walkway.

Harrison's eyes watched her from the shadows where he sat on the porch swing.

"What the hell are you doing here?"

"I came to take you home with me."

"Well, forget it." She snatched her clutch off the ground and snapped it shut.

He jumped off the swing, blocking her way to the door. "Please, Mariella. We have to talk."

"About what? The huge jerk you were tonight when you felt me up right in front of my brother, your sister, and my date? I have nothing to say to you!"

"Then don't talk. Just listen."

Slamming her arms down at her side, she scoffed. "There's nothing you can say at this point to—"

"I love you."

She wondered if this was how it felt when people were shot in the heart. She looked down, sure a gaping hole had just been punched through her chest.

"Did you hear me? I said I—"

She shoved him and jammed her key in the lock, her shoulders coming up to her ears to block out his voice. "Don't."

He caught her arm and pulled her away from the door, prying the key out of her grip, shoving it into his pocket. "Why won't you listen to me?"

"Because it's not true!" She tugged her hand out of his grip, but he wouldn't let go.

"How do you know?"

"Because I know you!" Tears welled in her eyes as she tried to retrieve the key from his pocket. "Harrison, don't do this to me. I can't handle any more."

He trapped her hands against his chest and hugged her close so she couldn't move. "Listen to me, Mariella. I *love* you."

"You're just saying that because you don't want to see me with someone else."

"That's not why I'm saying it. Yes, I hate the thought of anyone else dating you or touching you, but this is deeper than that. This is about us."

He caught her face and forced her to look at him, but she shut her eyes.

"I've tried to leave, but I can't. This time's different. Maybe I've changed. Maybe it has to do with my dad passing. I don't know. But I've made it halfway back to the city three separate times, and I can't get there without feeling like I'm leaving something behind." He pressed his forehead to hers and whispered, "It's you, Mariella. My heart's stuck here because you're here. I'm in love with you. I've always loved you, but it's gotten too big. It's more than wanting you. I need you."

Eyes pressed tight, she shook her head. "No, Harrison. When you love someone, you don't leave. Not once. You tough it out, every time, and figure out a way to make it work."

"Mariella, listen to me." He kissed her eyes, wishing he could rewrite history. "That wasn't our time. Everything that happened, needed to happen so that I could become a better man for you. You deserved more than anything I could have offered, and I knew that the moment you walked into the bedroom at Jenn Moore's party."

She shook her head, rejecting his words, but he persisted.

"You've always been too good for me. God only knows why you liked me, because I could never figure it out. But I did love you, Mariella. Even back then. I loved you so much, it killed me to leave you. But I never wanted to hurt you. I wanted you to be happy and with someone who could give you everything you deserved, but I wasn't strong enough to stick around and watch it happen. My home life was a nightmare, and I needed to save myself. I thought I was also saving you from me." He kissed her cheeks. "Don't you see? You were the only person who made me happy, but I loved you so much I knew I needed to let you go."

She wiped her eyes, the old cracks of her heart breaking under the strain of too many painful memories. "I could have gone with you. I would have—"

"No. I needed to figure out how to survive on my own. It wasn't always easy, and there were a lot of times when I thought of giving up."

"Nothing's changed."

"Everything's changed. I've been doing a lot of thinking, and I finally know what I want. I finally have the courage to go after it. Mariella. I want you more than anything else in this world. I need to know we have a future together and you haven't thrown me away."

"What about New York? Your job? Your apartment?"

"We can figure that out as we go. I only need to make it to New York on occasion. I can work from anywhere."

"But you hate it here. You'll get bored and eventually resent me."

He laughed. "Never with you."

"You did before."

"No, Mariella, I got scared. My entire life was framed around my dad's endless disappointment. I had this twisted desperation inside of me that needed to earn his praise. But I never could. No matter how hard I tried, I never got a *good job, son,* or an *atta boy.* All I got were daily reminders of what a screw up I was and his promise that I'd never amount to anything. I needed to get away from him so that I could think for myself and escape his endless criticism."

"You could have told me." She'd had an idea, but to hear him actually express it in words made her wonder why he waited so long.

"I never wanted you to know how awful it was. I never wanted you to look at me with pity. That would have destroyed me."

If he only knew how much she worshipped the ground he walked on. "Still, you could have talked to me. I could have listened and maybe helped you."

"You did help me. You have no idea how many nights the thought of your smile alone kept me alive. When I was with you, he didn't exist. You made me feel like a king. I could be someone else with you, someone I liked being. I needed to get far enough away from my dad to figure out how to be that man all the time."

She lowered her lashes. "New York."

"Yes. It was loud and fast and distracting enough for me to get through an hour without hating myself. Eventually, the hours stretched into days and then weeks and months."

"And years."

He nodded, his eyes dark with regret. "I'm sorry it took me so long to figure things out. But I know what I need to do now. I know what I want, and I'm ready to start my future —with you."

She sucked in a jagged breath, her heart jolting at his words. "You're sure?"

"Yes." He kissed her lips. "But I need you to promise you'll be patient when I mess things up."

"You won't mess up."

"Yes, I will. Mariella, I didn't come from a

normal home, and I don't know how to do normal family things, but I want to try. I want to make a normal life with you."

"Normal's overrated," she joked, leaning up to steal another kiss.

He caught her face and looked her in the eyes. "I mean it. Sometimes I get moody about memories I can't change. When things get tough, my first instinct is to bolt."

"Promise you won't—"

"I promise, as long as we're always honest with each other and we trust each other, I'll always come to you when I'm unsure. I'll never leave you again." He laughed. "Hell, I couldn't at this point if I tried. I want to be with you more than I want my next breath."

"You have no idea how long I've waited to hear you say that."

He kissed her again and whispered against her lips, "I'm sorry about tonight."

She drew back and looked up at him. "You are?"

"No, not really. It got us here. But I regret upsetting you, and I might have to find that dessert spoon and murder your date with it."

She laughed. "Please don't."

He looked away, true fear twisting his expression.

"Harrison, what is it?"

"I have to tell you something else…about my dad."

"Okay."

He released her and paced the porch, stopping to stand in front of the swing. "I can't remember the sound of my mom's laugh, but I remember her screams. I still have nightmares of her crying." His brow pinched as he met her stare. "I never want to hurt anyone the way he hurt her, the way he hurt us. Especially you."

"Oh, Harrison." She crossed the porch, closing the distance. "You're not him."

He stopped her from hugging him, his eyes glistening with unshed tears. "I still have a lot of unresolved anger to work through."

She forced her arms around his neck and made him look at her. "There are people you can talk to. I know you, Harrison. You would never raise a hand to anyone in anger."

"I punched your brother."

She gaped at him. "What? When?"

He shrugged. "Recently. But he started it."

"How?" Her brother was not a fighter.

"He accused me of using you."

She tried not to smile, but how cute was he? "You were defending my honor?"

"Something like that. That's when I started

admitting to myself that I was hopelessly in love with you."

"Then I guess it was worth it." Cupping his face in her hands, she pressed her brow to his and whispered, "I forgive you for beating up my brother."

"Actually, it was sort of a tie fight."

She frowned. "Really? You're bigger than Giovanni by a lot."

"I know, that's what I thought, but he's a scrappy thing when he has to be." They laughed and he asked, "Do you still love me?"

"I never stopped loving you."

"Promise you never will."

"Only if you promise the same."

"It's a given."

His mouth lowered to hers and he finally kissed her the way a woman was meant to be kissed. Her feet lifted off the ground as he slipped a hand under her skirt and over her ass.

"One other thing." He nipped at her ear, hitting that secret spot that drove her wild. "I don't want you to date that guy anymore."

She laughed, tipping her head back to give him better access to her throat. "It's handled."

"Good." He carried her to his car and pressed her into the door, unable to pull himself away from her long enough so they could get inside. "I *need* you."

Tempted to have him right there against the car, she considered the location of her parents' bedroom windows and how likely they were to be sound asleep. Then the car alarm went off and they both jerked apart.

He scrambled for his keys and shut off the siren just as the lights in the house flickered on. "Quick, get in!" she said, jumping into the car.

Harrison raced to the driver's side and climbed in. "Do you think we woke them?"

"Who cares? Go!" It had been weeks since she had sex, and there was no way she was postponing to get invited inside where her mother and father would no doubt hold the next inquisition.

Harrison peeled away from the curb and sped through the streets of Jasper Falls, hardly slowing at the traffic lights as he raced to the hotel. The side doors were locked at this hour and there would be no slipping discreetly past the front desk, but she was beyond caring. Her only goal was to get up to Harrison's room and into his bed.

The front doors leading into the lobby parted, and she walked quickly, trying not to make a scene, only Harrison's foot caught on the mat and he cursed, falling down to his knee. It was the same place she'd tripped the day their paths crossed again.

"Oh my God, are you okay?"

His head bowed over his leg as if he were in pain. "Help me up?"

She reached for his hand only to have him tug her closer. Then he smiled up at her, something cool and heavy sliding over her finger. "Gotcha."

An enormous emerald cut diamond glinted up at her. "What the hell is that?"

"A show of commitment. I told you I was serious."

She looked at the ring then back to him. "Did you rob a jewelry store?"

"Do you like it? We can exchange it if you'd prefer something else."

Her mind wasn't computing. An hour ago she was on a date with another man. She and Harrison had just made up. They were on their way to have sex. Crazy monkey sex. Now there was a diamond on her finger.

"I'm confused. Is this…" She was embarrassing herself. Of course it wasn't an engagement ring. It couldn't be. Because that would be insane.

"Marry me, Mariella."

Or maybe they were just that nuts. "Seriously?"

"We waited long enough. It's our turn to choose, and I choose happiness. I choose you."

He chose her.

She looked over at Leon, the night time desk clerk, her eyes filling up with tears as he mouthed the word *wow* and waved her back to the question at hand. She looked down at Harrison, her tears spilling down her cheeks as she nodded, staring at the man who had always been her first choice. "Yes, I'll marry you."

Harrison bolted to his feet and lifted her into a bear hug, kissing her hard and carrying her to the elevators. Leon rung the desk bell, cheering them on, and yelled, "I'll send up champagne!"

The moment Harrison broke the kiss, she looked down at the ring. "This is stunning."

"You're stunning." He nibbled her ear and she melted into him. "Mariella Montgomery. I like the sound of that."

So did she.

EPILOGUE

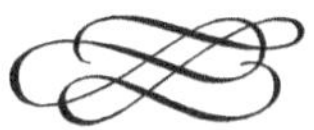

"*D*o you think the crepe station is still open?"

There was nothing more awkward than trying to pee while wearing a forty-pound wedding gown as your very pregnant sister-in-law held up your train. "Erin, you have to lift it higher. I don't want the train to fall in the toilet."

Erin huffed, lifting the skirt and suffocating Mariella in a nest of tulle and crinoline. The quiet bathroom filled with the slow trickle and Mariella finally felt some relief.

"Great. Now, I have to pee too."

"Well, you're going to have to wait. And don't you dare threaten me with a stye. It's my wedding day. I have stye immunity."

"Fine."

Once Mariella's bladder was empty, they shoved the dress down and shuffled out of the stall in a cloud of white. Erin swatted the material into place, challenged by her inability to fully bend over with the size of her protruding belly.

"Just go to the bathroom and I'll get the rest," Mariella said, as Erin bounced impatiently and crossed her legs.

"Thank you." She rushed into the stall, and Mariella continued to adjust the sides and back of her dress.

"This is an ordeal. How the heck did they do this all the time in Victorian days?"

"Oh, please. This is the first time you've gone since the start of the wedding. I think I've been in here six times in the last hour, all the while your niece has been stomping out the beat to Queen's 'We Will Rock You' on my bladder."

Mariella inspected her makeup in the mirror as the toilet flushed. Erin huffed out a breath, her large belly putting her back at an awkward angle as she waddled out of the stall.

"You're still as beautiful as ever."

"I better not have missed the crepes. There are only so many joys in life during the third trimester."

Mariella rolled her eyes. "Go."

It was her first moment alone all day and she took a few seconds to slouch her shoulders and catch her breath. The ceremony had been perfect, traditional, and done at the same church where her parents were married.

The moment her dad ushered her through those tall doors and her eyes set on Harrison, everything nervous inside of her seemed to settle. They said their vows, exchanged their rings, and she finally became Mrs. Harrison Montgomery. Life was perfect.

The door to the bathroom opened and Mariella straightened, fixing her dress and glancing into the mirror with a smile.

"Oh." Perrin King paused inside the door, realizing the bathroom was occupied.

Mariella never expected the other woman to attend her wedding, but as her boss's wife there was really no way around the invitation. "You can come in. I'm almost finished."

Perrin drifted into a stall and Mariella did a final inspection of her gown only to realize part of the lace train was hooked on a pearl, causing the back to rumple and hang wrong. She tried to unhook the material, but her corset was too tight, and she couldn't bend that way.

Perrin emerged from the stall and silently

washed her hands, her eyes peeking through her lashes as Mariella struggled with her dress. "Do you need help?"

Giving up, Mariella sighed. "My maid of honor abandoned me for a French pancake."

Perrin laughed. "Let me see."

She inspected the back of Mariella's gown and carefully detached the lace.

"Your dress is gorgeous."

"Thank you. It was my Nona's. Well, most of it. She weighed like eighty pounds when she got married." And why was she telling her this?

Perrin smiled. "Women were so thin back then."

"Tell me about it."

A strange silence seemed to wedge right between their words as they awkwardly ran out of things to say. Realizing it might be her only chance to set things straight, Mariella blurted, "I'm so sorry about everything that happened between us and Bran."

Perrin's eyes widened in startled relief. "Oh, please. I think we both dodged a bullet there."

"But I never would have gotten involved with him had I known he was a two-timer. I just…want you to know that."

"I…" Perrin awkwardly shifted and looked

down at her wedding ring. "Bran was a jerk. He played us both."

Mariella nodded. "And now you have Gage."

It took some time for Mariella to realize much of her and Perrin's issues stemmed from assumptions. She'd always assumed Perrin would think the worst of her, so she repeated that narrative in her head as a form of penance, which only enhanced her guilt.

Turned out, Perrin only ever said nice things about Mariella whenever she spoke to her relatives or the staff at the hotel. Her misjudgment of the situation just went to show how much harder people were on themselves.

A smile stole over Perrin's face, wide and genuine. "And now you have Harrison."

"Yes, I have Harrison." Life was perfect.

When someone knocked on the door, they both turned. A masculine hand curved around the wood, Harrison's wedding band showing on his ring finger. "I'm looking for my wife."

"I have to get back," Perrin said, tossing her paper towel in the trash. "Congratulations."

When she opened the door to leave, Harrison scoped out the empty bathroom and slipped inside. "Everything all right?"

"You're always meeting me in ladies rooms."

He closed the distance, his hands falling to her hips as his mouth pressed to her throat. "Have I told you how amazing you look in this gown."

His nose nuzzled her ear and she shivered. She was wearing the earrings he bought her.

"How many hours until we can officially begin the honeymoon?"

She wasn't wearing a watch and hadn't set eyes on her phone all day. Everyone she knew was on the other side of that door. "We haven't even cut the cake yet so you better cool your jets."

"I'll tell Mauricio to hurry things along."

Mariella had wanted a big, traditional wedding, so the hotel made sense for the reception. Plus she got a killer discount on everything from the flowers to the DJ because she worked with the vendors regularly.

Mauricio coordinated every detail, which could have been weird if not for Sophia, his beautiful Polynesian girlfriend he picked up in the Virgin Islands. If Mariella had gone with him, they never would have met so they all agreed everything happened for a reason. And after months of living at the hotel and getting acquainted with the staff, Harrison finally let his jealousy of the other man go.

Sort of. Every now and then he could get territorial over dumb things, but Mariella loved that side of her husband. She loved knowing she could drive him mad with a flick of her lashes. Loved knowing how a little jealousy could lead to incredibly possessive sex that always affirmed how much he needed her.

Their relationship had always been an intense and somewhat private affair, one most people didn't know existed. But Harrison never intentionally hid his feelings. Most days he struggled to contain them, not fully understanding how he could feel anything so deeply for someone else.

He and his sister had made incredible strides. Harrison helped Erin all the time, and no one was surprised when he asked Giovanni to be his best man.

Mariella's family adopted the Montgomerys as their own, and while they didn't always know what happened at holidays or why certain traditions held meaning, they were learning and enchanted every step of the way.

"Do you think we have time for a quickie?"

"Are you kidding? It takes twenty minutes just to get the bustle adjusted on this dress."

"Damn." He kissed her lips and stepped back. "I guess that's okay. The DJ sent me to find you anyway. It's time for the father-daughter dance."

A bolt of excitement shot through her, and she rushed out the door. When her father had been in the hospital earlier that year, she worried she might never have the chance to dance with him at her wedding or tell him how much his love and guidance meant to her all these years.

When they reached the ballroom, her eyes found him—bowtie already undone and a glass of red in his hand as he laughed hard at something Uncle Frank said.

She caught Harrison's arm and paused. "Look at them. Two best friends."

"Brothers," Harrison corrected.

She scanned the crowd for Giovanni and found him carrying two plates back from the crepe station, one glowing, very pregnant wife in tow. Harrison followed her stare and smiled at the two of them.

"I'll wait with them while you dance with your dad."

"Okay. You and Erin are next."

As soon as she set foot on the dance floor,

her father's eyes found her. He passed his glass to Uncle Frank and met her in the middle as the DJ played the classic "Daddy's Little Girl" by the Mills Brothers.

"You look beautiful, Mariella."

"Thank you, Daddy. For everything."

His acceptance of Harrison hadn't come easily, but once Harrison made a commitment, there was no going back. The men in her family gave him a second chance and found commonalities with her husband more than differences.

It wasn't that her father and Giovanni ever hated Harrison. They just really loved her and loathed to see anyone break her heart, which Harrison had done.

But just as her husband's struggles had made him stronger and kinder, their journey helped them grow as a couple. They understood the value of their love was immeasurable, and the history of their connection too complicated to explain or ever fully write down. They knew what they shared, knew how precious it was, and knew nothing could ever come close to matching their bond. And for that, she was grateful.

It might have taken Harrison more than a decade to tell her he loved her, but once he found the courage and the words, he made sure to tell her every day.

"He makes you happy," her father observed.

"Incredibly so."

"Good. Then I won't have to kill him."

She laughed and kissed her dad's cheek as the song ended. "I love you, Daddy."

"I love you more, *bambolina*. Enjoy your night."

The DJ called Harrison and Erin to the dance floor. Harrison reluctantly escorted his waddling sister away from her crepes so they could dutifully dance.

"They hate this." Giovanni chuckled, as Mariella took the seat beside him.

She barely ate a bite of her dinner so she picked at one of the many assorted plates at Erin's setting. "But they'll appreciate it later, when they see the video. Look how adorable they are."

Jason Mraz's voice came through the speakers, poetically coloring all their beautiful imperfections as they danced to "I Won't Give Up." Tears welled in Mariella's eyes, so taken by the perfect picture they made.

Over just a few months, Harrison had transformed into an amazing brother and friend. Erin once told Mariella she now had everything she needed—a family that loved and accepted each other through thick and thin.

Her brother's hand closed over hers. "I never did thank you."

"For?"

"Bringing another best friend into my life. He's awesome, Mar."

She glanced back at the dance floor and smiled. "I know."

The only person who had trouble seeing Harrison's greatness was Harrison, but she supposed that was the way it worked for most people. "If only we saw ourselves through other people's eyes."

"The right people."

She nodded, once more wishing Harrison and Erin's childhood could have been different. "They're with the right people now."

The rest of the guests joined them on the floor, luring Mariella and Harrison into the middle. Everything swirled in a beautiful blur. Her Clooney and McCullough relatives surrounded them in a sea of smiles, and the night floated on a cloud of love.

Sometime toward the end of the evening, she realized she was the last of their generation to get married—the last of her cousins. Next would come the children—probably

Frankie then Hannah, then possibly Tallulah and all the rest would follow.

What felt like an ending to some was actually just the beginning to others. Everything always came full circle, again and again.

Watching her older relatives smile and enjoy the night, she wondered if they realized this too. She wondered if that was the secret that kept them laughing after so many years. No matter how many ups and downs came, they would somehow survive because they had each other. That's what family was all about—having someone there to catch you when you fall and help you up when you're on the ground.

She thought back to the day she stumbled into Harrison's life again, falling head over heels for him just like she had before.

"What's that smile?" Harrison spun her across the dance floor, pulling her close.

"I was just thinking how humiliated I was the day I fell in the hotel lobby."

"Right at my feet," he joked, then kissed her nose. "Do you know what I was thinking, ten seconds before you came tumbling through that door?"

"What?"

"I was thinking, *God, send me a sign that I should stay,* and you literally appeared."

When the cake had been cut and the flowers bowed from the centerpieces in wilted blooms, the lights turned on, but the magic didn't end. Her parents were the last to leave, and Mariella felt strange abandoning the hotel staff to clean up the mess. Typically, the staff pulled together after big weddings.

"Let's go for a walk," Harrison said, pulling her into the hall and toward the back doors of the hotel.

"But…"

"You're the bride, Mariella. They've got this."

She reluctantly followed him out of the ballroom.

The crisp night was warm with barely a breeze. The town was decorated in splashes of gold and orange for the autumn months ahead. All the stores were closed and only O'-Malley's remained open at this hour, but even its parking lot was empty on account of most residents being at the wedding.

Harrison held her hand as they walked slowly down Main Street. A car drove by, blearing its horn and someone yelled out the window, "Kiss the bride!"

Harrison dipped her back and kissed her soundly, earning several other honks as the car drove away.

They laughed and continued on their stroll. As much as she wanted to get out of this dress, the quiet walk was nice. It gave them a moment to catch their breath after a long, busy day and let it all sink in.

"I have to grab something at the office."

Harrison's office looked nothing like the old hardware store. Jasper Falls wasn't much for fancy, so this was the town's first experience with any sort of financial advisor. Most people didn't know what a financial advisor did, but those who employed his services benefited greatly. Her aunt Maureen had been one of his first clients.

"She'll be your best advertisement," Mariella had told Harrison. "Her mouth gets more miles than a billboard."

As soon as he made the McCulloughs money, everyone wanted a piece of his advice. The people of Jasper Falls might not be as fancy as his New York clients, but Harrison was content.

She sat on the desk in the dim office and waited for him to find whatever he was looking for. There was something especially magical about sitting around in a wedding gown, and she decided she was in no rush to take it off, certain she'd never have the chance to wear it again.

Harrison closed a desk drawer. "Got it."

"It?"

He held up a small box. "Your wedding present."

Mariella cocked her head in confusion. "But we already did that. You got me flowers, and I got you cufflinks."

"This goes with the flowers." He stepped between her knees, bunching up the froth of her dress, and held out the box.

"Jewelry?"

"Better. Open it."

She lifted the lid and a plain silver key sparkled from within. "Is it a key to your heart?"

He chuckled. "You already busted that lock wide open. Come with me."

He pulled her off the desk and locked up the office. They walked down Main Street and turned left where the old grain factory used to be. The road was dark and in need of street lights, except for one house up ahead.

She rarely drove down this road, being that it was off the beaten path, so she wasn't sure where he was taking her.

"Do you see it?"

She scanned the open fields and dark mountains along the horizon. "See what?"

He turned her shoulders, pointing her eyes directly at the light up ahead. "There."

"It's a house."

"No." His arms closed around her waist, and he pressed a kiss to her shoulder. "It's more than that. It's a home. *Our* home."

Her jaw unhinged and she turned to face him, then looked back at the home. Two stories with a wraparound porch. Lights lit every window and there was even a chimney. "It's ours?"

He smiled. "It's all ours. Do you want to see inside?"

"Do I?" She grabbed his hand and ran up the hill, her dress frothing and swishing as she laughed into the night. Winded and panting, their footsteps thumped up the fresh wood of the porch steps.

Everything was brand new and absolutely beautiful. The siding was cedar and the porch lights were copper. It looked like something out of a storybook.

"You had this built?"

He nodded. "Your cousin Braydon was a lot of help."

She was shocked her family had been able to keep such a secret.

"Unlock the door." He handed her the key.

Her heart raced as she slipped the metal

into the slot. The scent of cut wood and fresh paint welcomed her as the door glided open.

She gasped when he swept her off her feet and lifted her to his chest. "I heard it's tradition to carry the bride over the threshold."

She looked up at him, more enchanted than she ever dreamed possible. Her hand softly cupped his cheek where stubble had grown and she whispered, "Just promise you won't let go."

"I promise."

He carried her into their home and her gaze caressed every molding and every detail. The rooms weren't yet furnished, but it was clear he'd thought everything out so the house would be furniture ready by the wedding.

He set her down in what she supposed was the living room. "Do you like it?"

She stared at the polished floors and suddenly saw Harrison kneeling on a carpet, putting together a castle made of connecting blocks. A little girl in fairy wings and a tiara hung off his back, blowing raspberries into his cheek as a little boy anxiously waited to drive his truck over the drawbridge of the castle.

Laughter filled the air as they softly encouraged each other and worked together to build something beautiful. She could smell something cooking from the kitchen and hear music playing.

"Do you like it?" he asked again and the vision faded.

Smiling, she shook her head in awe and met his stare. "No, Harrison, I *love* it."

She could see their future in that home, happy and full of love. Despite his fears, Harrison was going to be an incredible father, nothing like his own.

She laced her fingers with his. "You're a good husband."

Her words were simple, but his eyes registered the praise and he kissed her. Pulling away slowly, he whispered, "Let me show you the rest."

"I can't wait."

Keeping hold of his hand, she followed him toward the unknown, toward their future, trusting him to never let go.

THE END

Want more Jasper Falls?
Read Side Squeeze (Jasper Falls 6) Now!

Claim your FREE book when you subscribe

to Lydia's newsletter!
Click here to sign up for Lydia Michaels'
Newsletter.

Are you follow Lydia Michaels?
Stalk her on TikTok, Instagram, Facebook,
Goodreads, and BookBub!
TikTok @LydiaMichaels
Instagram @lydia_michaels_books
Facebook @LydiaMichaels
Goodreads
BookBub

Show Your LOVE
*If you enjoyed this book, please don't forget to
leave a review.*

LYDIA MICHAELS' READING ORDER

<u>MCCULLOUGH MOUNTAIN</u>
Almost Priest
Beautiful Distraction
Irish Rogue
British Professor
Broken Man
Controlled Chaos
Hard Fix
Intentional Risk

<u>THE ORDER OF VAMPIRES</u>
<u>Original Sin</u>
<u>Dark Exodus</u>
<u>Prodigal Son</u>

<u>THE SURRENDER TRILOGY</u>
<u>Falling In</u>
<u>Breaking Out</u>
<u>Coming Home</u>

STAND ALONES
<u>La Vie en Rose</u>
<u>Simple Man</u>
<u>Sugar</u>
<u>Breaking Perfect</u>
<u>Hurt</u>
<u>Protege</u>

About Lydia Michaels

Lydia Michaels is the award winning and bestselling author of more than forty titles, a certified life coach, and transformational speaker. She is the consecutive winner of the 2018 & 2019 *Author of the Year Award* from *Happenings Media,* as well as the recipient of the 2014 *Best Author Award* from the *Courier Times*. She has been featured in *USA Today, Romantic Times Magazine, Love & Lace*, and more. As the host and founder of the *East Coast Author Convention,* the *Behind the Keys Author Retreat,* and *Read Between the Wines*, she continues to celebrate her growing love for readers and romance novels around the world.

In 2021, Michaels released the groundbreaking, non-fiction series, ***Write 10K in a Day,*** to commemorate her career in the publishing industry. She looks forward to many more years of exploring both fiction and non-fiction writing, teaching about the craft, and learning from the others in the author community.

Lydia is happily married to her childhood sweetheart. Some of her favorite things include the scent of paperback books, listening to her husband play piano, escaping to her coastal home at the Jersey Shore, cheap wine, *Game of Thrones*, coffee, and kilts. She hopes to meet you soon at one of her many upcoming events.

You can follow Lydia at www.Facebook.com/LydiaMichaels or on Instagram @lydia_michaels_books

Read By Mood
Billionaire Romance
Falling In | Sacrifice Of The Pawn | Calamity Rayne | Blind

Contemporary Romance
Wake My Heart | The Best Man | Love Me Nots | Pining For You |Almost Priest| My Funny Valentine | Side Squeeze | Almost Priest | Beautiful Distraction | Irish Rogue | British Professor | Broken Man (LGBTQ) | Controlled Chaos | Hard Fix|Intentional Risk

Emotional Favorites
La Vie en Rose | Simple Man | Wake My Heart | Sacrifice of the Pawn | Crush
Romantic Comedy
Calamity Rayne

Erotic Romance
Breaking Perfect | Protégé | Falling In | Sugar

First in Series
Almost Priest | Falling In | First Comes Love | Wake My Heart | Crush | Original Sin

Paranormal Vampire Romance
Original Sin | Dark Exodus | Prodigal Son

LGBTQ+ & Menage Romance
<u>Broken Man</u> (MM) | <u>Breaking Perfect</u> (MMF) | <u>Crush</u> (MMF) | <u>Hurt</u> (Non-Consensual) | <u>Protege</u>

Sexy Nerds & Second Chances
Blind | <u>Untied</u>
Teacher Student, Workplace, and Age-Gap Love Affairs... Oh my!
<u>British Professor</u> | <u>Pining For You</u> |<u>Breaking Perfect</u> | <u>Falling In</u> | <u>Sacrifice of the Pawn</u>

Single Dads & Single Moms
<u>Simple Man</u> | <u>Pining For You</u> | <u>First Comes Love</u> | <u>Controlled Chaos</u> | <u>Intentional Risk</u>
-
Dark Tortured Hero Romance
<u>Hurt</u>

Non-Fiction Books for Writers
<u>Write 10K in a Day</u>: Avoid Burnout